Stars and Waves

Roberto Maiolino

Published by Clink Street Publishing 2021

Copyright © 2021

First edition.

ISBN:
978-1-914498-07-7 - paperback
978-1-914498-08-4 - ebook

To Cesare

Acknowledgments

Many people have been helpful during the writing of *Stars and Waves* on several fronts, from input on the technical and scientific aspects, to comments on the several human facets of the novel. I want to specially thank Asa Bluck, Steven Brereton, Giorgia Busso, Sara Cazzoli, Cathie Clarke, Romeo Ghiriti, Nadia Gorlova, Anais Gonneau, Valentin Ivanov, Nikku Madhusudhan, Manuela Magliocchetti, Filippo Mannucci, Alessandro Marconi, Annelies Mortier, Raffaella Schneider, and Alberto Sesana.

I owe special thanks to Philippa Donovan, whose tips helped raise the novel to a whole new level.

Finally, I am especially grateful to my family. Not only for their advice on the novel, but also for putting up with me being often absent-minded while thinking about the plot and, consequently, lagging behind in conversations. Sorry! Emilia has been the person who really provided the most extensive feedback and comments, improving the novel a lot. Clara has been a fantastic aide, not only in improving the style of the novel but by also providing excellent ideas. Her rubber stamp was the key step in finalising each chapter. I'm also extremely grateful to Gemma, not only for her suggestions, but also for the many 'Well done!' and smiley faces on her annotated copy, which were truly encouraging :)

CHAPTER 1

Stars dancing around each other, born in cosmic cradles, dying in apocalyptic blasts. Vast, greedy black holes devouring matter. Beautiful swirls of glowing gas and powerful jets approaching the speed of light. Matter and energy in continuous transformation…

His contemplation of the night vault was interrupted by the squeaking of the enormous dome behind him, as it adjusted its position to follow the movement of the telescope inside. It was tracking Messier 13, a star cluster in the constellation of Hercules, now high in the sky.

While waiting for the data acquisition to be completed he was lying on the lawn in front of the observatory, hands clasped behind his head, admiring the wonders of the revolving heavens.

Since he was a child, his musings on the starred sky had gone well beyond simple delight, beyond the glittering appearance that most people seemed to enjoy.

He would still be a shepherd in that secluded village in Siberia if it was not for her. "You are gifted," his teacher used to say, beaming, "there's a bright scientist inside you. We just have to nourish him." She fed his unquenchable thirst for knowledge with books that his companions would not even glance at. Despite all the difficulties associated with his humble origins, he managed to persevere in his studies, excelling at university, thriving and becoming an internationally recognised scientist.

Yes, thriving.

But humiliation can change a man.

Many would have overcome it, but for him, that single event had become a permanent stain.

He squeezed his eyes shut. Wipe it away, erase it! No – it had sunk too deep. Opening his eyes again, as the night sky glowed above him, he sought comfort from his old shimmering friends.

Looking at the myriad of stars was like going back in time. Stars and galaxies appear to us as they were thousands, millions or even billions of years ago. No matter how fast light can travel, it still takes timespans, inconceivable to the human mind, to reach us from any part of the universe.

Going back in time.

Thirty years would have been enough. He would behave differently. He would not make the same mistake.

The dome squeaked again, like a child whining for attention. It was probably right, the scientific camera's exposure should be nearly finished by now, he should start heading back to the telescope and its control room.

Grunting, he got up, joints clicking, and started walking towards the control room located next to the 54-metre-high dome. The large slit of the dome was wide open in front of him, revealing the majestic BTA-6 telescope of the Russian Special Astrophysical Observatory. From his position, he could see the telescope's huge monolithic concave mirror, whose six-metre diameter had made it the largest telescope in the world until 1990. Since then it had been superseded by many other telescopes worldwide, yet he still looked at it with glinting eyes.

He entered the control room, stuffed with screens and electronic panels. The telescope operator was dozing on his reclined chair, feet on the main console, with its four large monitors and three keyboards. He was a graduate student, making some money by working as a telescope operator a few nights per month. Trainers, loose clothing, and black dishevelled hair poking out of the hood into which he had sunk.

"Nikolai, be careful, please! One day you're going to accidentally hit some key while sleeping with your feet on the console."

Nikolai awakened, and jumped out of his chair. "I'm sorry, Professor Kasparov."

"No, you must excuse me," Vladimir Kasparov said, shaking his head. "The fact is… you know how much I care about this telescope."

"I know, Professor. It won't happen again," responded Nikolai, straightening up in his chair and placing his hands on the keyboard in front of him, without actually typing anything.

"That's fine," said the Professor. He grabbed his logbook and said, "It's now time to move to the next target, the stellar globular cluster Messier 12, and start another exposure."

Kasparov bent awkwardly over his desk, too tall and skinny to reach it properly. He was part of the telescope staff and also an extensive user of the telescope, mostly for research into stellar globular clusters – large and dense agglomerates of hundreds of thousands of stars, which look like sparkling puffs in the sky. In front of him was the latest issue of the *Monthly Notices of the Royal Astronomical Society*. Although Kasparov had relegated himself to the outskirts of scientific research, he kept up to date with the most recent publications.

He ran his hands through his white hair and started reading from where he had stopped just before leaving the control room – an article entitled 'Monitoring of a sample of 30 nearby stars: detection of seven new exoplanets' by Laura Bellini and Julia Russell, from the University of Cambridge. Kasparov quickly skimmed through the article. Exoplanets, aka planets orbiting other stars. Hundreds of new exoplanets were discovered every year.

He was about to move to the next article when a page caught his attention. The page reported a table listing the stars that had been observed, along with the main results for each of them. The name of one of them took his breath away.

70 Ophiuchi

A star in the constellation of Ophiuchus, the 'serpent bearer' in Greek mythology. Coincidentally, his next target, Messier 12, where the BTA-6 telescope was now pointed to, was also in this constellation.

He kept staring at the table. Still. Heart pounding fast.

Then, with a gleam in his eyes, he pulled the keyboard towards him. He copied the email addresses of both the authors of the article and started typing a message.

He had just hit 'send', when Nikolai tried to catch his attention. "Professor Kasparov, we seem to have a problem."

Kasparov was motionless, staring at the screen of his computer. 'Message sent'. His finger was trembling on the mouse.

"Professor?" insisted Nikolai.

Kasparov slowly moved his gaze towards him.

"The first images of the new target are completely blank," explained Nikolai.

Kasparov raised an eyebrow. He stood up and went to take a look at the screen displaying the images delivered by the scientific camera – totally black.

"Must be the shutter of the camera, stuck again, or a loose wire," he said. "Although…" he paused a few seconds, his forehead furrowed. "I'll go and take a look. I can probably fix it quickly."

"But Professor," complained Nikolai, "you know the safety regul–"

"Oh please!" interrupted Kasparov. "No need to remind me about the regulations, those are for inexperienced people. I've done this many times. Don't worry."

"Ye— Yes, I know that you are very familiar with this telescope… probably more than anyone else…"

"And you also know that asking for assistance would mean waiting hours for the technicians to come. We would hardly get any observations for the rest of the night." Kasparov's face flushed. "Observing time on these large telescopes is precious. I don't really want to waste half a night, especially such a clear one!"

Nikolai pursed his lips.

"Please park the telescope in the horizontal position," requested Kasparov.

"Fine, I will override the automatic control system," replied Nikolai.

Kasparov grimaced, as he did every time he was reminded of the new telescope control system. The BTA-6 telescope's

Technical Committee had recently approved an upgrade to the telescope software control system, prompted by an apparently 'very convenient' offer by an American company. Kasparov thought this had been a waste of money. He deemed the previous system just fine. Funding for science was under strain everywhere across the globe and Russia was no exception. As if that was not enough, in recent years the Russian government had diverted most astronomy resources to the space sector, claiming that the future of astronomical exploration was through telescopes in orbit. This had resulted in further draining of funds from ground-based telescopes, such as the BTA-6. In such a grim climate it was really inappropriate to spend money on fancy but unnecessary control systems. Kasparov made no secret of his reservations.

He left the control room, closing the door behind him, passed through a few narrow corridors and entered the huge expanse inside the dome. The interior of the vast dome always gave him the impression of entering a cathedral. A cathedral erected to serve science and human knowledge.

The telescope, dimly lit only by the glow of the Milky Way's billions of stars filtered through the dome's slit, was in a nearly vertical position. It was still pointing to Messier 12, now close to the zenith, the highest point in the sky.

The huge, concave mirror of the telescope was facing up. Fanning out from its perimeter, eight massive steel tubes supported a large metal ring 26 metres above the mirror. Inside this ring, four smaller tubes held the large scientific camera at its centre. The camera collected the light focused by the large mirror and sent the resulting images to the computer in the control room. Externally the camera looked like a black cylinder, more than two metres long, with a large lens on the side facing the mirror, and electrical wires sprouting out of its sides.

The whole telescope structure was moving rigidly while slowly tracking the movement of Messier 12 in the sky. The low humming of the gears and motors was echoing inside the dome.

The telescope stopped its movement and remained still for a few seconds. Nikolai had finally halted the tracking and given the command, Kasparov thought.

The telescope started to lean, faster and faster. The sounds of the gears and the accelerating motors became louder and high-pitched. The telescope kept tilting until it reached a nearly horizontal position, as if observing something on the nearby mountains.

Everything was now still and silent.

Kasparov scanned the whole telescope, back and forth. It was rare to see it lying down. Although more than 40 years old, it was still a stunning piece of technology. In this position, the large, curved mirror was nearly vertical. The long tubes attached to its edges were nearly horizontal and were holding the camera at a height of about ten metres above Kasparov's head.

He approached the tall mobile scaffolding, parked on one side, which was used for maintaining the telescope and its instrumentation. He moved the scaffolding towards the telescope until its top reached the camera. He then blocked the scaffolding wheels, put on the safety harness and started climbing to the top. When he was at the height of the camera he hooked his harness to the scaffolding frame, leaned onto the camera and started checking the various wires and connectors. Everything appeared in order.

Placing one foot on one of the tubes holding the camera, he started to inspect its front side.

He froze – hearing the telescope's motors engaging.

The telescope started to rotate horizontally. Kasparov grasped the camera to avoid the ten-metre fall. The telescope kept moving fast and hit the scaffolding. While still clinging to the camera, which was swiftly moving together with the whole telescope, he watched with horror as the scaffolding gradually leaned over, pushed by the telescope's frame. It kept leaning… it toppled. But its fall was halted by Kasparov's harness, still firmly hooked to it. The weight of the scaffolding was pulling Kasparov down. He would not survive the fall if his grip slipped.

"Nikolai!" he yelled.

The telescope wouldn't stop spinning and the scaffolding, dragged by Kasparov's harness, was clattering, rattling and hitting all kind of hardware on its way. While still gripping the camera with his left hand, he managed to free his right hand to reach a Swiss knife inside his pocket. He unfolded the blade with his teeth and swiftly cut the harness. The scaffolding crashed loudly onto the ground.

Suddenly the telescope stopped.

Nikolai, that clumsy student, must have finally realised the mess he had caused, Kasparov thought. He panted with relief. Still clinging onto the camera, he looked down at the pieces of scaffolding scattered over the ground, ten metres beneath him.

"Nikolai! You could have killed me! Come here immediately and help me!" yelled Kasparov.

The control room, as well as most of the offices in the building, were insulated very well to cope with the chilly winter nights, which also resulted in perfect soundproofing. To enable communications, the inside of the dome had an intercom that was continuously connected with the control room. So, surely, Nikolai must have heard the loud noise, the clattering of the scaffolding being dragged and its crashing onto the ground, as well as Kasparov's cry for help.

Silence. Absolute silence.

No reply from Nikolai through the intercom.

Kasparov twisted his head in an effort to look at the dome's entrance door, expecting Nikolai to appear at any moment now.

The door remained firmly shut.

He began to sweat.

The telescope started moving again, this time higher, towards the zenith. Was Nikolai trying to kill him?

As the telescope continued towards its vertical position, Kasparov's grip slipped. He desperately tried to find other parts of either the camera or the telescope to grab, but any new grasp would quickly become ineffective as the telescope's frame kept tilting, moving him higher, higher and higher. It was like riding a giant wild beast.

As the telescope reached its final, vertical position he lost his grip. He fell... but managed to grab two wires that were hanging out of the camera.

He looked down. He was now 25 metres above the telescope's large mirror. He could see the reflected image of the starry sky, and himself, dangling high in the air.

The telescope was now still.

No sound of steps approaching. No hint of a human presence beside him.

Kasparov looked at the wires that he was grasping. They were thin but apparently strong enough to hold his weight.

His hand felt a vibration coming from the point where the wires were attached to the camera. The connectors were giving away. One broke, leaving the wire limp in his now dangling hand. Kasparov quickly grasped the only available wire with both hands.

The connector attached to the remaining wire started cracking under the strain of his weight. He looked around frantically. There was no other point within reach that he could grab.

The second connector came off.

He hurtled into the mirror of his beloved telescope.

The fall only lasted a few seconds. He saw his image, reflected by the huge mirror, getting larger and larger, with the starred vault petrified behind him.

Strangely the impact was not painful. Just sudden blackness.

Lying on the mirror, and the glittering night sky reflected in it, it was as if Kasparov was floating in space, among his adored stars. His head was next to the silvery Milky Way, now crossed by a scarlet stream.

CHAPTER 2

Her head hit the window hard.

It was not the pain, but the loud sound that woke her up.

She was so tired after her recent observation period at the telescope, that she had fallen asleep in her seat, only to be abruptly awoken by her head bumping against the window as the aeroplane touched the runaway.

Laura struggled to lift her backpack from the luggage belt and put it on her shoulders. She glanced at the tourists around her who were comfortably pulling their wheeled suitcases. Her envious glare soon turned into a smug grin. All these people were visiting Florence as tourists, rushing about, seeing nothing. She had been lucky to live in this gorgeous city for four years when she was an undergraduate student and was able to savour its atmosphere and hidden beauties. The intimate glimpses of the cathedral from secluded alleys. The concealed gardens adorned by elegant statues and flooded by the scent of roses. The tiny ice cream shop that she found when she got lost… Their pistachio gelato was sublime.

"Laura!" called a young woman, beaming at her while jumping up and down and waving with both arms from behind the barriers in the Arrivals Hall.

"Sofia!" Laura screamed back while speeding up her pace.

They hugged each other, lingering for a moment.

"I'm so happy you could pass through Florence before going back to Cambridge," said Sofia.

"I'm glad too," responded Laura. "Thank you for offering me somewhere to stay for a few days"

"Of course! I miss the time when we were roommates so much."

Sofia grunted as she helped Laura lift her backpack and squeezed it into the small boot of her car. "You must have been at the telescope for a long period," she commented, pushing hard onto the boot's door as it would not close

Laura nodded, "Yes, long… far too long."

Sofia was now speeding up on the road connecting the airport to the city. "So, where have you been for your scientific research this time?" she asked.

"The TNG telescope," replied Laura.

Sofia looked at her cluelessly.

"It's on the top of La Palma, one of the Canary Islands," explained Laura.

"I must confess I'm a little bit jealous. I know that astronomical observations are complex and demanding, but they take you to such remote places, surrounded by breathtaking landscapes, far away from any human settlement," said Sofia with a dreamy expression.

Laura smiled. She closed her eyes and visualised the immense, deep, revolving fresco visible from those sites, the night sky exploding with the most vibrant contrasts and gleaming with the softest shades. The vastness of the heavens above her was what made her blissful when visiting astronomical observatories. But her smile disappeared as she remembered the difficulties of the last observations at the telescope. "I couldn't really enjoy it this time."

"Why not?"

"It was an odd observing run," responded Laura with a grimace

"Odd? In what sense?"

"For the first few nights, the telescope didn't respond to the commands of the operator. It behaved like a defiant child." Laura narrowed her eyes. "The telescope would simply refuse to point at the selected stars, it just moved to apparently random positions. Initially I couldn't get any data." She shook her head. "I was exasperated. And I was not the only one. The telescope operator and the engineering team had no idea what was going on." She paused and sighed. "On the third night, they decided to completely shut down the computerised control system of the telescope. This meant that the telescope had to be guided manually from inside the dome, making the observations much more difficult and challenging... but at least I could get enough data for my PhD project."

"You do look exhausted."

"Yes, I must admit that I am very tired," said Laura, closing her eyes and letting her head fall back on her seat. She opened her eyes slightly and frowned, "Tired and confused."

"Confused?"

"Yes... well... the rebel telescope has not been the only oddity this week." Her lips twitched. "I received a strange message a few days ago."

Sofia raised an eyebrow.

After a few moments of hesitation, Laura pulled out her smartphone and started browsing through her mail.

"Here it is:

Dear Dr Bellini and Dr Russell,"

She paused, "The person who wrote this message didn't bother checking that I'm still a student and that Julia is a professor, or maybe he simply wrote the message in a rush." Laura shrugged her shoulders. Then she started again.

"Dear Dr Bellini and Dr Russell,
I read your recent article on the detection of seven
new exoplanets with great interest. I found it
extremely exciting!
I would like to share with you some data that I obtained
30 years ago, which I'm sure you'll find intriguing.
I could call you or we could even meet in person.
Please let me know your availability as soon as possible.
Best regards,

> *Prof. Vladimir Kasparov*
> *Resident Scientist at the Special*
> *Astrophysical Observatory, Russia"*

"I cannot really see anything 'strange' about that message," commented Sofia, "I'm not a scientist, but to me, it actually sounds quite encouraging."

Laura shook her head. "Technologies and instrumentation evolve very fast in our field. I can hardly believe that such old data, taken 30 years ago, can be of any interest for my project. I was not even born 30 years ago," said Laura with a laugh, "and exoplanets had not been discovered yet. I initially thought it was a scam or a prank. But I've checked online: Kasparov really is a professor at the Special Astrophysical Observatory in Russia. So he is a scientist, but… I've looked at his publications – he has never worked on exoplanets. There isn't a single article published by him on the topic. He has always worked on stellar atmospheres and stellar evolution. I cannot understand what the connection might be."

Sofia shrugged, "Shouldn't you take a look at his data before judging?"

"I did try. But here's another strange thing about the story: Julia and I replied to Kasparov's email, expressing our interest and availability to talk, and we gave him our contact details, but guess what? He never called. I sent another couple of messages asking him to share some information – he didn't reply." She turned to face Sofia. "Isn't it puzzling? I mean, this Russian professor first contacts us with great enthusiasm, to the point of even offering to meet with us in person… and then he completely ignores us."

"Well, perhaps he is just a peculiar person," Sofia suggested. "On the other hand, I must say that, since I met you and your friends, I have learnt that scientists can be a little bit… how shall I put it… bizarre?" she said laughing.

Laura had heard this joke from Sofia several times, but this time, absorbed by her thoughts, she did not laugh with her. "If I have to be completely honest," she said, "the weirdest thing is neither the story of his old data nor his lack of response."

"No? Then what?" asked Sofia.

They had just entered the city centre, but Laura wasn't looking around her. She was staring at a spot on the windshield and tapping her fingers on her lap.

"What is so weird?" insisted Sofia.

Laura sighed, "I have hardly ever found anyone even marginally interested in my results. My work is not in the mainstream, I think my colleagues barely glance at my articles, I'm sure nearly no one really reads them," she paused, "so… the sudden enthusiasm of this stranger… there must be something wrong."

"I'm sure that's not true. Lots of colleagues must appreciate your work," said Sofia with a comforting tone.

Laura looked down and shook her head. "I'm at the end of the second year of my PhD and I haven't achieved much. I simply have to face it, I don't really have the skills for scientific research."

"Laura! You're too harsh on yourself! You are just too tired. I'm sure you only need a good night's rest."

But Laura did not respond.

They were now crossing the Arno River in the late afternoon. Laura looked at Florence's jagged skyline, with its mixture of medieval and renaissance buildings. She looked at the unique Ponte Vecchio, the old bridge, crowded with small ancient shops. Her green eyes reflected back at her in the window. Her bob looked more like a mane, but she was far too tired to care about her looks.

They entered San Frediano, one of Florence's medieval quarters, where Sofia found a parking spot.

"We have to leave the car here. I recently moved into a flat in the pedestrian area, just a few blocks from here," said Sofia, while helping Laura with her backpack.

Their footsteps on the worn stones echoed within the narrow streets. The late sunbeams hit the top of the ancient buildings, casting dense amber hues throughout the alley.

Laura stopped to watch the flight of swallows swiftly swooping across each other above their heads, their chirps high-pitched. She smiled.

"What?" asked Sofia, looking first at Laura and then up, trying to spot the point Laura was staring at.

Laura closed her eyes, "I had nearly forgotten this melody. It sounds like a warm welcome home."

Sofia beamed. "I'm glad Florence feels like a second home for you. Even though you come back so rarely from Cambridge… By the way, what is the conference here that you mentioned?"

Laura's smile faded away and her stomach turned. "Yes, there's a conference on exoplanets here in Florence. It already started a few days ago. Tomorrow I will only attend the last day. My supervisor, Julia, suggested not going straight back to Cambridge after La Palma, but that I should attend this conference and present some of my results."

"It does sound like a good opportunity for you," commented Sofia.

Laura nibbled her lower lip. Taking a deep breath, she said, "Yes, but you know how it is for me. Giving presentations at conferences, in front of a large audience, is something I'm not really comfortable with."

"Still? I thought by now you had overcome that problem," remarked Sofia.

"Yes – no, not really," Laura squeezed her eyes shut, "the mere thought of talking in front of one hundred astronomers makes my stomach churn."

Sofia opened her mouth slightly, looking at Laura, but her lips just trembled in hesitation and no words came out.

They approached a small green, wooden door. "Here we are!" Sofia exclaimed while pulling a keyring out of her purse. They walked up a flight of narrow, stone stairs.

"It's small," apologised Sofia while opening the door of her flat, "but it's comfortable."

The colourful, multi-ethnic furniture and decorations contrasted with the uneven white walls, the dark wooden beams on the ceiling and some weathered stones protruding from the old, medieval structure of the building.

"I see that now that you have your own flat you have given free rein to the architect inside you," said Laura with a grin.

"Maybe", responded Sofia, feigning an uninterested tone. Then she opened a door. "Although small…" she said, letting Laura in, "I also have a room for guests."

As Laura entered, her gaze focused on one single thing: a bed.

Sofia swung the window fully open, letting the refreshing air of the summer evening flood the room. It was facing a small busy square, full of restaurants and wine bars.

Laura pushed her bag into the room and collapsed on the bed.

"Take some rest," said Sofia, "I'll call you in about one hour. I want to take you to a very nice and tasty *trattoria* nearby for dinner." Then she left the room, closing the door behind her.

Laura remained in bed, staring at the ceiling. Her thoughts were brought to the message from the Russian professor. She had to admit that, although weird, it had triggered her curiosity and created expectations. His lack of response had been frustrating. She was tempted to check if, in the meantime, he had replied, but she was too tired.

Her eyelids drooped.

Her phone rang. The sound floated in the air and mixed with the indistinct chattering of people dining at outdoor tables wafting in from outside. The phone rang two more times – but Morpheus had already embraced her.

CHAPTER 3

The zodiacal light plume emerged from the ocean like a giant brush that had just painted the firmament. Most people had never had the chance to see the beauty of the zodiacal light. This glowing strip in the sky, produced by microscopic sand particles on the plane of the solar system which reflect the light of the sun. Visible only rarely, in clear skies, far from cities and far from any light pollution.

He was sitting on the rim of the Caldera de Taburiente, an immense crater – 8 km across – formed out of a collapsed volcano millions of years ago, on the island of La Palma. It was now filled with low clouds, some of which were swirling out, pushed by the light breeze of the night. It looked like a gigantic cauldron in which some magic elixir was simmering.

Pedro was part of the TNG telescope staff. He was responsible for archiving all datasets obtained with the telescope and also for delivering the data to the visiting astronomers after their observing run.

Despite the spectacle around him, he was looking down at the clouds inside the Caldera.

He picked up a small porous stone next to him and examined it in his palm for a moment. Narrowing his eyes, he clenched the stone in his fist and then threw it in front of him. The stone hovered over the Caldera for a few seconds, seemingly lifted by the breeze, then it plummeted and vanished in the clouds beneath him.

He stared at the point where the stone had disappeared, as if somehow expecting it to return at any time… as if wishing that events could be reversed.

He was jolted from his thoughts by the sound of steps on the volcanic gravel approaching from behind.

Thomas, the TNG telescope operator, sat down next to him.

A stronger gust of wind moved the clouds and unveiled the wide, deep interior of the crater. It was crossed by water streams and waterfalls. Diverse species of plants and animals had developed in the unique microclimate inside it.

"Isn't it fascinating?" said Thomas.

"What?" asked Pedro.

"That such an apocalyptic, prehistoric event has eventually turned into this paradise."

Pedro nodded.

"I mean," Thomas continued, "when I look at this immense crater... I always find it amazing that nature could generate such an infernal catastrophe and then the same, identical laws of physics could transform it into this heavenly sanctuary of life."

Pedro hinted a smile. "Yes, it's really amazing."

He lifted his gaze to scan the horizon. From their high position, he could see the ocean surrounding the island in all directions. Some feeble hint of twilight was still visible, enough to illuminate the domes of the observatory scattered on the outer, more gently sloping surface of the extinguished volcano. All of them with their slits wide open and their telescopes already busy exploring the night sky. Among them the TNG telescope. Pedro felt his stomach twist.

Thomas stretched his back by pulling his arms above his head. "It has been a long week. I'm glad that my shift is over," he said. "Gosh, it's never happened before, the telescope behaved so weirdly, like a bucking animal!" exclaimed Thomas, shaking his head. "It wouldn't respond to any of our commands. It affected the entire programme of that poor student from Cambridge, Laura Bellini. At the end of the observations, she looked quite frustrated."

He glanced at the TNG dome, now glowing with red hues from the rising moon, which had just peered out of the ocean.

"Operating the telescope manually from inside the dome was exhausting and inefficient. I hope she got enough data for her thesis," added Thomas.

Pedro said nothing. Motionless.

"Pedro? What's going on with you? I've just told you that I've gone through a hell of a week... I would expect a little bit of sympathy from a colleague!"

Pedro covered his face with his hands and sighed, "The fact is that I'm not sure we're going to be colleagues for much longer," he said.

"Wh– What? Are you leaving?" stuttered Thomas, pushing his feet deeper into the gravel.

"I may lose my job," said Pedro sharply. His lower lip was trembling.

"But wh– why?"

"Laura's data." Pedro sighed. "There's no trace of it in the archive. I checked it today. Vanished."

"What? But your archival software has always worked perfectly, like a Swiss clock."

"Yes, always, until today. I don't understand how it could have happened."

"But... so... all datasets obtained by Laura last night are lost?"

"Not only last night's data. All datasets that she has taken during the past week and also during her previous visits in the past six months... all wiped from the archive."

"But... how... how is that possible? Anyway, there's a backup copy in the headquarters' central archive in Rome, isn't there?"

"I've checked. Disappeared from the central archive too."

Thomas gawped.

Pedro wrapped his arms around his knees and hid his head between them.

"I don't understand," he said, "it's a mystery. It's not a global fault of the archival system. All the other observing programs are unaffected. Only Laura's program has been hit."

He lifted his head, frowning. "I cannot think of any bug in the archival software that would specifically target Laura's project. And why should any bug affect data only now? There has been no upgrade of the software since last year."

"Are you sure that the system hasn't been hacked?"

"You know it's impossible for any hacker to enter the system!" responded Pedro with a scolding glare, "And anyhow, a hacker would have wiped the entire archive, why would anyone surgically erase only one specific program? Competing scientific interest?" he questioned with a sarcastic tone.

Thomas raised an eyebrow.

Pedro shook his head and sighed. "The director will hold me accountable for this... *I am accountable* for this mess."

"But what could have you done to prevent it?" Thomas tried to comfort him. "This story is so absurd... the whole week has been absurd!"

Pedro turned to face Thomas for the first time since he had arrived. "How much is a night at the TNG telescope worth?" asked Pedro.

"I'm not sure..." Thomas hesitated, "the cost of a single night at modern, large telescopes is in the range of $40,000 to $60,000... I'm not sure specifically for the TNG telescope..."

"Higher than my monthly salary. I would gladly give several months of my salary if this could compensate."

"Does Laura know?"

"Not yet. This morning, soon after the end of her observations, she left in a rush for the airport. She mentioned something about having to go to Florence to attend a conference... hectic life these students. I hadn't discovered the issue yet at that time." Pedro closed his eyes. "I'll have to inform her soon, before she discovers it herself when she tries to download her data from the archive."

Thomas' forehead furrowed. "First the wild telescope, then the vanishing data... if I wasn't a scientist I would say that Laura's project is cursed."

They both remained silent for a while.

Pedro's thoughts were interrupted by the flash of a powerful laser, shot by one of the telescopes. Hitting the upper layers of the atmosphere, the laser had created an artificial star that could be used to correct the effects of atmospheric turbulence, which would otherwise blur astronomical images.

They both looked up at the far end of the beam.

"I always try to see the artificial star at the end of the beam. I know it's too far high to be seen by the naked eye, yet I always try," Thomas said.

The corners of Pedro's mouth curved up. "So do I." Then he added, "Staring as the laser beam fades into eternal distance feels hypnotic and soothing, doesn't it?"

"It does... it does."

Pedro kept staring at the beam for a while.

The laser went off, breaking the spell. A few seconds later the laser was shot again, but now aiming at the centre of the Milky Way.

"They must be observing the supermassive black hole at the core of our galaxy", Pedro said.

He let his gaze drift down along the Milky Way's silvery strip until it reached the dark rim of the crater. The evening breeze had now ceased and the low clouds inside the Caldera were a soft, steadily glowing layer under the shine of the night vault.

Everything was still. Peaceful.

But tonight none of this was of any comfort to him. He stood up and took a deep breath. "Time to share the bad news," he said, "I will start with Laura."

Thomas nodded, "I think the boss can wait a little longer, he's already had enough troubles to deal with this week."

CHAPTER 4

It was a clear, fresh morning. The night had wiped away the mugginess in the city from the previous day. The taxi passed the medieval city walls through Florence's southern majestic gate. Then uphill along a boulevard flanked by high cypress trees and gorgeous villas of different styles, built over the last few centuries.

The beauty and calm of the surroundings was in striking contrast with her physical turmoil and the feeling of her shrunken and churning stomach. The tiredness after the lengthy period of observations at the TNG telescope, together with the tension for her forthcoming presentation at the conference, were a toxic blend. Nausea. She had not had any breakfast, making her even weaker.

The taxi ran past the university's department of physics, home of so many fond memories of when she was an undergraduate student there. She recalled when she was first taught about the wonders of physics. She loved physics. The fact that everything can be explained in terms of a few fundamental laws. Finding out about the discoveries that became part of the history of physics, often gave her goosebumps. Among these, the detection of gravitational waves, which had left her sleepless the night it was announced in a press conference broadcast around the world. Just a graph: two oscillating curves tracing the gravitational waves resulting from the merging of two massive black holes. Laura regarded that simple graph as the Sistine Chapel of physics. Gravitational waves, ripples in space and time produced by any accelerated body. Propagating everywhere and through everything. Making every single particle, every single atom, resonate and vibrate in harmony. The discovery had added a new dimension to the human perception of the universe, offering a radically new way to explore the cosmos.

Her dream would have been to dedicate her graduate studies to gravitational waves, but events brought her to different shores. She was offered a PhD project on exoplanets at the University of Cambridge. Laura wasn't totally convinced by the topic. Although fascinating, there were already several large research groups who had discovered thousands of exoplanets, and she was not sure how she would fit in such a competitive area. After two years of her PhD, doubts still lurked inside her.

She was jolted from her memories by the gleam of the small white domes against the clear blue sky of the early morning. The taxi was passing by the astrophysical observatory on the top of a hill overlooking Florence. The small telescopes inside those domes were now only used for educational activities and public outreach. Inside the offices of the observatory, Laura pictured dozens of astronomers in front of their screens, busy uncovering the mysteries of the cosmos by deciphering data coming from several large telescopes scattered around the globe or floating in space.

As soon as the taxi reached the top of the hill, the view opened out over the gorgeous Tuscan countryside, the multicoloured slopes surrounding Florence. On the ridge of the first hill, in front of the astrophysical observatory, lay a tiny village, which seemed painted on the landscape of vineyards, olive trees and cypresses. It was a cluster of ancient villas and rural houses, in pastel shades, that had preserved their original beauty across the centuries. Among them, in the distance, Laura promptly spotted the outline of one specific villa, their destination, Il Gioello, 'The Jewel'. This was where Galileo Galilei spent the last ten years of his life, after the Roman Catholic Inquisition had tried him for his theories that placed the sun at the centre of our planetary system, and sentenced him to lifelong house arrest. The villa had been recently converted into a centre for conferences in physics and astronomy.

The cab stopped in front of the main entrance gate, a large wooden door, now partly open to let in the last few participants of the conference. Laura entered, slowly, as if entering a private house, as if Galileo was still living there. The entrance led directly into a large garden courtyard. Three sides of the court were surrounded by a colonnade. The side opposite to Laura had a low parapet and opened onto the countryside. Galileo had walked in this courtyard in his last days, nearly blind, pondering over the fantastic implications of the 'new sciences', as he secretly continued his experiments and astronomical observations, despite being forbidden by the Church to pursue any of his studies.

"Good morning. I would like to collect my badge," Laura said, as she approached the registration desk.

"Good morning. Name?" asked the young man behind the table, while pulling a box towards himself.

"Bellini, Laura Bellini."

"Oh, yes, finally! We were getting worried. You are the second speaker on the programme this morning and we haven't seen you the whole week," said the man with a hint of rebuke in his voice. "The session is about to start. Here's your badge and this is the programme."

Laura looked at the programme. The opening talk of the morning was scheduled to be a review presentation by the famous Professor Arthur Cecil-Hood, an authority in the field of exoplanets. Her skin crawled as she saw that she was scheduled to give her short presentation right after Cecil-Hood. The contrast would make her talk even more underwhelming, she thought.

She cautiously entered the main conference room. Most participants had already taken a seat. There were about one hundred of them. She sat in the back row. The first slide of Cecil-Hood's presentation was already projected onto the large screen, with its title displayed in large capital letters: 'A universe of new worlds: the discovery of hundreds of new exoplanets, from exo-Jupiters to exo-Earths'.

"Good morning everyone and welcome to the last day of this exciting conference," the chairman of the session announced loudly, to quieten the hubbub from people still settling.

"We start this morning session with a review by Professor Arthur Cecil-Hood."

A man in his early 60s walked onto the stage. Suit and tie, greying hair, moustache and goatee. With a clear, loud and deep voice, he confidently went through the slides of his presentation. It wasn't really a review of the field, he mainly presented the results from his own team. But it was an engaging and exciting presentation, with several fantastic new datasets from some of the best observatories. He and his team had really discovered hundreds of new planets orbiting other stars, with masses and sizes spanning from Jupiter-like to Earth-like. The presentation was followed by prolonged loud applause.

The chairman of the session stood up. "Thank you, Arthur, for such an exciting presentation. I'm sure there are many questions."

Sure enough, many in the audience had their hands up, but rather than asking questions, most of the delegates praised Cecil-Hood's results and his achievements.

Ten minutes later there were still many hands up. "I'm afraid that we cannot take any more questions, as we need to move on with the programme. You will have the chance to ask Arthur further questions during the coffee break. We shall now move on to the next presentation, by…" he looked at the programme, squinting his eyes and adjusting his spectacles "by Ballimi… er, Ballini, Laura Bellini."

While walking towards the stage she looked at the first slide of her presentation, which was now projected onto the large screen, with the title: 'An algorithm to detect candidate exoplanets from noisy data'.

"Wow, that's an exciting title," whispered someone in the audience, followed by some chuckling.

Her legs were trembling. She tripped on the steps of the stage. The laser pointer slipped from her hands twice. Then she tried to start, avoiding eye contact with the audience.

Her voice was quivering. "I will… I will present an algorithm… an algorithm that I have developed, that can potentially extract information from data in which the signal is weak," she attempted a smile, "you know... low-quality data, datasets that aren't so good, or simply data in which the signatures of interest are very faint... and my algorithm can potentially enable the detection of an exoplanet where other, standard methods may fail. I will show the application of this method to some data that I collected in the past two years and where the signal is..." she coughed "... indeed weak."

As she went on describing her algorithm, she glanced towards the audience. Several people were checking emails or browsing through the internet on their laptops or their phones. The chairman of the session was distracted, looking outside the window.

"These are some of the datasets that we have collected, for the following stars: 61 Cygni, Sigma Draconis, 61 Ursae Majoris, 70 Ophiuchi, 61 Virginis..." The laser spot was trembling on the screen.

"By applying my algorithm to these datasets I have tentatively detected the presence of exoplanets around some of these stars, as illustrated by this slide. Unfortunately, the modest quality of the data does not allow us to extract much information on the properties of these exoplanets... their masses can be anywhere between Earth-like and Jupiter-like, depending on the actual inclination of their orbits."

Laura concluded her presentation with a brief summary, followed by a lukewarm polite applause, which awakened the chairman.

He stood up, cleared his throat and asked, "Any questions?"

No hands were being waved, in contrast with the previous presentation.

Then after a few seconds, Cecil-Hood raised his hand. Laura flinched. Without even waiting for the chairman to give him the floor, he started to speak, "Very interesting presentation. However those datasets are REALLY..." mocking air quotes "... modest quality," and with a sarcastic tone he added, "I would advise you to put more effort into collecting higher quality data than in developing algorithms." His remark triggered giggling in the audience.

Laura gulped. Was that a question? She opened her mouth slightly – no sound came out. Then, nearly stuttering, she said, "We do… we do have more data on these stars, data that I haven't had time to process yet… in fact, I'm just back from an observing run at the TNG telescope, during which I have obtained more data… so the overall quality will improve."

For a split second, it seemed to Laura that Cecil-Hood's face betrayed a mixture of interest and concern. Then his expression returned to his usual, arrogant smile, as he watched her descend the stage.

She dashed out of the conference room with glistening eyes. Behind her, in the distance, the chairman was introducing the next speaker.

Could it have gone any worse? Do not cry, please! Do not cry! She was telling herself while fighting back tears.

She was now by the edge of the courtyard, alone. Soon people would start spreading across the area for the coffee break. The hilly countryside around Florence was open in front of her. Fields of olive trees and vineyards spread all across the surroundings. Some of the olive trees were massive, knotted and twisted. They must have been a few hundred years old. The landscape was probably not too different from when Galileo was living there. Shame flushed her face. Galileo had endured an inquisition, had his theories mocked, and was eventually arrested, silenced and banned from undertaking any further studies. Her self-confidence problems were tiny in comparison. She lowered her head – those thoughts did not help, on the contrary.

A loud round of applause came from the conference room, meaning that the last presentation of the morning session was over. People started pouring out into the patio and courtyard while chattering. The intense aroma of coffee and croissants was pervading the air. Delicious in other circumstances; now it was simply making her stomach churn.

To avoid everyone's gaze, she snuck out of the courtyard and into an isolated corridor. As she pretended to look at a poster, a voice came up beside her. "Miss Bellini?" She closed her eyes, not being in the mood to talk to anyone. Turning, she saw that it was the last person she had expected would come to talk to her.

"Or, should I say Dr Bellini?" asked Professor Arthur Cecil-Hood.

"Not yet," she replied.

"I believe we have never met before," he said, while offering his hand.

"Actually, we met briefly at a conference last year… but you probably don't remember."

Cecil-Hood ignored Laura's last remark. "Your presentation was very…" his eyes flickered "… interesting," he said.

Laura had learnt long ago that, within the ultra-polite British code of conduct, 'interesting' was often used as a euphemism for 'very dull'. But Cecil-Hood had a strange spark in his eyes, which gave her some hope that he had really found something interesting in her presentation.

"I understand that you have collected more data on those stars, which you haven't analysed yet. I would be very glad to help, possib–"

Cecil-Hood was interrupted by a voice coming from behind him, "I'm sure we can handle our data without taking any of Professor Cecil-Hood's precious time. He can certainly wait for our data to be published." The voice came from an elegant woman in her late 50s with short, silver-grey hair.

Cecil-Hood's face was twisted by a grimace of pain, as if the daggers coming from her blue eyes were penetrating the nape of his neck.

While turning towards her, his face made a goofy attempt to transform his grimace into a grin. "Oh, Julia, of course, I didn't mean to interfere… just trying to see if I could be of any help."

Julia did not reply, her tense glare piercing him.

Then, without removing her eyes from him, as if to keep him nailed in his position, she said, "Laura, there is a poster further down the corridor which is of interest for your project."

"Oh… yes… of course, thanks… I'll go to take a look at it. It was a pleasure to meet you, again, Professor Cecil-Hood," said Laura while swiftly leaving the two.

Julia waited until Laura was out of hearing range and then, in a heated tone, said, "Arrogant and sarcastic as ever, aren't you?"

Arthur attempted to reply, "I was just giving some advi–"

But Julia continued without letting him finish his excuse. "The focus of Laura's presentation was her new algorithm, not those test datasets. She is aware that the signal in her data is weak and admitted so explicitly. There was no need to humiliate her."

"Humiliate? Humiliate! You, YOU are talking to me about humiliation!" Arthur replied, now with anger in his tone.

Julia's eyes changed from flaming to drilling. "So it's all about revenge! Personal revenge towards me. You are still holding events from over 30 years ago against me."

"Revenge towards you? But I didn't even know that she was a student of yours!"

"Of course you knew, my name was on the first slide of her presentation." She paused and then continued, "Anyway, for the record, I did not humiliate you at all. It very simply did not work out between us. I acknowledged it and you failed to acknowledge it. Period." With that she strode away.

***

Julia reached Laura at the end of the corridor. Upon seeing her, Laura started with an apologetic tone, "Julia, I'm terribly sorry for my horrible performance this morning. You wanted me to come to this conference with the specific purpose of advertising our work and I have disappointed you…"

Julia interrupted her with a warm and kind tone, "Don't be silly. You haven't disappointed me. You did great. You presented all the results clearly and rigorously, that's what matters." Then she continued with a concerned expression, "But you really look unwell!"

"Yes, I'm not at my best today. My body still feels like it's come off the night-shift and I'm probably still exhausted from the challenging observations at the TNG… also," she continued with a knot in her throat and misty eyes, "I guess the tension for this conference didn't help."

Julia couldn't help hugging her. "Take a cab, go back to your hotel and have a good rest," she said.

Laura nodded, her head still buried in Julia's shoulder. She stepped back, wiping her eyes, and looked at the far end of the corridor. In the distance, Cecil-Hood was sipping coffee and talking with a swarm of colleagues that had surrounded him.

"How do you know Cecil-Hood?" Laura asked.

Julia looked at Cecil-Hood for a few seconds. Then she said, "I met him in Cambridge, long ago, when I started my PhD. Everything was new and fascinating. It was an easy game for Arthur, also a PhD student, self-confident and a few years older than me, to ensnare me into a relationship." She sighed, "But it did not last more than a year, as I realised that he was not the kind of person that could be my companion for life." She shook her head, "Arthur did not take it lightly. Being dumped was not something he would accept easily. Apparently, it hit him so hard that it is still wounding his pride and his ego."

With widened eyes, Laura looked again at Cecil-Hood, who was now gesturing with his hand and speaking more loudly, in response to the growing interest of the colleagues around him.

"Why…" she paused and frowned. "Why is he so interested in our datasets? To the point of offering his help to analyse them?"

"I've been wondering the same thing," commented Julia.

"Maybe he realised he had been a bit harsh on me and wanted to be kind?" proposed Laura.

"Ah! You don't know Arthur. He would never offer any of his 'precious time' just to be kind. If he is willing to invest some of his time it means that he has some vested interest. He must be expecting to get something out of our data, something that he deems particularly intriguing."

Laura waited silently for a few seconds. Julia was frowning and motionless, staring at Cecil-Hood.

Then Laura broke the silence, "So, I'll take your advice and leave to get some rest. I'm staying at a friend of mine's."

"Yes, please, go and have some rest," Julia said, jolted from her thoughts. "I guess I'll see you in Cambridge next week."

"Yes. As I mentioned to you, tomorrow I'm going to San Gimignano to spend the weekend with my family, but I'll be at the Institute on Monday morning."

"Of course, they are so close to Florence that you shouldn't waste this opportunity to visit them."

As Laura was walking away, Julia called out to her, "Laura, have you heard back from that Russian scientist?"

"No, nothing at all."

"Weird. He sounded so keen to talk with us."

Laura shrugged. Then she walked to the conference main room to collect her bag. She pulled her phone out of her pocket to call a cab and only then did she notice that there was an unanswered call. It was from the previous evening, from a foreign number that she could not recognise. She frowned. After a few second of hesitation, she decided to call it back. An automated voice message started playing. It was in a foreign language that she could not understand. She hung up and searched the internet to check what country the prefix was from – Russia!

CHAPTER 5

Professor Arthur Cecil-Hood was admiring the view of Florence from his window. The hotel was located on one of the hills surrounding the city. The last feeble tints of dusk were blending with the warm lighting of the city and its monuments.

The intense scent of wisteria cascading around the open window was filling his nostrils.

He was staring at Santa Croce, the magnificent church holding the tombs of prominent artists and scientists such as Michelangelo and Galileo, to name just two. Not far from it, dominating the city, was the dome of Florence's cathedral —Brunelleschi's dome. A masterpiece of architecture, art and engineering. At that time, carpenters did not have scaffolding high enough to sustain the structure during its construction, so it was virtually impossible to build such a high dome. But Brunelleschi managed to overcome the technical constraints and made the impossible possible. He designed the dome as an ingenious system of concentric rings that made the huge structure self-supporting while being constructed, with the void gaping beneath the carpenters. Such an innovative architectural system was not implemented at the expense of the dome's beauty and elegance. When Michelangelo left Florence and headed to Rome to build Saint Peter's Cathedral, he waved to Brunelleschi's dome with the words "I'm going to Rome to build your sister, who will be bigger than you, but not more beautiful." Quite so, Arthur thought.

He, Professor Arthur Cecil-Hood, had not yet produced any masterpiece. No. He was internationally recognised as a leader in his field but had not achieved any outstanding major discovery that would warrant him a place in the history of science. At the age of 62, he was now approaching retirement.

But he might now have one last chance.

What he had heard that morning was deeply disturbing and deeply exciting at the same time. Yet... stupid! Idiot! Couldn't his arrogance refrain from prompting him to make his usual sarcastic comments? Openly and in front of a large audience! He had attracted attention to what should have remained below the radar. Everything would now be more difficult.

Attempting to approach Julia and her student again would not be practical, he had totally messed up that chance. He could not wait for their data to be published.

But there was another option. Yes, another option.

He trembled. The air of the evening was becoming cooler. No, it was not cooler, he admitted to himself. The fact was that he was getting uncomfortably close to the boundaries of scientific research ethics. Close to the red line that no scientist should ever cross.

He narrowed his eyes. He would also have to admit that he had been wrong. Most people would not even remember after so long. After 30 years. But that person… that person would remember, for sure. A blow to his pride. But he was ready to admit that he had been mistaken, ready to subdue his ego for a moment, if that was what was needed to achieve his goal, to grab this last chance.

Whatever that implied, ethical or unethical, pride or humiliation, that was the only viable option.

Reluctantly, he searched an online directory. He found the contact details he was looking for and started writing the message.

CHAPTER 6

Laura was lying on her bed, facing the ceiling, eyes wide open.

She heard keys rattling, unlocking the apartment door, followed by quick steps approaching her room. Sofia appeared at the door, without entering. She looked at Laura, her forehead creasing. "How did it go?" she asked.

"I'd rather not talk about it," replied Laura, flatly, while still staring at the ceiling.

Sofia waited by the entrance for a few seconds, staring at her without saying a word. Then she went to sit on the bed next to Laura and pulled something out of her purse. "These may cheer you up," she said while waving two colourful pieces of paper.

Laura raised an eyebrow.

"I managed to get two complimentary tickets for a concert this evening. They're playing Bach's *Brandenburg Concertos*," said Sofia.

Laura narrowed her eyes. Sofia had connections everywhere and could always find free tickets to an event… or at least friends who let her in at the back door.

Laura sighed, "Thanks, but I don't think I feel up to it at the moment. Not only, but tomorrow morning I have to leave early to take the coach to San Gimignano."

"They're playing in the Accademia," interrupted Sofia.

"You mean *the* Accademia?"

"Yes and–"

"Give me twenty minutes to take a shower and put something on," Laura interrupted, jumping out of bed.

"…it's part of an initiative by the Florence City Council aimed at organising concerts and events in venues traditionally associated only with the visual arts…" but Sofia was talking to the air, as Laura was already in the shower.

***

As they arrived in front of the Galleria dell'Accademia, the usher urged them to enter and take a seat, as the concert was about to start.

They entered the main hall, which was now holding several rows of chairs, all of which taken by the audience. The event was apparently fully booked. She had no idea how Sofia had managed to find two tickets. Laura did not want to know.

While the usher was guiding them to their seats, Laura couldn't help stopping in front of one of Michelangelo's *Prigioni*. Four unfinished sculptures, representing four male slaves, still enshrouded in the blocks of marble out of which they were partially carved.

These sculptures revealed how Michelangelo gave shape and created nearly living bodies out of dull, blank pieces of stone. He did not see a plain block of marble, as all common people would, his mind could picture the body living inside it, which his talent set free. Laura noticed a Latin inscription at the base of the half-carved marble block. This must have been part of an ancient Roman building, which had been reused by Michelangelo for this sculpture. Matter in transformation, as everywhere in the universe, but here shaped into superior forms by the human intellect across the ages.

The hostess prompted Laura and Sofia to take their seats, apparently the last two available ones.

From there Laura could see Him clearly, standing majestically at the end of the hall. Michelangelo's *David*. Magnificent. Breathtaking. He was the real reason she had accepted Sofia's invitation. She came here often when she lived in Florence, spending hours in awe, admiring this masterpiece. *David*. Splendid, noble, glorious, and at the same time peaceful, unassuming and humble, despite the feat he had just achieved. Triumph without glamour. This young man had just used his intellect to defeat the giant Goliath.

Laura interpreted this sculpture as human intellect defeating gross stupidity, which so often rules the world. This statue gave hope, hope to small people like her, that they can change things, even gigantic things that may appear unmovable and oppressive.

The members of the orchestra started taking their seats around the base of the statue. Soon Bach's heavenly music soared around Michelangelo's masterpiece.

As Laura was contemplating David being lifted by the divine harmony, she was distracted by the gaze of an elderly man who was sitting in the row in front of her and who had twisted his head sideways in an effort to look at her. As she looked back at him, he smiled. Laura snapped her head back to the orchestra. From the corner of her eye, she saw that he was still beaming at her. She noticed his thick glasses with a thick purple frame and his abundant and uncombed fluffy white hair. If it wasn't for these peculiar features she would not have recognised him, as at the conference he had been dressed very casually, with a chequered shirt, shorts and sandals. Here he was dressed up, with a grey suit and (tartan) bow tie, probably out of respect for the place, or the concert, or, most likely, both. Laura responded with a shy smile. The man nodded and turned to face the orchestra. She tried to focus on the concert, but her gaze kept shifting towards that curious stranger. Bach's music now sounded like a plain sequence of disconnected notes.

**

The first part of the concert finished with a standing ovation. The audience was in awe. It was not clear what they were clapping for, whether the orchestra's performance, Bach's genius or Michelangelo's talent. Probably a blend of them all.

People started to drift towards the refreshment area. Laura noted that the elderly man with purple glasses and the tartan bow tie was slaloming between chairs and people in an attempt to reach her, and finally succeeded.

"Miss Bellini, it's a pleasure to meet you here," he said with a German accent.

"Good evening, Professor… umm…"

"Schneider, Gerard Schneider. Don't feel embarrassed about not knowing me, I'm retired, emeritus at the University of Heidelberg. I still like going to conferences to keep myself up to date, but not often, so I don't think we've previously met." He adjusted his spectacles and continued, "Anyway, I just wanted to congratulate you for your presentation this morning. The results that you showed are truly interesting."

Laura simpered, "Maybe you are confusing my presentation with that of some other speaker."

"Not at all, I remember very well.'

"Then it seems you were one of the very few in the audience who found my results of any interest."

"Don't put yourself down," he sighed, shaking his head, "many discoveries and great minds had to pass through down periods, were not recognised, or even humiliated… shall I recall Galileo? Also in more modern times some important theories and discoveries of remarkable scientists were ignored or even ridiculed at the beginning. Einstein's theory of relativity is a classic example. It has also happened outside the fields of physics and astronomy. Just think of Darwin, widely mocked for his theory of evolution. Geniuses have also been humiliated well beyond the boundaries of science…" he said, glancing at the orchestra, where a few of the musicians were sorting their music sheets in preparation, "Bach's original sheets of this divine music were allegedly sold as butter paper."

Laura looked at the orchestra for a few moments in silence. "I appreciate that you want to cheer me up… but I think you're exaggerating a little bit," she said while giving him a half-smile, "you're comparing me with people who have not only changed the history of science, but also transformed society and our human spirit".

"Yes, sorry, I didn't mean to overstate," replied Schneider with a grin, "I just meant to emphasise that, not infrequently, good scientific results are deemed unimportant, unfairly disregarded or even ignored." A shadow of concern crossed his face, wiping away his grin. "Scientists are humans and, as all human beings, sometimes tend to conformity. Scientific results following the dominant research directions get much more attention and praise than the alternative, new views. This is what has sometimes limited progress in science: refraining from thinking outside the box."

Laura looked at him intensely and raised an eyebrow.

Schneider continued, his features softening, "Junior scientists like you have much to offer. They approach research with a fresh mind, much more open to new ways of investigating the universe. Their research spirit has not yet been narrowed, not yet channelled through the mainstream research paths."

Laura's forehead creased. "Well, I can confidently say that I'm not in the 'mainstream' of scientific research, but I'm not sure it's really doing me any good."

Schneider smiled, "I'm sure we think alike. The only difference between us is that you believe not being in the mainstream is your weakness, while I believe it's your strength."

Laura looked into Schneider's small, yet penetrating eyes. She, an inexperienced student, realised that, unexpectedly, she had much in common with this retired professor, whose quiet wisdom had matured throughout a lengthy career. Their conversation was on a different level, above the multitude of active and hectic professional scientists, too busy and too focused on their research to ponder about any of this.

From the side Sofia broke the profound silence between the two, "Sorry to interrupt with more mundane matters, but if we want to take advantage of the interval to grab a cup of coffee then we may need to move on."

Sofia's words jolted Laura from her trance, "Sorry, how rude of me, Professor Schneider, this is Sofia, a friend of mine. She is an architect."

Schneider beamed at Sofia, "Nice to meet you. You must be quite in your environment here," he said, gesturing around the whole Accademia.

Sofia beamed back, "Quite so."

Then, as they were walking towards the cafeteria, Schneider turned to Laura again.

"Anyway, I didn't mean to bore you with a philosophical discussion. I just wanted to tell you that I'm sure your data contains some delightful surprises. I think you want to contact Professor Vladimir Kasparov."

Laura's ears pricked up. "Actually he has already contacted me and my supervisor."

"I'm not surprised, he must be very excited."

"Can you tell me what it's about?"

Schneider grinned, "I don't want to spoil Kasparov's surprise."

***

Laura could not fully enjoy the rest of the concert and the sight of the masterpieces in the Accademia. Professor Schneider's words kept resonating in her mind.

What was in Kasparov's data... and in her own data?

Did her datasets really contain something particularly interesting that she could not identify herself? What had attracted the attention of Professor Schneider during her presentation that morning? She mentally scanned her slides: the description of her new, dull methodology, some noisy data, half-baked results reporting the potential detection of a few exoplanets, amid hundreds of new and far more exciting exoplanets reported by Professor Cecil-Hood in his presentation earlier that morning. She shook her head – nothing, she could not spot anything remarkable, nothing that could potentially be of great interest.

The only explanation was that Kasparov must have had some additional information, the key to properly interpreting her data... or was it something else?

CHAPTER 7

Most of his colleagues were active in research and teaching, and had to fly straight back home. But being retired, Professor Gerard Schneider could take advantage of the trip to visit some museums and wander the old narrow streets of the city centre. Or, perhaps, having been to Florence many times, he would take a short train ride and visit the Italian Riviera, a narrow coastal strip on north-western Italy where high mountains dive into the Mediterranean Sea. This was a coastline studded with picturesque, colourful old fishing villages clinging onto steep, high cliffs.

The train was now chugging through the countryside of the north-western tip of Tuscany, between the shore and the Apuan Alps. Gerard noticed the white peaks of the mountains. From this distance, they looked as if they were covered in snow. But it wasn't snow. These were marble quarries, the source of some of the finest marble in the world, since ancient times. Michelangelo would personally come here to select some of the marble blocks for his sculptures.

This reminded him of his conversation with Laura Bellini at the Galleria dell'Accademia the night before. He was sure that, with the help of Kasparov, she was going to be thrilled by what was hidden in her data. That morning, before departing, he also took the liberty of sending a short message of encouragement and congratulations to Kasparov, but he did not want to interfere much more. And anyway, enough about science, for the next couple of days he had planned only leisure, on the Italian Riviera… although, he grinned, science was leisure for him too.

His first stop was Portovenere, a beautiful, small harbour laid on a ness, overlooked by a medieval fortress. Next to it, the 'Gulf of Poets'. It was where Lord Byron used to spend most of his days when visiting the Riviera to find inspiration for his romantic poems. It was also where he went swimming, sometimes even crossing the large creek to reach Lerici, the village on the opposite side, where yet another British poet, his friend Shelley, lived.

But Portovenere was not Gerard's final destination.

He reached Riomaggiore, the first of the Cinque Terre. These were five small fishing villages, located on such steep, high cliffs and with high mountains just behind them, that they were originally only accessible by boat.

Amber to carnelian – crowded houses painted in all the warm hues. Sapphire blue – the sea, with its foamy waves crashing onto the majestic silvery cliffs. Emerald – the vegetation sprouting from the terraced mountains. Gerard was overwhelmed by the colours, almost dizzy from them.

He started his walk along the Via dell'Amore, the Love Path. This was a narrow track carved out of the steep coastal cliffs, connecting the first two villages. It was supposedly once used by lovers in the two villages to meet each other, to avoid their parents' scolding glares. The view was breathtaking. About 40 metres beneath the path, waves violently crashed on the rocks, adding a light tint of drama to the beautiful landscape. The salty smell of the sea blended with the aroma of the Mediterranean vegetation. Intoxicated by beauty and nature, he took a deep breath.

He sat on a low parapet made of stones flanking the path. He became pleasantly mesmerised by the rhythmic splashing of the waves beneath him and the foam patterns that formed in the deep water.

Next to him, he noticed a small flower that had stubbornly grown out of a crack in the parapet. He got closer to admire the various shades of violet of its petals. He had always been fascinated by how some of the most beautiful forms of life could sprout out of the harshest environments.

Suddenly, the petals started to curl, the stem to droop. The flower quickly withered onto the rock. Gerard rubbed his eyes in disbelief. Had he just witnessed a paranormal phenomenon? Having been fully taken by the rapid transformation of the flower, he had not realised that it was now hot. Very hot. Too hot to be real. He realised that the heat was not outside, but within him. His body was burning up inside. This was not possible. Was the beauty of the place sending him into raptures, like the romantic poets, to the point of experiencing a sort of passionate fever, yielding to hallucinations and internal turmoil?

No, this was real. The flower was really lying wrinkled and lifeless on the rock. And he was really hot… and in pain. Unbearable pain. What was suddenly happening inside him? He tried to scream for help, but his throat was burning too. The heat was spreading throughout his entire body. The burning inside was overwhelming. He was losing consciousness, his weight tilting on the parapet.

The last thing he felt was the refreshing sea spray, before crashing onto the rocks.

CHAPTER 8

Laura squinted her eyes as the blazing afternoon sunlight reflected off the wheat fields. This was her homeland, but she was no longer used to such a flood of light.

The car was winding along the twisted road, through the gentle hills scattered with some cypress trees.

She needed this. To recharge. To wipe away her blue thoughts with these golden wavy slopes.

The loud sound of cicadas was overwhelming, touching thousands of chords, bringing to life memories from her childhood.

She looked at the man at the wheel, smiling. Then, with a touch of humour in her voice, she commented, "Dad, you're wearing the same shirt as when you took me to the airport, one year ago. It seems like you haven't changed it since."

"Well, I think I have a total of three shirts, so the likelihood of you seeing me in the same shirt is pretty high."

"Yes, the same three shirts for the last twenty years. Daaaaad! You are neglecting yourself."

"Oh, come on, we live in the countryside, I don't really need to dress up or follow any fashion trends, and as far as my job is concerned, its dress code," he said laughing, "doesn't leave much scope to the imagination."

Laura's father was a chef. Born in Sicily, he had travelled across most of Italy before settling in Tuscany, where he met and married Laura's mother. His cuisine was a delicious blend of Sicilian and Tuscan flavours, sprinkled with inspiration from the whole of Italian culinary tradition.

Deciding that it was pointless to argue any further, Laura changed the subject. "So, naughty little Emma didn't bother to come to the coach station with you to pick me up, did she?"

"Actually, I'm to blame. I left her home to look after some stuff in the oven. But the official version," he grinned, "is that she didn't come because she's offended that you missed her 18th birthday."

"I know," said Laura with a grimace, "I'm so sorry. And I'm sorry that I haven't been back home for so long." She looked down. "Is Emma really angry at me?"

Her father laughed, "Emma angry? Emma? Angry?" he laughed even more loudly, "You *have* been away for too long!"

Laura's home, her real home, was a refurbished farm, on top of a hill in the countryside between the medieval town of San Gimignano and the Etruscan town of Volterra, south of Florence and north of Siena. As the car came to a stop in the yard in front of the house, a dog approached the car, barking, jumping and wagging its tail. A young woman came out of the front door, arms open, giggling and screaming. Emma, Laura's sister.

Laura's mum had passed away giving birth to Emma. Laura was never sure whether to feel sorry for Emma because she could not know Mum, or be glad for her that she did not have to go through the pain of missing her. One thing was for sure, while passing away her mum must have transferred all her energy to Emma, as Emma was the most lively and joyful person Laura knew.

Emma jumped on Laura, hugging her vigorously and yelling with joy, "I've missed you so much!" Then, in fake anger, she complained, "You naughty girl, you haven't been home in so long, you even missed my 18th birthday party."

"I know," said Laura apologetically, "the past year has been so dense with observing runs, confer–"

"I don't care," interrupted Emma with a mock snotty tone, "too bad for you." Then she smiled and, with a wink, she whispered, "You don't know what you've missed… and *someone* was even more disappointed than me that you were not there…"

Laura whispered back, "You shall tell me later," with a knowing smile.

***

Laura and Emma spent most of the afternoon chatting about their parallel lives, everything they had experienced over the past year apart, both insignificant and profound.

Later in the evening, Laura enjoyed the sun setting on the mellow hills while swinging on a hammock stretched between an oak and a pine tree. Blank mind, just enjoying the warmth of the last sunbeams. The sound of cicadas was slowly softening, but still accompanying her rocking.

It occurred to her that she had promised the TNG telescope operator to submit a report of her observing run by the end of the week. She pulled herself together with a sigh and opened her laptop, wincing as she saw three unexpected messages.

The first message was from Pedro, the archive manager of the TNG telescope. He was informing her that, because of an inexplicable glitch of the archive, all the data acquired by her during the last six months had been lost, including the data obtained during her last observing run. Laura gasped. She trusted the telescope archival system. But now she had to admit that Julia had been right when she suggested making a copy on an external hard drive. "It is always useful to have an additional local copy of data," she had said. Laura suspected that the real reason was that Julia was not entirely comfortable relying on the archival system. She preferred the 'old way'. Laura reached inside her bag and extracted a hard drive, which she had used to copy all the data from all observing runs, including the last one. Julia had been quite visionary. Laura quickly wrote a note to Pedro, reassuring him that fortunately she had a personal copy of all the data obtained during all her observing runs. This would come as a relief to him, she thought.

The second message was from the organisers of the conference in Florence:

> *Dear participants,*
> *it is with profound sadness that we inform you that our*
> *colleague and friend Professor Gerard Schneider passed*
> *away today in a tragic accident.*

*During the conference this week, we were all lucky enough
to enjoy the last few days of his lively and enthusiastic
contributions to astronomy.*

The message went on with an extensive obituary, outlining
Professor Schneider's career and his scientific achievements.

Goosebumps covered her skin. She had met him last night,
when they had that odd conversation in front of Michelangelo's
David. She was probably the last scientist who had interacted
with him before his death. His words were now echoing in her
mind. 'Junior scientists like you have much to offer…'

Laura spent a few minutes staring at the sunset.

The high-pitched cry of a passing swallow broke the spell.

The third message was from a student at the Special
Astronomical Observatory in Russia, where Professor Vladimir
Kasparov worked, and was addressed to both Laura and Julia.

Dear Ms Bellini and Prof Russell,

*I am a student at the Russian Special Astronomical
Observatory and I was working in collaboration with
Professor Kasparov.*

*I am aware that he contacted the two of you in relation to
your research project and some old data that he obtained
a long time ago.*

*I regret to inform you that Professor Kasparov died earlier
this week.*

*I must say that the circumstances of his death are quite
puzzling. The police are charging a friend of mine with
manslaughter; they are also considering the possibility
of murder.*

She quickly closed the laptop and, trembling, put it back into her bag.

The long shadow of a cypress, cast by the setting sun, slowly enshrouded the bag.

Then, she reached in, pulled the laptop out again, took a deep breath, and continued reading.

But I think the death of Professor Kasparov is far more mysterious, and I have reason to believe that it may actually be linked to your research project and the data he wanted to share with you.

I would be most grateful if you could share all possible information about your recent project, which apparently had attracted Professor Kasparov's interest just before his accident. Your project may hold the key to solving the mystery surrounding his death and help get my friend out of prison.

I would be grateful if we could talk about this over the phone. I tried reaching out to you, but was unsuccessful. Of course, it would be even better if you could visit me at the Special Observatory, so that we could discuss your project and the potential connections with Professor Kasparov's death in detail.

Looking forward to hearing from you.

Sergei Vasiliev
PhD Student at the Special Russian Observatory

Laura blanched.

She read it again… *death… murder… your research project…* A chill passed through her bones.

She raised an eyebrow as she saw that Julia had already replied. Julia was a brilliant scientist, and, like many brilliant scientists, she was extremely curious, always eager to learn more. The potential existence of intriguing data somehow connected to their research project was something she would not resist investigating.

Laura opened Julia's response mail and quickly skimmed through it '…very sad …unfortunate …we will be there on Tuesday.'

Wh– What? 'We'? Julia had taken it for granted that she would fly with her to Russia to help with such a messy story involving the mysterious death of a scientist. No way! She would talk to Julia as soon as they were both back in Cambridge.

She was still looking at the screen, frowning, when Emma arrived and jumped on the hammock, making Laura's laptop jolt on her lap. "Look at this tattoo that I got on my ankle!" she said while the hammock was rocking and shaking.

"Be careful, Emma!" yelled Laura grasping the laptop with both hands.

"I'm sorry. I didn't think I was being too careless," Emma frowned, looking at the sunset. "Not long ago you enjoyed swinging with me on the hammock."

"I'm sorry. I'm just a little jumpy."

"What's the matter? You looked so relaxed and peaceful until a few minutes ago."

"I've just read a few distressing messages."

"Distressing?" asked Emma, trying to peek at Laura's laptop.

"I prefer not to talk about them," said Laura curtly, with a touch of irritation in her tone, and swiftly closed the laptop.

Emma glanced at her with a worried look.

Laura took a deep breath and, with a calmer tone, said, "Nothing… it's just that during the last few days there has been a sequence of disturbing events. Altogether, they have upset me a little bit."

Emma leaned towards her. "What kind of disturbing events?" she asked.

Laura decided to skip over her shameful performance at the conference the day before and only tell the few facts that she had just learnt by reading her emails, "Briefly… many of my datasets have been accidentally erased from a telescope archive. A Russian professor, who attempted to contact me about my project, died in obscure circumstances. Another German professor that I met yesterday evening also died in an accident today."

"Wow... what are the odds?" Emma whispered.

"What do you mean?" asked Laura frowning.

"What are the odds that, in just a few days, three unusual events happen, and all of them are somehow connected with you?..." she responded. "You must have done something," she added with a half-smile and with a pinch of jokiness in her tone.

Laura's jaw dropped. She rewound her own words in her mind... *my... me... I...* in her ingenuity Emma had identified one single feature in common to all those recent, strange events: *herself*.

Emma was right, what were the odds?

"I think you should take a proper break," her sister said, interrupting her thoughts, "and not look at your emails."

"You're right," Laura responded shaking her head, "it was a mistake, those messages have ruined my day."

"I think Dad's dinner will fix it," said Emma, nodding towards their father, who was setting the outdoor table in the distance.

Laura's expression softened. "I expect so," she said. Then she looked at Emma disapprovingly, trying to hide her smile, and added, "Let's see this tattoo."

Emma revealed her ankle with a proud expression.

Laura raised a brow. "Isn't that a little bit excessive?" she commented, "What did Dad say?"

"I don't think he's noticed it yet," responded Emma, followed by a cunning smirk.

"But look at this other tattoo," said Emma with excitement, while exposing a more intimate part of her body.

Laura's eyes widened. "Emma! But... but what if the two of you split up?" she commented in disbelief.

Emma looked up, narrowing her eyes. "Good point," she said. Then she shrugged.

Laura shook her head.

"Hey! There is more important stuff to think about now," exclaimed Emma, looking at their father in the distance, who was bringing out a casserole with some steaming food in it.

"Enough chitchatting, the two of you," he said loudly, "and come over here, dinner's ready."

"I'm not that hungry," said Laura, walking with Emma towards the table.

"Don't worry, it's a light dinner… just a few things I threw together," he responded while arranging some dishes.

Laura sat down with a smile and ended up feasting on everything that was on the table. *Arancini* stuffed with spiced *ragù* and peas, or with spinach and buffalo mozzarella. Crispy *bruschetta,* fragrant with garlic, dripping fruity olive oil from the last crop. Steaming *parmigiana* with the aroma of fried local aubergines and melting parmesan cheese. A platter of matured sheep cheese, *pecorino*, spread with chestnut honey. Another platter of locally produced *prosciutto*, sliced so thin it melted in her mouth, and *finocchiona* (fennel salami). Finally, crunchy Sicilian *cannoli* freshly stuffed with delicious ricotta.

After the 'light' dinner she went back on the hammock to sip liquorice liqueur, while looking at the twilight spotted with the glow of the first, brightest stars.

She was slowly slipping into dreamland when Emma woke her up with a thrilled voice, "Bedtime story!" she said, waving a book in front of her.

Since Emma was a baby, Laura was the one who would read her bedtime stories in the evening, as their father was always home late because of his job. At that time, Laura was still young enough for the bedtime story to have a soporific effect also on herself, and she often fell asleep next to Emma.

After they had grown up they had preserved the same evening habit. Now that Laura was living far away, whenever she was back home she was glad to repeat the same childish ritual, as if needed to reaffirm their profound bond.

Laura smiled, rolling her eyes, pretending that this was a nuisance. "Of course…"

CHAPTER 9

Perfect.

The timing could not be better.

Saturday night. The Institute was deserted.

Even students close to their thesis submission were taking a break at pubs or having fun in Cambridge. Laura had extended her trip to the weekend, so there was no risk that she might show up.

He darted along the dark corridor, passing by the offices of the cosmologists. He had always felt a mixture of awe and reverence for their area of research, cosmology. Understanding how everything came to be and how everything will end. The ultimate goal of the human mind and the human spirit.

After a few more steps he reached Laura's office. The door was not locked. Under the light of an angle lamp on Laura's desk, he grabbed all the notes that Laura had in her drawers and on the shelves, and started taking pictures, just as Thuban had instructed him.

He did not understand how any of these notes could be of any interest to Thuban. Actually, he didn't know anything about Thuban apart from his code name, and that he was impatient to obtain information about Laura's research and findings.

'Anything, anything you can find out about her research, her data, her findings. Anything!' was his last message.

Thuban was the Arabic name of a star in the Draco constellation, the constellation of the dragon. The ancient Arabs had been pioneers in astronomy, and many stars still kept their original Arabic names. It was fascinating, but the star associated with the code name of his mysterious contact sounded quite eerie to him. Thuban means 'snake' in Arabic.

If that was not enough, Thuban was particularly interested in stars that Laura might have observed in the constellation of Ophiuchus, the constellation of the 'serpent bearer' in Greek mythology.

He was not sure what to think. All of these names associated with snakes, dragons and ancient mythologies. A chill passed through his bones. Was Thuban part of a cult worshipping some ancient evil divinity?

Thuban was a star with yet another peculiarity, often forgotten. It had been the polar star between the fourth and second millennium BC, when civilisation was born. Did Thuban believe he was the ancient guide of human civilisation?

Whatever the possible explanation, it was highly disturbing to him. But it was too late to have second thoughts, he was now too heavily involved. No way back.

He then accessed Laura's desktop computer. It was far too easy. Laura had simply kept the same password that was given as default by the IT managers to all new users at the Institute, with the recommendation to 'change it as soon as possible!' It seemed that she had not expected anyone to ever have any interest in entering her account.

He rapidly skimmed through the various folders. The datasets on Laura's computer were the same that she had published in her recent article, nothing new for Thuban. Any new datasets obtained during the last few months must have been stored in the telescope archives, and Laura had not downloaded them yet.

He sent the content of some folders to Thuban, unsure whether they would be of any interest. He also sent the photos of Laura's notes along with a short report. Then he swiftly left the Institute.

He wondered when Thuban would read his report. He had assumed that Thuban was based in the UK, but in principle, he could be anywhere. Communications had always been through written messages, so he had never had any chance to hear his voice and guess his location from his accent.

***

Thuban sipped from a glass while reading the report. No recent data on Laura's computer. Had the only copy of the new data been on the telescope archives?

The stakes were too high. Additional action must be undertaken.

Thuban stood up and looked outside the window, in deep thought. Venus was as shiny as ever.

CHAPTER 10

Laura was awakened by Venus shining in through the open window of Emma's bedroom. She had fallen asleep next to her sister, with the book still lying open on her chest.

Quietly, she got out of bed.

Venus' aura was so bright that she could walk out of the house without switching on any lights.

The chant of a multitude of crickets was blending into a mellow melody. She walked barefoot through the fields, stroking the soft wheat ears with her hands.

Vega was now the brightest star in the sky. Her redder brothers, Sirius and Arcturus, were already dormant below the horizon, so she could freely diffuse her sapphire light over her glittering siblings.

A thin ruby slice of moon was peeking out behind San Gimignano's medieval towers in the distance. On the opposite side of the horizon, Volterra recalled her ancient roots.

A light breeze gently stirred a glowing sea of fireflies, creating waves of light, slowly passing by her. Just like gravitational waves, which in that very moment were passing through her, making every molecule, every atom in her body vibrate in harmony. Waves coming from celestial bodies at cosmic distances and waves coming from the swinging trees around her. Her own pulsing heart and the blood flowing in her veins were creating waves, which, no matter how weak, were dispersing everywhere and resonating with everything. The waves from her first heartbeat had reached Vega by now, and would continue travelling, reaching the fringes of the cosmos.

No matter what would happen to her, her waves would keep travelling forever and everywhere. She was expanding over the entire universe, and the whole universe was passing through her. Truly.

CHAPTER 11

Lieutenant Corelli struggled to remove the last strip of police tape, under the eyes of a tourist couple. The Love Path had been closed to the public since the day before. While the woman in front of him was impatiently tapping her flip-flops with her arms crossed, he was sweating in his uniform, although the early morning sun was still gentle and had not yet lifted the freshness lingering from the previous night.

Eventually he decided to simply cut the tape.

"Can we pass now?" asked the tourist, annoyed.

Corelli stood up, grunting and glaring at her. Then he turned to face Captain Esposito who was a few metres away, leaning on the parapet and looking down the cliff.

"Captain, can we let people pass now?" he asked.

Captain Esposito glanced at him and replied, "Yes, we're done."

As Corelli nodded at the two tourists, they sighed and strode past him. Are they truly going to appreciate the breathtaking walk? He thought.

He approached Captain Esposito who was staring at the spot where the crashed body had been found. The last few stains of blood were being washed away by the waves. She shook her head.

"Is something perplexing you, Captain?" Corelli asked.

"This death," she sighed, "it doesn't make sense."

Corelli tilted his head. "It's certainly not the first accident of this type that we have had. This area is as wonderful as it is perilous. Especially during the summer season we are used to dealing with quite a few casualties. Inexperienced climbers, reckless swimmers, careless strollers... you name it."

"Yes, I know, but this doesn't seem like the other accidents."

"Why?" Corelli joined her in looking down at the scarlet spotted rocks. "That elderly man probably leaned too far to see the cliff and watch the splashing waves. Raptured by the view, he may have lost his balance and fell."

"Maybe. But have you read the autopsy report?" she asked, now facing him.

"Erm," he hesitated, "yes… well, I skimmed through it… a crashed skull, a few broken bones, multiple concussions, nothing unexpected from a 40 metre fall."

"Have you read the part about the burns?" she asked frowning.

"Yes, there was something about burns, so what?" he shrugged, "We continuously see tourists with sunburns. They're often too late to realise how strong the sun can hit over here."

"Those were not ordinary sunburns! The whole body was burned and… deep inside it."

Lieutenant Corelli twisted his mouth to the side, thoughtful. "Well, it took a few hours for the corpse to be discovered. Yesterday was a very hot day. Dark surfaces can reach very high temperatures under the blazing sun, we know that very well from the asphalt, sometimes even exceeding 80 degrees. Some of those rocks down there are quite dark and may have created a sort of oven around the body."

"I thought about it too, but look," said Captain Esposito pointing down, "the poor man crashed in a recess, between very high rocks. The direct sun rays do not really make it in there for most of the day, maybe only very late in the afternoon," she added while glancing to the West. Then she looked down again squinting her eyes. "You can even see some seaweeds in that recess, they wouldn't survive if that spot became terribly hot during the day." She turned her back to the sea, frowned and concluded, "No, that cannot be an explanation for the burns *on and inside* the corpse." She sat on the parapet and leaned backwards on her arms.

Corelli glanced at the cliff just behind her, raised an eyebrow and cautiously sat next to her. He casually stroked his chin and then he gave her an inquisitive look.

"No Corelli, I don't have an explanation," she responded to his untold question.

They both stared in front of them, in silence, for a while. They were facing the opposite side of the path, flanked by a steep wall of earth and rocks, scattered with some small plants and shrubs that had stubbornly grown on the uneven terrain.

A family of tourists approached. While following their parents, the two playful children were attempting to climb the steep terrain siding the path.

Corelli sighed and then addressed them with an annoyed but loud tone, "Don't climb it, it's dangerous!"

Their mother turned and scolded them, "Children! Behave, please!"

The two brothers grunted. One of them whispered "Fun sucker," and kicked a small stone on his way back along the path.

His brother checked that neither of their parents was looking and defiantly jumped onto the rough, steep terrain again. Having climbed half a metre, he grabbed a tuft of grass to pull himself up – the grass strands crumbled in his hand.

The child lost balance, fell badly on his back and started crying. His mother screamed and hurried to assist him. Corelli also darted towards the sobbing child on the ground.

"Sweetie, are you alright?" asked the mother while laying a hand on his cheek. In the meantime Corelli was scanning his body and his movements, trying to figure out if there was any serious injury.

Captain Esposito approached from behind. She kneeled and inspected the child's hand. It was still partly clamped, holding what was left of the grass strands – a bunch of green, dry flanks.

The father arrived, lifted the child and pulled him into his arms. As he embraced him, the child calmed down with a last few sobs. "He's fine," said the father, "he is just scared," his eyes shifted to Corelli, "as you may guess it's not the first time."

Corelli nodded and smiled.

Captain Esposito was still intensely looking at the grass flanks on the child's hand, some of which were being lifted by the sea breeze and floating in the air.

As the family was leaving, with the child still moaning in his father's arms, Captain Esposito approached the sparse vegetation on the side of the path. A shrub in front of her appeared flourishing, dense with ruby flowers and emerald leaves – but as she got closer, she realised that they were all withered. As she stroked one of the leaves, it crumbled in her hand. They were like autumn, dry and crispy leaves, but green and still attached to their twig. Another small plant next to it had grown several blue berries, but they were all wrinkled – like raisins.

"Have you noticed that over here all of the vegetation has withered?" Captain Esposito remarked.

Corelli approached her. He grabbed a grass tuft, which disintegrated in his hand. "Yes, indeed… sort of dried out. It must have happened recently as the leaves are still whole and green." He inspected the leaves more closely. "It has been a dry season. I think last time it rained was a few weeks ago, and we have had unusually hot weather recently," he commented.

"Right. But still… these are plants that can withstand very dry climates and can endure long periods of drought." Captain Esposito narrowed her eyes. "And anyway during lengthy dry seasons grass leaves turn yellow while withering, while all these tufts are all bright green."

Corelli shrugged.

Captain Esposito walked a few metres along the path, while inspecting the vegetation flanking it. She stopped and pinched the leave of another shrub. It was healthy and sturdy. She pulled at it – the twig bent, not giving away its leaf.

Turning to Corelli and, raising an eyebrow, she said, "And, how come that the vegetation has suddenly withered *only* in *that* spot?"

CHAPTER 12

Cambridge welcomed her with a clear sky. Flamingo tints were emerging out of gorgeous gothic pinnacles and blending with the light azure hues.

Although she missed her family, the short visit to her homeland had recharged her, and she was now feeling more upbeat and relaxed than in the previous days.

"Laura! Welcome back! We've missed you so much!" exclaimed Jessica, one of Laura's housemates, soon after she entered the house that she was sharing with four other female students.

"How was your observing run on La Palma?"

"Well, it was quite unus–"

"And how was the conference in Florence?"

"Not real–"

"Fantastic! We'll get together with the other girls in the pub tonight. I'm going to gather them all."

"Jessica. I'm actually somewhat tired after the trip and I would prefer to rest this eveni–"

"No way. You just need a shower and then you'll be all right. It's going to be great. Just give me a couple of minutes to text them all," interrupted Jessica with her thumbs already tapping on her phone.

A couple of hours later, Laura was sitting in a pub by the river Cam, at a table with six friends of hers. Each of them with a pint of beer, a bag of crisps and their phones in front of them. Laura was watching them, each busy texting or scrolling.

Her gaze lazily wandered over the pub. She spotted a lonely student sitting at a table. Thin, black hair, glasses with a thick frame. He had a pile of scientific papers in front of him, which he was reading while taking notes.

Laura left the table of friends and walked over to the lonely student.

"Hi, Jack. May I?" Laura asked, raising her voice to be heard over the pub's murmur, but also to distract the student from his deep reading.

Jack raised his eyes, with a shy and nervous smile.

"Erm… Hi Laura, nice to see you! I didn't know you were back. Yes, of course, t– take a seat," he stuttered.

Laura sat in front of him.

"How was your trip? And the observations?"

"Well, awkward at best," Laura told Jack about the issues with the telescope and the story of her data disappearing from the archives.

"Fortunately I have a copy of all my data taken during the past year on a hard drive. It's always with me in my bag, but tomorrow I'll leave it in my office. It's now the only copy, I cannot risk the hard drive being accidentally lost or even stolen." She paused for a few seconds. Then, as though talking to herself, she said, "Actually it's safer if I leave it in Julia's office tomorrow. I share my office with other students and it's never locked, I cannot risk someone taking it by mistake. At some point, I should make another copy, but there are so many datasets stored on the disk that it would take several hours to make a backup copy, and I'm not sure if I've got the time. Julia has planned for the two of us to go to Russia on Tuesday."

"Russia? What for?" asked Jack, dropping the paper that he was holding and leaning forward.

She twisted her mouth to one side, while watching the threads of bubbles rising to the top of the beer in front of her. "It's another weird story. It's about an astronomer at the Russian Special Observatory, Professor Vladimir Kasparov, who was very interested in our project and who said he had some old data he wanted to share with us. Unfortunately, he died in an accident. An accident whose circumstances are not clear…" she paused, still staring at the bubbles, then she repeated, "Not clear."

Jack was scrutinising her without saying a word.

"Anyway," she said, jolting from her trance, "we are going over there to visit someone who wants to discuss our project and its possible link with Kasparov. Julia is really eager to look into this. I don't know, I'm conflicted. On the one hand I'm curious to know more about Kasparov, his data and the possible connection with our project; on the other hand I must say that I'm not comfortable with the whole story, which has some worrying aspects – a person over there has been accused of murder." Her mouth twitched.

Jack did not comment, keeping a serious expression. His dark, deep eyes were staring at her.

Then Laura broke the silence, "What about you? What are you up to?" glancing at the pile of scientific papers in front of him.

"Oh, well, I'm writing up an article on our latest results. We have detected water in the atmosphere of an exoplanet, and I'm reviewing the previous few detections recently obtained by other groups," pointing at the papers in front of him.

"Fantastic, congratulations!" exclaimed Laura.

Jack was a student in the same institute as Laura, also working on exoplanets, but in a different group. His research did not consist in finding new exoplanets but in characterising their atmospheres. The principle of the technique was very simple: observe exoplanets that were transiting in front of their sun, which required accurate knowledge of their transit time. The stellar light partially filtered by the exoplanet's atmosphere would have the imprint of the atmosphere's composition. In reality these observations were very challenging. However, by exploiting this technique various molecules had been detected in the atmosphere of a few exoplanets.

"You know… I must admit that your research project is far more exciting than mine," said Laura, while tilting her head in the effort of looking at his notes upside down.

"Don't say that. Your project is fantastic too. You are developing new, innovative techniques to find exoplanets. You should be proud of that!" exclaimed Jack.

"Yeah, maybe. Anyway, I'll leave you to your papers. See you at the Institute tomorrow. Lunch time?" smiled Laura.

"Yes, of course, tomorrow, lunch time."

Laura returned to her friends' table to finish her beer. All her friends were still texting and swiping through their phones. None of them even noticed that Laura had left the table.

It was time to call it a night. "Girls, it's been a lot of fun, but I need some rest."

Jessica distractedly lifted her gaze. "Yes, ok. It was fantastic to be with you again!" she exclaimed, gushing.

ılıılı

As he saw Laura leaving the pub, Jack pulled out his phone and sent a short message:

> *They are heading to Russia to discuss their project with some astronomers over there.*

He was about to put his phone back in his pocket, when it buzzed back. Thuban:

> *I already know that.*

Jack wasn't very surprised by the rude tone of Thuban's message, he was more surprised that he had replied so quickly.

He sent another message:

> *Laura's data has been erased from all archives, but she has a backup copy on a hard drive.*

This time there was no reply from the other side.

CHAPTER 13

"Baked."

"What?" exclaimed Captain Esposito bewildered.

"I think they were baked in an oven," explained the forensic police expert, kneeled next to a shrub, as he collected some leaves and berries in plastic bags, "I'm taking some samples to the lab for a detailed analysis, but I'm pretty sure the outcome won't change."

"Oven? But…" Captain Esposito couldn't find the words. She just gestured her arms around her, spanning from the deep cobalt sea to the imposing mountains in front of them, as to remark how ridiculous the 'oven' scenario was.

The expert raised his eyebrows and shrugged. After quickly sorting his tools back in his bag, he saluted the captain with a polite smile. His face did not hide a slightly annoyed expression, perhaps wondering why he had been summoned so urgently for a botanical consultation. As if to avoid any further questions from the captain on such a dull subject, he quickly walked away along the Love Path.

Captain Esposito didn't really have more questions to ask him. She walked to the parapet and leaned to watch the waves violently splashing onto the cliff. She could hardly see any blood stain remaining on the rocks where the body of the retired German professor had been found.

Lifting her eyes, she slowly scanned the horizon. It looked immense, but she felt she was facing a wall. Her investigation had reached a dead point. There was no plausible explanation, no alternative trace to follow.

Maybe it was time to give up. She should simply stop trying to make sense of such nonsense.

CHAPTER 14

"You aren't too thrilled about this trip, are you?"

Laura's eyes widened, as if Julia had read her mind.

She kept looking at the landscape from the window of the Airbus 320, while shifting on her seat.

"Actually I'm curious to find out what was in Kasparov's data too–" Laura said.

"Yes, there might be something really interesting for your project in his data," Julia interrupted with a glitter in her eyes, "Kasparov was not a fool, he knew what he was talking about," she added.

"Yes, I agree. However… how can I say this…" Laura hesitated as she tried to find the right words. Despite having lived in the UK for two years, it was not always easy to translate the nuances of her thoughts into a language that was not her mother tongue. She turned to face Julia, "I mean, there has been a death, maybe a murder, possibly somehow connected to our project. That makes me a bit uncomfortable."

"Don't be worried," said Julia with a reassuring tone, "it was simply an accident. There is no way that anyone would commit murder for some astronomical data. The student who has contacted us is obviously shocked by the death of his supervisor and must have a distorted view of the facts, he is certainly overinterpreting some events. Anyway, this trip is not only for that story. I will take this opportunity to visit a collaborator and friend of mine, Igor Levkin, who works at the same observatory. It will be good to touch base with him on a few joint projects, some of which, by the way, are also of interest to you."

Laura nodded and tried to relax in her seat. Then she pulled a scientific article out her bag and started reading.

Julia leaned towards her slightly to glance at the title. "That's the article reporting the latest detection of gravitational waves, isn't it? The one resulting from the merging of two neutron stars?" she asked.

Instinctively, Laura drew her paper away from Julia. Then she loosened her grip and said, "Ye– Yes, indeed."

"You shouldn't be ashamed of having other scientific interests. Intellectual curiosity outside one's area is praiseworthy. Breadth of knowledge is a virtue," said Julia. Then she leaned back on her seat and sighed, "I wish more colleagues would look outside their narrow research topic." Then she turned to face Laura. She smiled and, nodding towards the article in Laura's hand, said, "I know that you are not enthusiastic about your PhD research project…"

"That's not tr–" Laura tried to object, but Julia halted her by gently raising her hand, indicating that she wanted to finish her sentence.

"Let's just say that deep down inside, your true research interests are elsewhere. Is this a fair statement?" said Julia.

Laura did not respond.

"It's too late to change your research project. But despite all this, you have done very well," said Julia with a serious expression, without a hint of complacency. "Well beyond expectations. Although you may sense that you have not achieved much, the hard work that you have done *will soon pay off*. You are intelligent, with a brilliant and inventive mathematical mind. The PhD project is providing you with the required training in the scientific method. It doesn't matter if afterwards, you decide to change your research area, at that point you will be a junior scientist ready to stand on your own feet."

Laura opened her mouth to say something, but eventually, she just blushed.

***

At the Arrivals Hall of Mineralnye Vody Airport, a well-built young man was waiting for them frowning and holding a sign with their names. Blond, short hair and pale blue eyes, which were searching the whole hall trying to spot them. He finally recognised them as they approached him. His concerned expression turned into a smile, "Welcome! I'm so glad you could come, and especially on such short notice!"

His English was excellent, but with a very strong Russian accent.

"Nice to meet you… Sergei, I guess," Julia said, reaching out for a handshake. "I'm Julia. Julia Russell."

"Yes, sorry, I am Sergei, indeed."

"It's a pleasure to visit you and your institute, and to be of any help in such a situation. It must be very distressing for you."

"Thanks, I really appreciate it."

Then his gaze moved to Laura, beaming. He hesitated a moment and then extended his hand.

Laura responded with a timid smile, "I'm Laura. Nice to meet you."

"Of course, I had already recognised you, well the two of you, from your photos on your institute's web page," he said grinning.

Laura's smile turned into a grin too.

Sergei grabbed their luggage and nodded toward the exit, "Please, follow me. My car is just outside the building."

The trip from the airport to the observatory took two long hours and so gave Sergei the chance to brief Julia and Laura about the events.

"…the commands sent to the telescope, as recorded by the system, really seemed intended to make Professor Kasparov fall. The whole sequence of movements appeared aimed at hurting… actually at killing Professor Kasparov. That's why the police are considering allegations of…" he hesitated a moment, "… allegations of murder."

"Do you think your friend, the telescope operator, may have had any reason to hurt Professor Kasparov?" asked Julia, who was in the passenger seat next to Sergei, "I mean not really killing him, but maybe in a moment of rage…"

"I won't believe it!" Sergei replied curtly, with a heated tone, "I can't imagine Nikolai doing anything like that."

Julia had touched a delicate nerve, thought Laura, who was listening from the rear seat. She hoped that her supervisor would be a little bit more sensitive with their host. When Julia was in 'investigation mode', either in science or in any other situation, her impetus to find out more sometimes overrode her British tact.

"Yes, of course, sorry," Julia commented, "I'm just trying to understand the reasoning behind the police's allegations. Was there any animosity between the two of them? Any argument?"

Sergei's mouth twitched. His gaze shifted twice towards the side mirror opposite to Julia, although no car could be seen anywhere on the country road.

Julia kept looking at him with an inquisitive expression.

Eventually he replied, "Well…" he hesitated a few more seconds and then continued, "Professor Kasparov often complained that Nikolai was somewhat sloppy when operating the telescope. My supervisor was particularly sensitive about 'his' telescope. I happened to witness him scolding Nikolai a few times. But he was never too harsh." Laura noticed the muscles in his jaw tightening as he continued, "Anyway, I cannot believe that this may have been a reason for Nikolai to hurt Professor Kasparov."

Julia did not give up. "The human mind is a maze of hidden emotions. You never know what subconscious streams of sentiments may develop inside it."

This time Sergei did not comment, but knitted his brows.

"What's Nikolai's version?"

Sergei opened his mouth as if trying to find the words.

As he did not answer, Julia prompted him, "Can we talk with him?"

Sergei hesitated, "Ye– of course… sure, we can visit him tomorrow… where he's being detained."

Laura, who had been listening silently, froze when she heard the word 'detained'. She held her breath, worried that she and Julia were playing with fire in a foreign country.

Julia's expression was instead unperturbed, steady and focused on her questioning. "I must admit it's a strange story," she commented, "but what does this accident have to do with our research project?"

"Although I am a PhD student, I have also undertaken some duties. I've been developing and maintaining software for the processing of data produced by instruments attached to the BTA-6 telescope. In order to properly assist users and quickly fix their issues, I've been given the privilege to access some of the accounts used for data analysis. Professor Kasparov's account was one of these. Soon after his accident, the police asked me to access his account. We noticed a message that he had sent to the two of you just before the accident. The police did not seem to care much, but I thought, and I still think, that his interest in your project and the claimed link with data that he had obtained 30 years ago are somehow related to his death."

Julia raised her eyebrow. "Sergei, I don't mean to offend your deduction skills, but I'm sure that the fact that Professor Kasparov sent a message to us just before his accident is only a simple coincidence. I don't see any other element linking his death to our project."

"That's not the whole story. I'll show you something at the observatory that will convince you."

Julia and Laura looked at each other, frowning.

No one spoke a word for the rest of the trip.

From time to time Julia shifted her gaze to look at Sergei, as if trying to extract additional information by inspecting his expression.

From the rear seat, Laura looked at him through the rear mirror. Every once in a while Sergei looked back at her.

Laura was not sure what to think. There was something weird. Well, the whole story was obviously odd enough. But she sensed something even stranger going on, though she could not pin down what it was. Sergei's obsession with trying to link Kasparov's accident to her project was a little bit freaky. But she had to acknowledge that Sergei seemed truly upset by the events, and for good reason. His supervisor had died in mysterious circumstances and his friend had been detained and accused of murder. No wonder he was distressed. But there was something else unusual that she could not quite identify. Maybe it was just his accent. It was the first time that she had heard such a strong foreign accent accompanied by such fluent English, the contrast was striking. But Julia did not seem to be bothered by this. So, Laura decided to relax in her seat and enjoy the view of the Caucasian landscape flashing by.

One of the mountains in front of them was higher than the others. Laura noticed a tiny, peculiar protuberance on the very top of it.

Only half an hour later did Laura realise how titanic the 'protuberance' actually was.

CHAPTER 15

Arthur was extremely excited. Thrilled.

The information provided by that British student had been precious. Resolutive. It had a cost, on several fronts, but it had been worth it.

Kasparov was dead. Qualms wiped away.

Thanks to the new information, he now knew when it would happen. Exactly. Exact date. Exact time.

On June 10th. At 06:17, Universal Time.

CHAPTER 16

A layer of ash grey clouds was idling just above the top of the mountain. Cold light rain was slowly drizzling, as if suspended in air, as if suspended in time, shrouding the colossal dome. The mountain was still mourning the death of Vladimir Kasparov.

Sergei parked in front of the dome. As Laura got out of the car she had to lean backwards to see the full height of the structure. She had visited other large telescopes, but the BTA-6 had been designed according to a different concept, which had resulted in both the telescope and its dome being much larger than its counterparts around the world.

Laura followed Sergei and Julia. She lagged behind and hesitated a second before entering the dome building.

The telescope was in its vertical position. Julia and Laura stopped in front of it, scanning its whole extent, from the bottom frame, holding the six-metre wide mirror, all the way upwards along the steel tubes. Once they had reached the top, their gazes halted for a few seconds, looking at the scientific camera, which was now 25 metres above the telescope's mirror.

Sergei looked at them. "Quite a fall, isn't it?" he said in a bitter tone, "Follow me. I want to show you something."

They passed through the control room.

"The police tapes have just been removed, so things are still as they were when the accident happened."

Laura got goosebumps when she noticed, on one of the desks, a copy of the *Monthly Notices of the Royal Astronomical Society* opened at the page of her recent article.

"This way," prompted Sergei while holding a door open.

The door led to a staircase. Julia stopped in front of it and gave Sergei an inquisitive look.

"Downstairs," he prompted again.

They walked down four flights of stairs and arrived in the basement of the building. Sergei led the way through a dimly lit corridor with a low ceiling covered in cobwebs. They passed next to a few metal cabinets, in the style of the 70s, covered with dust. The plaster of the walls had several cracks and had peeled off in many places, leaving faded bricks exposed. Large stains of mould were visible on the walls' lower parts.

Sergei stopped in front of a door. It had a faded sign on it:

АРХИВ

It was a simple wooden door, broken at the level of the lock, with jagged splinters.

"This door leads to the storage room where old instruments are kept and old datasets are archived. It's usually locked." He pointed at the broken lock. "A few days ago, after the death of Professor Kasparov, someone broke into it."

"Worrying," said Julia, pretending to be concerned, "but I still fail to see a clear link with the accident."

"You will see," interrupted Sergei, opening the door by simply pushing it.

"They haven't fixed the broken lock yet?" asked Laura, furrowing her brow.

Sergei shook his head and rolled his eyes.

Laura inspected the door more closely. "The door is made of plywood," she commented, "it must have been very easy for the intruders to force it, a simple screwdriver was probably enough."

"You're right," responded Sergei, "as you may have guessed, the observatory staff didn't put much effort in safeguarding what's inside here," he added, sighing.

As they entered, a smell of dampness and dust filled Laura's nostrils. Sergei switched on the lights. It was a vast area. On one side there were decommissioned scientific instruments, old electronic racks and other disassembled hardware chaotically stacked. He pointed at a very large instrument that had gathered a thick layer of dust. "That's the instrument that was on the telescope about 30 years ago, and which was used extensively by Professor Kasparov. I'm pretty sure it is the same instrument he used to obtain the data mentioned to you in his message."

He walked past the instrument. Julia followed him, slowing down to scan Kasparov's instrument. Laura stopped in front of it to observe it more closely. It was a metal cylinder about two metres in diameter, painted red, with several dangling wires. On one side it had a hole with a large lens in it. Laura knelt to peek into the instrument through the lens. Darkness. She looked more closely inside the lens, squinting her eyes. As her eyes adjusted to the darkness inside, she could see something – a strange shape. She got even closer, nearly touching the lens with her nose. The twisted shape inside the instrument became sharper, it seemed to her it was moving… it had a pale hue – a deformed face! She jumped back in horror. Panting, and heart pounding out of her chest, she found herself on the floor, staring at the dark hole of the instrument.

"Laura, are you coming?" called Julia from a distance, "What's the matter with you? You look pale. And what are you doing on the floor, are you unwell?"

Laura shook her head, gulping, still looking at the instrument. "I'm fine… but…" she shook her head once more, "I'm coming."

As Julia turned, Laura frantically crawled towards the instrument again, held her breath and looked into the dark lens again. She winced as she saw that the twisted human face was still there! But it had something glittering on top of it. She recognised it – her necklace. She was looking at her own image, distorted and inverted by the lens, reflected by some optical surface inside the instrument. Closing her eyes, she tried to slow down her breathing. 'Calm down, Laura,' she told herself, 'this story is upsetting you, but you are overreacting.'

She kept inspecting the inside of the instrument and, although she could only see part of it, she noticed that it was quite different from any other instrument she had seen before.

"Laura! We're waiting for you", Julia called with her hands on her hips.

"Yes, sorry, I'm coming," said Laura, standing up and walking towards Julia and Sergei.

"That instrument," she said while approaching Sergei, "it seems that it was developed with an unusual concept. I guess it was how astronomical instruments were built in those times."

"Quite the opposite," responded Sergei, "Professor Kasparov explained to me that it adopted a totally different and very ingenious design, conceived by one of the best optical engineers of all times. It was developed in tight consultation with Professor Kasparov himself in order to optimise its performances for specific astronomical observations. The lenses and highly sophisticated optical elements were manufactured by the best Russian company in the sector at that time. Professor Kasparov regarded it as a masterpiece of optics. The instrument had some drawbacks, it was not easy to use for many astronomers, which eventually resulted in it being removed from the telescope after only a few years of operations. But it was extremely efficient for some kinds of astronomical observations. Professor Kasparov claimed that it was superior even to most current instruments and he often complained that it had been decommissioned."

Laura raised her eyebrows, casting one last glance at Kasparov's instrument. She turned and only then realised that Sergei and Julia had stopped in front of several long rows of metal shelves, which occupied most of the vast basement area. Laura approached the closest of them and noticed that they were filled with strange objects. She pulled one out, blowing the dust away. It was a sort of round plastic container, about 30 centimetres in diameter, a few centimetres thick, and with a hole in its centre. "What are these?"

"Magnetic tapes. Data tapes on reels," answered Julia, approaching her. She opened the plastic case, extracted the large reel contained inside it, and pulled out the end of the magnetic tape for Laura to see. Laura inspected it more closely and touched it gently, as if she had been introduced to some exotic animal.

"When I was a student, scientific datasets were stored on these tapes," Julia explained. "Of course, they are no longer in use, but some of the old datasets are still stored on them." She scanned the rows of metal shelves. "All the data stored on the thousands of tapes archived in this place could now easily be contained in your smartphone."

Laura noticed that each tape was labelled with a name and a date. A copy of the same label was on the shelf, to identify the slot reserved for that tape.

She pointed at one of the labels and asked, "I guess these labels give the name of the observer and the date of the observation associated with the data on the reel"

Sergei nodded, "Yes, all the tapes were carefully archived with this system."

Julia looked back at the broken entrance door. "Did the intruders steal anything?" she asked.

Sergei didn't say anything. He moved toward a darker area and signalled for Julia and Laura to follow him. They entered the aisle between two rows of shelves packed with reels, each of them classified with labels. The smell of dampness and dust became stronger as they walked down the narrow, dimly lit corridor. They reached a point where several tape reels were scattered on the ground. Some of their cases were broken and plastic splinters crunched beneath their shoes as they approached. Two of the shelves were empty, despite being labelled. Julia and Laura got closer to the empty shelves, trying not to step on the many tapes amassed on the floor. Most of the labels were half peeled off, curling with age and yellowed. The writing was so faded that it was difficult to read, especially with the dim lighting of the aisle.

"Kasparov!" exclaimed Laura.

"Yes, 'Kasparov' is the name on most of the empty slots," confirmed Sergei, "and the dates are all about the same."

"You're right," confirmed Julia while scanning the labels, "most of them are associated with observations taken 30 years ago."

"Yes, the intruders' search was very much focused. Aimed specifically at the datasets Professor Kasparov was referring to in the message he sent to you just before… just before his death," commented Sergei.

"Are the police aware of this?" Laura asked.

"Yes, I pointed it out to them, but they did not seem to care," Sergei replied with a frustrated expression. "They did pretend to take fingerprints, but I suspect they haven't even analysed them, assuming that they found any recent ones at all. They barely understood what I was talking about when I tried to explain to them the possible link with the scientific data. I don't think they got my point at all. Honestly, also the Observatory staff didn't seem to care much. As you can see, they didn't even bother to sort out this mess," pointing at the tapes scattered on the floor, "nor to fix the broken door. They consider anything stored in this place as old stuff with no value."

Julia looked at the tapes spread on the floor. "I guess that none of these tapes are from Kasparov's program."

"Right," Sergei answered, "they are all from other programs. Either the intruders pulled them out and dropped them on the floor amid their hectic search for Kasparov's data, or they wanted to remove some of them from the shelves so as to create a decoy and to distract attention from the main focus of their search. If the latter was the case then it was a useless attempt, as their aim is pretty clear," said Sergei, who had now bent down to randomly inspect some of the tapes on the ground. "The only missing reels are the data from Kasparov's program 30 years ago. I've already checked the whole lot," he added.

Julia continued scanning the faded labels of the many missing slots on the empty shelves. Laura flinched every time a piece of plastic cracked beneath her feet and was nervously looking around in the narrow aisle – its ends were difficult to see.

Sergei was now sitting on the floor, trying to sort the scattered tapes in different piles. He stopped and looked at one of the tapes in his hand. "Actually…" he said while inspecting the tape more closely, "it seems that the intruders, in their haste, forgot something. This tape is part of Professor Kasparov's lot. It must have been mixed up with the others and thrown on the floor by mistake."

Julia knelt to look at the reel more closely. "Do you have any way to read the tape?" she asked.

"Yes, there's a tape reader at the entrance of the room, which might still be functioning. It can be used to transfer the tape's content on a... more modern device," Sergei said, grinning.

Julia glanced at Laura. "Maybe the two of you could take care of reading the tape and inspecting its content. I don't think I can be of much help with that. In the meantime, if you don't mind, I will visit a colleague and friend of mine, Professor Igor Levkin. He has an office in this building, doesn't he?" Julia asked, looking at Sergei.

"Yes, on the first floor. There aren't many rooms, you'll find his office easily."

CHAPTER 17

Betelgeuse.scan.3.1.fits
Betelgeuse.scan.3.2.fits
Vega.scan.6.1.fits
Aldebaran.scan.5.1.fits
....

The names of the files being read from the tape were slowly scrolling on the green-light monitor of the old, massive computer in front of them. It was a primitive system, thought Laura. The contrast with the modern, ultrafast and much smaller computers in the control room, just a couple of floors above them, was striking. Descending those few steps to the basement had transported her to a remote epoch, before she was even born, when scientific research was much more difficult and progressed at a much slower pace.

"So, you work on exoplanets," said Sergei, breaking an awkward silence that had been lasting for several minutes, while the two of them were looking at the sequence of file names appearing on the monitor.

"Yes. I have developed a method… well… improved a method to identify exoplanets, and I'm applying it to some datasets that I have obtained at various telescopes."

"You don't sound terribly excited," Sergei commented.

Laura didn't comment. "What about you?" she asked.

"Well, I use data obtained with instruments similar to that one," nodding at Kasparov's dusty instrument lying in a corner, "just a bit more modern," with a hint of a sarcastic smile, "to investigate the chemical composition of a sample of stars."

"You don't sound thrilled either," Laura pointed out. Sergei did not comment.

A hint of regret crossed Laura's face. Her eyes left the screen to look at him and, with a mellow tone, she asked, "What happens now? I mean, now that Professor Kasparov... now that your supervisor has passed away. How badly does this affect your thesis? Who will supervise you?"

"The PhD thesis was already at a very advanced stage," he replied dismissively, looking at the monitor. Then, noticing Laura's concerned expression, he turned to her and clarified, "I'm sure I can complete the thesis in a few months without any additional help."

Sergei did not appear concerned to Laura. It was not clear to her whether he was pretending not to be concerned in front of her, or if he was pretending to himself, as a sort of self-defence. She decided it was inappropriate to pursue the topic further.

Both of them turned to look at the green monitor again, where the names of the files were still slowly scrolling. Sergei was resting on the reclined chair.

Laura was wondering why they were staring at this list of meaningless filenames, when something caught her attention. "Wait!"

"What?"

"70-Ophiuchi.scan.15.1," murmured Laura, pointing at the name of one of the file names on the screen.

"Yes, it must be one of the many stars observed by Professor Kasparov on those nights, so what?"

"It's one of the stars in my sample."

"Is it one of those published in that article of yours, the one that Professor Kasparov was reading just before he died?"

"Yes, it is. Although in that article we have only reported data obtained up to about six months ago. Since then we have obtained additional datasets on 70 Ophiuchi, but I haven't had time to analyse them yet."

"Do you have that data with you?" asked Sergei, pulling himself up on his chair and leaning towards Laura.

"No. They are on a hard drive in Julia's office, in Cambridge. That's the only copy available."

Laura explained the odd disappearance of all the data from all archives.

"What are your findings?" asked Sergei, intrigued.

"Well, based on its periodic motion, we can infer that 70 Ophiuchi has a planet – an exoplanet – orbiting around it. The exoplanet's orbit was poorly outlined. We could only estimate that the exoplanet's mass can be anything larger than five times the mass of Earth." Laura noticed Sergei's forehead creasing. "I know, not very illuminating," she added.

"Would your more recent data help to characterise the exoplanet and its orbit around 70 Ophiuchi?" asked Sergei.

"Probably… yes, I'm pretty sure," Laura clarified.

"It seems Professor Kasparov observed this star 30 years ago, and quite a few times, as implied by the sequential number '15' in the file name," said Sergei, pointing at the monitor, "and probably more times after this. It's too bad that this tape only contains this single file of 70 Ophiuchi. Do you reckon the file might contain anything useful to help us figure out why Professor Kasparov was so excited? And possibly also useful for your project?"

Laura rolled her eyes at such a silly question. Looking into the file was the least they could do after this lengthy search. Sergei probably thought that opening and looking into Professor Kasparov's files was disrespectful, so he was somehow seeking Laura's complicity.

Laura played along, "It's difficult to say until we know what's in it. Can you open the file?"

Sergei smiled, "I suspect it may be difficult to extract data from files in such an old format, but I'm sure we can work it out."

***

"May I?" she asked while knocking on the half-open door.

"Julia! So nice to see you!" Igor Levkin turned away from the monitor to beam at her, "I've been so thrilled about your visit since I received your message a few days ago."

"Yes, I reckoned that with a short visit here I could kill two birds with one stone," Julia said, smiling back, "I thought

I could touch base with you on a few projects and…" her expression got grim "… look more closely at this story about Kasparov and his interest in some results that a student of mine has recently obtained."

Igor's smile slipped. "A terrible accident. It has been such a shock for all of us. For me, in particular, I must say… he was a close friend of mine."

"I'm so sorry," she paused for a few moments. Then she asked, "Do you have any idea why he was interested in our results?"

"No clue. He had never worked on exoplanets."

"What do you make of Sergei's claim that his death might be somehow connected to our project?"

"Ah, yes, Sergei shared his thoughts with me," Igor said with a bitter smile, rolling his eyes. "Nonsense. Just the vivid imagination of a student who has been reading too many novels."

Julia shifted her eyes to look at the rain hitting the window, "Yes, maybe," she agreed. She kept staring at the patterns that the drops were forming on the glass. Then she turned to Igor and asked, "Can you tell me more about Kasparov? He seemed to be a somewhat peculiar character. His scientific publications reveal that he was a brilliant scientist, but I've never seen him at any conferences or any scientific meetings. I haven't seen him involved in any international projects."

"Vladimir was indeed an outstanding astronomer, intelligent, and exceptionally knowledgeable. But for the last 30 years he had exiled himself to this site, within these walls. He would not go to conferences, he did not want to have any external collaborators."

"So a very shy character, was he?"

"I wouldn't say shy… I would say… ashamed."

"Ashamed? Why? What for?"

"I don't know. He wouldn't talk about it, not even with me, his closest collaborator, probably his only collaborator."

Julia frowned and tilted her head with an inquisitive look.

"The only thing I know is that this was triggered at an international conference that he attended about 30 years ago. Something happened there, I don't know what, he would never talk about it. The fact is that he never recovered."

Julia rested her hand on her chin, focusing on the rain on the window. "30 years ago is the same time when Kasparov… Vladimir," clarified Julia looking at Igor, "when he obtained the data that he claimed was relevant to our project… probably the same data that has now disappeared from the archive."

Igor rolled his eyes again, "Julia, it's just a coincidence. That theft of worthless stuff in the storage room is probably the work of some silly fellow who expected to find something valuable. They must have been disappointed, so they made a mess and took away some stuff just as a souvenir of their wild night."

"You're probably right… probably," Julia commented with a thoughtful expression. "Do you know anyone who could help to figure out what happened at that conference 30 years ago?"

"Not really. At that time I was still a graduate student and, as far as I know, Vladimir was the only one attending that conference from here."

Julia twisted her mouth to one side.

"However," he added, narrowing his eyes and scratching the nape of his neck, "there's something that may help." He stood up and walked out of the office with a 'follow me' gesture.

While leading the way through the corridor, he explained to Julia, "Some time ago, while searching for some notes in one of his drawers, he accidentally pulled out a conference group photo, which had been buried under layers of scientific articles. He did not want to comment and quickly tossed it back into the drawer. I sensed that the photo was making him uncomfortable."

They reached a door with 'Профессор Владимир Каспаров' painted on it. Igor opened the door, which was unlocked. "The police have just removed the tapes from Vladimir's office," he said.

The room was stuffed with so many books, articles and sheets of paper that the furniture was barely visible. Julia wondered whether the police had really attempted to extract any clues out of this mess.

Igor approached a set of drawers beneath the desk. "If I recall correctly, it was in this one," he said, while opening the bottom drawer. He searched through a mass of articles and sheets of paper. Then he pulled out a photo, "Yes, it was this one."

Julia approached him and looked at the faded photo. There were probably around a hundred people lined up in four rows on the stairs of a building. On the bottom of the photo was the title of the conference, 'Fifth Annual Conference on Stellar Spectroscopy. Paris'. It was dated 30 years back. Julia wondered why Kasparov had kept this photo if it was associated with bad memories.

"It's common to many of us," commented Igor, as if reading Julia's mind. "We store things away that remind us of bad feelings, but we don't bin them. Some scars are deep and we cannot… we don't want to entirely get rid of them."

"This is him," he said pointing at one of the faces in the photo, "30 years ago."

Julia looked at Kasparov in the picture for a few seconds and then scanned all the other faces. At first sight, she could not recognise anyone. She inspected the photo more closely. Her eyes widened and she pointed out a face, "Schneider, a younger version of Professor Gerard Schneider."

"Do you reckon he can help?" Igor asked, with a hint of hope in his tone.

"Not any longer, unfortunately," replied Julia with a sad expression. Igor looked down and did not ask for further clarification.

Julia kept scanning the participants in the photo.

"Arthur?" she exclaimed. "Arthur was among the participants?"

Igor looked at the point of the picture where Julia's finger had stopped. "Oh, yes, that's Arthur Cecil-Hood. I'm sure he can certainly help," exclaimed Igor enthusiastically.

"Certainly not!" replied Julia curtly and frowning, "He surely would *not* be of any help."

Igor did not comment any further and pursed his lips, looking at Julia out of the corner of his eye.

Julia kept looking at the photo but couldn't recognise any more people. Until she spotted, half-hidden in the back, squeezed behind two other participants, a chubby face. "Smith. I think this is Roger Smith. Actually, I'm pretty sure about it," she said.

"Roger Smith? I don't think I've ever heard about him."

"He left academia long ago. He is now CEO of a major space technology company. I recognise him because he was part of a press conference on the occasion of the launch of a space X-ray observatory."

"Maybe... maybe, he can help?" Igor asked, this time more cautiously.

"Maybe."

"Which company is it?"

"SPACEWAVE, based near Tucson, Arizona."

Julia stared at the photo for a few more seconds while pondering. "Can I borrow this photo?"

"You can keep it. All the stuff in this office will soon be disposed of."

In that moment Laura and Sergei entered the office holding the magnetic tape reel.

"Anything interesting on that tape?" Julia asked.

"Apparently Kasparov observed one of the stars that is also in our sample, 70 Ophiuchi," explained Laura, "the tape contains a single file with a set of data, but certainly, he observed the same star many more times. Unfortunately, all the other files must have been stored on the other tape reels that have been stolen."

"Have you checked that there are no other tapes of Professor Kasparov's from that period in the archive, Sergei?" asked Igor.

Sergei looked at Julia and Laura. A hint of uneasiness crossed his face. "Ye–," his mouth twitched, "Da professor, proveril. Drugih dannih za etot period v arhive net."

Julia and Laura looked at each other, Sergei had replied in Russian. Laura shrugged, clueless. Julia frowned.

"I see," said Igor, "I may also take a look in the archive in the basement, but…" he paused, adjusting the spectacles on his nose, while his forehead creased, "if you couldn't find anything else, then I doubt I can be more successful."

"Does the data on that file reveal anything interesting?" asked Julia, looking at Laura.

"Not really," responded Laura. "With this data we can only gather basic information on the star's chemistry. Maybe in combination with the other datasets collected by Kasparov it would reveal something more. It's difficult to say".

"Can Kasparov's data on that file be of any use to us, in particular for your thesis?"

Laura shrugged. "Maybe. I can combine this data with mine. Maybe we can obtain some additional information, but I suspect it won't be terribly useful." She paused. "I fail to see what Professor Kasparov was thinking when he claimed that his data would have been very interesting to us. It must be something in the missing reels," said Laura, while looking at the reel in her hands.

Her gaze then shifted to look at the photo that Julia was holding. "What's that?"

CHAPTER 18

Bars.

Rusty, narrow and murky windows.

Damp.

Moist and musty, still air.

Laura felt like she was suffocating. She realised it was not due to the small room, with its tiny windows and mouldy walls, in which they were waiting to talk with Nikolai, the telescope operator… the *former* telescope operator. Deep inside, she knew that her discomfort was actually coming from the even remote possibility of being somehow connected with a crime, with a murder.

She was not the only one who was uneasy. Sergei was sitting on a chair in a corner, nervously tapping his foot.

The only one who did not look uncomfortable was Julia. She was sitting next to Laura by the table at the centre of the room. Legs crossed, bored expression, her gaze shifting between her watch and the door in front of them. "They said he would be brought here in a few minutes," she said with a hint of annoyance in her voice, while looking at Sergei.

"Erm, you know, 'a few minutes' here probably has a somewhat different meaning than in Cambridge." Sergei had an apologetic tone in his voice, as if he was personally responsible for the delay.

In that very moment, the door burst open. Two guards escorted Nikolai into the room. He was wearing a prison jumpsuit and was handcuffed. Pale, unshaven, a blank expression, with dark bags under his eyes. He was walking slowing and unsteadily, lost and unsure where to go. He looked at Julia and Laura and narrowed his eyes, as if trying to put them into focus. Then he noticed Sergei sitting in the corner and gave him a tense glare. Sergei responded with half a smile. He shifted uncomfortably on his chair and lowered his head slightly. Laura and Julia glanced at each other.

The guards prompted Nikolai to sit at the table, on the opposite side of Julia and Laura. Nikolai sat down while still glaring at Sergei.

"Nice to meet you, Nikolai," Julia began, "my name is Julia Russell. I'm a professor at the University of Cambridge." She innocently reached out to shake Nikolai's hand, but one of the two guards shouted something in Russian. Laura jumped in her chair. Apparently, they were not allowed to have any physical contact with the prisoner.

Julia nodded at the guard.

"And this is Laura Bellini," she continued with a calm voice, "she is a student, also at the University of Cambridge."

"What do you want?" Nikolai asked curtly.

"We are terribly sorry for the situation in which you are currently in. Sergei reckons we can be of some help," said Julia.

Nikolai did not blink. He kept staring at Julia.

Julia continued, "It seems that Professor Kasparov got very excited about our research just before his death, but we don't know why. We would like to find out whether he mentioned anything to you at some point that night." She paused. "If you could tell us what happened then we may find a clue and it might also be of help for your situation."

"I have already told the police everything, and look where I am now!" Nikolai yelled while leaning forward, with a mixture of defiance and distress.

"Nikolai, I fully understand that you are upset. But we are here trying to help. Professor Kasparov's death seems… maybe, linked to other events and possibly associated with our research, somehow…"

Laura looked at Julia, bewildered. It was the first time that she had heard Julia admitting that Kasparov's death might not be an accident and that it was possibly connected with them.

"So, if you would be so kind as to tell us what happened that night, we may be able to identify some clues."

Nikolai sighed and looked away. "There's not much to say. I didn't notice anything unusual until… until Professor Kasparov was dead."

Julia exhaled. She plastered a reassuring smile on her face. "Right, I see." Then she got closer to the table while keeping an eye on the guards, whose glare was getting tenser. "However, it could be that... something that was insignificant for you may actually be important to unravel the whole story." She leaned forward, knitting her brows. "On that night, I mean before the accident, did Professor Kasparov mention his excitement about our project, a project on exoplanets?"

Nikolai slowly shook his head. "Not really. Professor Kasparov did not usually talk much. He used to be excited even less. Come to think of it, I had never seen him excited at all."

"Did he mention some data that he obtained 30 years ago?"

Nikolai responded with a blank stare and a shrug.

Julia waited a few seconds, drumming her fingers on the table. Eventually, she asked a more open question, "Can you simply tell us your version of the events that night?"

Nikolai's face flushed, a muscle in his jaw twitched. "It's NOT my version! It's simply what happened!" he burst out, while glaring at Julia with flaming eyes.

While Laura flinched, Julia didn't move a muscle, keeping her eyes on Nikolai.

He looked away, towards the barred window, and sighed. Closing his eyes, he took a deep breath, and started, "We were both in the control room. The scientific camera broke down. Professor Kasparov decided that he could quickly fix it. I tried to warn him that it was against the safety procedures to undertake any maintenance of the telescope and its instruments at night, alone in the dome, without proper technical assistance. He would not listen. He had fixed minor technical issues with the telescope and its instruments several times in the past. He was very familiar with it. He considered the BTA-6 as a sort of beloved pet. That night he asked me to move the telescope to a horizontal position, so that he could access the scientific camera more easily. I did so. He left the control room, heading towards the dome. That was the last time I saw him, alive."

"What did you do next? I mean, after Kasparov left the control room," asked Julia.

"Nothing, simply nothing. I just made sure that the telescope was still idling, and just sat in front of the console, simply waiting… actually, I dozed off a little bit, I must confess, but what was I supposed to do? The telescope operator is not allowed to leave the control room, barring exceptional circumstances."

"Didn't you hear anything from the dome? I mean, from what I understand, the whole sequence of accidents, with the scaffolding falling onto the ground and… erm… probably Professor Kasparov crying for help, must have been quite loud."

Nikolai looked at Julia, narrowing his eyes. A vein popped out of his neck. He had clearly been asked that same question repeatedly and was probably not believed. Nikolai closed his eyes again and sighed deeply. "No, I didn't hear anything," he said, "the control room is well insulated. We do have an intercom, which is permanently connected to its twin in the dome… but it must have had some fault, because I didn't hear anything. After about half an hour I got a little suspicious that I was not hearing any noise from the dome. I was expecting to at least hear some clanging from Professor Kasparov's handling tools. I tried to ask him whether he needed any help through the intercom, but apparently it was not working. The weird thing, which I cannot explain, is that the intercom was working perfectly later on, when the police inspected the apparatus."

Laura's eyebrows twitched slightly. No wonder the police found it hard to believe Nikolai's story.

"And that's when, I mean when you failed to get any response from Professor Kasparov, that's when you decided to go to the dome?" Julia asked.

"Not yet. I was still torn on whether to leave the control room or not. I simply assumed that the intercom was faulty. But then I glanced at the monitor reporting the position of the telescope and then, only then, did I realise that the telescope was in its vertical position, pointing at the zenith. For some inexplicable reason, the telescope had moved, quite a lot.

I had the dreadful thought that this may have happened while Professor Kasparov was trying to fix the camera. So I rushed to the dome."

He paused.

"There I found a mess. Pieces of broken hardware scattered everywhere…" he paused again, looking down, "… and Professor Kasparov in a pool of blood, dripping from the telescope's mirror."

Julia and Laura looked at each other with a mournful expression, as if trying to find something comforting to say. Laura turned to look at Sergei, who had been listening from behind. His eyes shifted nervously from Julia to Laura and then to Nikolai. He visibly gulped and finally spoke, "Nikolai, my ochen' sozhaleyem o neschastnom sluchaye…"

Laura frowned and whispered to Julia, "Why is Sergei speaking in Russian again?" she had barely finished her sentence when Nikolai stood up, violently banged the chain of his cuffs on the table and with a red face burst out, "You! It's because of you that Kasparov is dead! If you had t–"

The guards grasped his arms and shoulders while shouting something in Russian. Nikolai was convulsively trying to free himself from the guards' grip. As he was not calming down, the guards started to drag him out of the room, while he kept shouting, "Because of you! He's dead because of you!"

His screams echoed behind the metal door for a few minutes, until they faded into silence.

***

The worn wipers squeaked on the windshield, mixing raindrops and dust into muddy stripes.

After leaving the prison, the car was filled with an awkward silence. Laura didn't know what to think. The whole meeting had been bizarre, with Sergei only having spoken a few words, and in Russian. Nikolai had angrily glared at him, with his final outburst accusing him of somehow being responsible for Kasparov's death.

Julia was looking at Sergei, who was pretending to focus on his driving. Her stare was a silent, but clear request for explanations.

Sergei only resisted for a few minutes, then he broke down, "I was there. I was there that night. At the telescope."

Laura looked at Sergei, eyes wide open. Julia kept staring at Sergei without changing her expression, as if prompting him to explain further.

"At night, the control room is supposed to always have three people: the 'astronomer', who is the scientist that has been allocated observing time on that night; the 'telescope operator', who guides the telescope; and the 'support astronomer', who is in charge of helping the astronomer with the observations, especially if the latter is not familiar with the instrument. Having three people in the control room is also a safety requirement." His voice was now trembling. "Experienced PhD students often volunteer for the roles of telescope operator and support astronomer, as this allows them to earn some money, and it is also good for their CV."

Laura could already guess the continuation of Sergei's 'confession'.

"I was the support astronomer for that night." He sighed while telling this part of the story, which had probably been weighing on his conscience. "But in the case of Professor Kasparov, the support astronomer was just a redundant formality. He was far more experienced than anyone else with the telescope and its instrumentation. He often referred to the BTA-6 as 'his' telescope. So yes, I was at the telescope that night, but I was not in the control room most of the time... there was really no reason for me to stay in there, Professor Kasparov would not let me help at all!" he said, while raising his voice and glancing at Julia, as if seeking approval. "I spent most of the night in the cafeteria, downstairs, mostly writing my thesis, sipping coffee and... napping."

He sighed.

"If I had been in the control room that night, at that very moment, I would have assisted Professor Kasparov when he tried to fix the camera, I could have checked what was happening in the dome when the intercom was not working… he might still be alive."

Laura now thought that Sergei's eagerness to find out more about Kasparov's death was not only to help Nikolai, but also, and more likely, to cope with his sense of guilt. An attempt to redeem himself.

Julia shifted her gaze to the road ahead, apparently now satisfied by the explanation, but not yet speaking a word. Laura didn't know what to say. She tried to find some words of comfort for Sergei, but nothing appropriate came to mind. Finally, she decided to break the awkward silence by totally changing the subject. "Julia, did you get any reply from that person in Arizona? The one that you recognised in that photo from the last conference attended by Professor Kasparov, 30 years ago?"

"You mean Roger Smith? The CEO of SPACEWAVE? Of course not. But I'm not at all surprised. However I have a Plan B. Next week we are going to Phoenix, Arizona, to attend the meeting of the American Astronomical Society. Tucson, where SPACEWAVE is based, is only a couple of hours' drive from there. So I propose that after the conference we visit the company and ask to speak with Smith. We may have a better chance to speak with him if we're onsite, at least it would be harder for him and his staff to ignore us. After all, one of their claimed missions is to engage more with the scientific community."

"That's a fantastic idea!" Sergei exclaimed with a revived expression, "May I please join you?"

Julia frowned. Her perplexed gaze prompted Sergei to explain further, "I will be attending the meeting of the American Astronomical Society too. I had planned to stay a few more days after the conference to visit Monument Valley and the Grand Canyon, I've never been there, in fact, I've never been to the USA before, but I would be glad to use those extra days to visit SPACEWAVE in Tucson, with you." Then he glanced at Laura in the rear mirror, who responded with the hint of a smile.

"Of course," replied Julia, while looking out of the window, away from Sergei, "you're very much welcome to join us. After all, you've been affected much more than us by this whole story, and it's thanks to you that we've become aware of several interesting facts linked to Professor Kasparov and his data." Despite the warm words, the tone of her voice was flat and cold.

Julia probably did not yet fully trust him, especially after discovering that he had omitted an important part of the story. Laura didn't share the same concerns. She looked at his sad eyes in the rear mirror. He must have been overwhelmed by the events. She could only imagine how it would feel to lose Julia. His behaviour was understandable, also given that he must have been devastated by his sense of guilt. She felt that she could trust him and would be glad to see him again in Arizona.

"Here you are," said Sergei, while pulling out in front of their hotel.

"Thank you very much," Julia replied with a polite smile. "See you in Arizona then, in about one week."

"I understand your flight departs tomorrow morning. May I invite you for dinner at a local restaurant?" asked Sergei, "Traditional cuisine," he added, while winking at Laura.

"No, thanks, but that's very kind of you. I'm so tired, and still stuffed from the heavy lunch we had today," Julia said, uninterested, while getting out of the car.

"Erm, actually, I'm getting hungry…" said Laura, looking at Sergei with a shy smile.

Julia rolled her eyes.

CHAPTER 19

Laura could not focus.

She had planned to dedicate the week, before going to Arizona, to start drafting the introduction of her thesis. But her thoughts were continuously dragged to the events of the previous week. That cryptic message from Professor Kasparov, to then discover that he had died in a strange accident, just after having sent that message to her. The odd conversation with Professor Schneider, then being told that he had died the day after in yet another odd accident. The unexpected interest of Professor Cecil-Hood in her data, to then find out that he had attended Professor Kasparov's last conference, along with Professor Schneider. She was anxious and uncomfortable about being somehow involved in such a weird story. Although concerned and even shaken by all these events, she was also intrigued. Eager to find out more. What was in Professor Kasparov's old datasets? Were they really of any interest? When she had received his message she thought that he was an odd person who had overestimated the importance of his data. But it would seem the people who broke into the BTA-6 archive basement valued that data just as much as Professor Kasparov did, maybe even more.

The week spent in Cambridge was unproductive and strange. Strange not only because of those thoughts, but also because of Julia. As soon as they were back in Cambridge, Julia had been in a good mood. She even looked excited. But just a few days later her mood changed abruptly. She barely said a word. Her expression was tense and absentminded. Something seriously distressing must have happened, but she would not talk about it.

Laura decided to spend most of the time out of the office, on the lawn by the River Cam, under the shade of her favourite willow tree. The sun rays, reflected in the ripples caused by the passing boats, caressed her face. She was hoping that spending some time in isolation would help her focus on her thesis writing. In vain. Those distressful and intriguing thoughts continued to whirl around her mind.

***

The screen on the back of the seat in front of her showed a map of the USA and the shape of the aeroplane approaching Phoenix airport. Less than 20 minutes to landing.

Trips with Julia had always been something Laura had enjoyed. They would spend most of the journey passionately talking about their common interests. The history of science was a recurrent theme. They were both keen to express their different views about the fundamental discoveries that had led to the current fund of human knowledge, arguing about how the brightest minds managed to understand the universe and reveal the laws of physics. Championing Isaac Newton versus Galileo Galilei was among their favourite topics of playful debate.

But there was none of this during this trip. Julia was silent, lost in thought. Unresponsive to any of Laura's attempts to start a conversation. Anxiety was clouding her features.

Laura decided she could not stand it anymore. She could no longer pretend that everything was fine and normal.

"Julia," Laura tried to catch her attention, "Julia?"

Julia finally turned her head to look at Laura, seeming as if she was woken from deep thoughts. "Yes?"

"Julia, what's going on? What's wrong?"

"What do you mean?"

"You know what I mean. You have been absentminded and worried about something for the last few days. You have barely spoken a word during this entire flight. You have continuously avoided eye contact with me."

Julia turned her gaze to look at the monitor as if pretending to be interested in the trajectory of the aeroplane on the map.

Then she sighed, "Right. I reckon that you shouldn't come with me to SPACEWAVE in Tucson."

"Why?"

"Something happened in Cambridge, which has got me very worried. Worried that we may be involved in something much bigger than us. I have probably underestimated the seriousness of the whole story. I now fear for your safety."

Laura leaned toward Julia with bewildered and wide-open eyes, silently prompting an explanation.

Julia cleared her throat, "A few days ago someone forced the door of my office, at night, and stole the hard drive with your data."

"What? Do you mean that even the last existing copy of my data is now lost?"

"Don't worry about that. Fortunately, I had made a copy of your data on another hard drive, which is in one of the drawers in my office. But that's not the point. Don't you understand? This cannot be a random theft. This cannot be a coincidence. Whoever broke into my office had a specific target – your data. This happened only a few days after someone broke into the BTA-6 archive room, in a remote region of Russia, to steal Kasparov's old data. And this is only a couple of weeks after Kasparov claimed a connection between the two datasets, just before his fatal 'accident'…" Julia hesitated a moment, then continued, "I'm afraid these are not rogue villains. I fear we're dealing with an organisation that is working on an international scale, or someone capable of orchestrating obscure activities across the globe. Unwittingly, we're part of something far bigger than us." She was nervously bending and twisting the fingers of one hand with the other. "I'm sorry that I had naively underestimated the scale and the gravity of this story. And I'm even more distressed that you're involved in this. That's why I don't want you to join me when, after the conference, I'll be visiting SPACEWAVE."

Laura was shocked and confused. "But… but then…" she stuttered, "why do you want to investigate any further? Why don't we simply forget this whole story? Why don't we just leave it behind us?"

"Because I'm not sure we can. I need to get to the bottom of this. I don't really know what these people are looking for and I'm not sure whether they have found it or not…" she looked down and added in a low voice, "Probably not."

Laura kept staring at Julia, puzzled. 'Probably not'? What did Julia mean? What else did Julia know? Something so disturbing that she didn't want to share it with her? She realised it was pointless to question Julia any further and decided to use her energy to argue on another front. "I'm not a baby. I can take care of myself. We are in this together and I want to find out more too. If you're going to SPACEWAVE, expecting to find some clues, I'm coming with you."

The aeroplane wheels screeched as they touched the hot asphalt of the runway. Laura felt goosebumps on her skin, not sure if it was due to the high-pitched sound or the fact that she had just committed to investigating a murder.

CHAPTER 20

The temperature was approaching 40 degrees Celsius.

Laura had followed all the presentations during the conference in Phoenix with interest. She had spent the coffee breaks outside the venue, enjoying the burning sun. She had also met with Sergei several times, although he was attending different sessions.

The conference had been enjoyed by Laura as much as it had been detested by Julia, who kept complaining about why such a major conference had been organised in early summer in Arizona.

Now they were heading southbound on Interstate I-10. Julia was driving, squinting her eyes despite wearing sunglasses. Her facial muscles were rigid, her head was pushed back against the seat, her arms were like two wooden logs attached to the wheel.

"You look tense, Julia", Laura said.

"Of course I'm tense! I've been staring at the burning, dark asphalt in front of me for the past hour! It's the only thing that doesn't blind me around here!"

Laura rolled her eyes and then turned to look at the desert flashing by. "So, what's the plan? Simply showing up at the reception of SPACEWAVE and hoping that they will let us talk with Roger Smith?" she asked, with a hint of sarcasm in her tone.

"Well, I sent another message a few days ago explaining that we are in Arizona, and this time I got an enthusiastic reply, directly from Smith's deputy, Grace Wilson, if I remember correctly," replied Julia while adjusting the sunglasses on her nose. "She said that they would be glad to welcome us and that Smith is eager to talk with us. So we have an appointment in a few hours."

"That's fantastic!" commented Sergei from the rear seat, leaning forward and enthusiastically grinning at Laura and Julia.

Laura did not comment. She found it strange that Smith had changed attitude so suddenly, from ignoring them to eagerly welcoming them. However, it was not something she wanted to dwell on too much. After all, people from various parts of the world had different attitudes and ways of dealing with situations. She had experienced this when moving from Italy to the UK. However, she was a little bit surprised that Julia was not baffled as well, or at least she did not appear so. Laura looked at her, but Julia's face revealed nothing.

***

"Dr Wilson will be with you in a minute," said the receptionist, giving them visitor badges.

SPACEWAVE, located in the Arizona desert, a few miles from Tucson, consisted of several large, modern buildings. Half a dozen enormous parabolic antennae for satellite communications were scattered among them. The whole area was vast and surrounded by a double barbed-wire fence, monitored by armed guards and CCTVs. Laura was not surprised by such a massive security system. Most space companies, especially those as big as this one, are also heavily involved in the development of military-grade satellites and devices.

They were now in the reception area of the largest building. A sliding door opened and an elegant woman walked into the hall with a speedy and determined gait. "Good afternoon and a warm welcome to SPACEWAVE," she said, beaming at them.

Laura was still feeling a little bitter about the seemingly hypocritical behaviour of the SPACEWAVE staff, who had initially totally neglected their request. But the friendly expression of this woman was truly welcoming.

"My name is Grace, Grace Wilson. I'm the Deputy President of SPACEWAVE," she said while shaking their hands. "I'm so glad to meet you, Professor Russell, Miss Bellini… and…" she looked at Sergei with a baffled expression.

"Vasiliev, Sergei Vasiliev. I'm a student at the Russian Special Observatory."

A shade of concern crossed Grace's face. Clearly, at this centre, which was obviously also receiving big commissions from the US Defence Department, there was considerable sensitivity about the nationality of visitors, Laura thought.

Julia intervened, "Yes, sorry, I did not inform you that our friend and colleague Sergei was joining us. I hope it's not much trouble."

Grace looked at Sergei for a few moments. Then she plastered a polite smile on her face and said, "Of course not, Mr Vasilev is very much welcome too." She continued warmly, looking at Julia and Laura, "You know, when I was young, before entering the space business, I was an astronomer too. In fact, my degree is in astronomy. Dr Smith is also a former astronomer. Even though we're now working in this space enterprise, we very much enjoy maintaining connections with the astronomical community and, more broadly, with the scientific community. Many of the space satellites developed by us are astronomical facilities or space observatories. Would you like a quick tour of the labs in which we develop and test these satellites?"

"That would be fantastic!" Sergei exclaimed.

"I would love that!" echoed Laura.

Julia scowled at them. She was clearly much more interested in going straight to their primary goal: asking Smith about Kasparov and that infamous conference.

"That's very kind of you," said Julia, "but I'm afraid we're short on time. Later on, I'll have to rush back to the hotel to join a videocon that I cannot miss."

"That's absolutely no problem," said Grace "we can provide you with a quiet office space so that you can join your videocon... and I suppose we do have an internet connection here," she added, smiling and glancing at a huge antenna parabola that could be seen in front of the building through the large entrance window door.

"This way, please." A large door opposite the entrance slid open as Grace approached it.

They passed through a sequence of wide corridors, all separated by large sliding doors. Laura noticed that each door had a red light next to it, which would turn green as Grace approached it, before granting access.

There were signs giving directions to various facilities:

Clean Rooms 1 and 2
Vibrations Test Facilities 3 and 5
Test Cryo-chamber
…

***

In a different building of SPACEWAVE, in a dimly lit room, a hand was slowly scrolling through the images of Grace, Julia, Laura and Sergei captured by the security cameras.

***

"You are probably mainly interested in the satellites and instrumentation that we are developing for astronomical observations," said Grace while entering a small room with various white packages on the shelves. She opened one of them and extracted a set of garments for the 'clean room' facilities.

"We're about to enter a Class 5 Clean Area. All satellites and any spacecraft parts must be kept in a protected environment that is as free from any dust and contaminating particles as possible."

In a few minutes, they were all covered in hooded white bunny suits, shoe covers, masks and latex gloves. Grace inspected the three of them to make sure they were all properly covered, with no exposed parts, except for their eyes. Then she approached a badge sensor, which turned green and a sliding door opened. Grace led them into a vast area, brightly lit, with white walls, ceiling and floor. In the centre of the vast clean room was a large satellite, covered in a sort of aluminium foil, with a large concave mirror in its centre. The whole satellite was sitting on a large platform. It was surrounded by several engineers, some of whom were in the process of fixing the satellite to the platform, while others seemed to be testing some sensors attached to various points of the satellite, including the mirror. Laura noticed that the large mirror did not have the typical silvery reflection, instead it had a golden hue.

"This is a space telescope that is planned for launch next year," Grace explained, "it is designed to observe the light of distant, primaeval galaxies and black holes, as well as nurseries of stars embedded in thick layers of cosmic dust. As you may know, infrared is the optimal light to observe both classes of astronomical objects. This space telescope is therefore specifically designed for infrared observations. As you can see, the primary mirror is coated with gold, as gold reflects infrared light much better than aluminium."

Laura looked at her golden image, reflected and distorted by the concave mirror.

"The satellite bearing the telescope is being clamped to this platform, which is a vibration test facility. During the launch, the satellite is subject to vigorous shaking and we have to make sure that it will endure the associated strong vibrations. The thrust of a launching rocket is so powerful that it is essentially equivalent to a bomb explosion, just more controlled and redirected properly. So you can imagine what it is like being inside a rocket during launch."

Laura's jaw went slack, although she could not really imagine what was like being inside a rocket, as fortunately she had never experienced being near an explosion.

Grace continued, "Satellites must be designed to withstand tremendous shocks. The platform will test this by shaking the satellite violently to simulate the vibrations during launch."

Sergei moved to inspect a tall tower of gigantic loudspeakers and horns, about ten metres high, facing the platform, with a twin tower on the other side.

"During the launch, the satellite is also swamped by soundwaves," Grace looked at Sergei and her voice got louder, as if warning Sergei not to touch anything. "Soundwaves so powerful that they can potentially break electronic devices, lenses and mirrors," explained Grace. She pointed at the loudspeaker towers. "Those massive loudspeakers and horns are used to simulate such extreme sound waves during launch and test the satellite's resilience in such harsh conditions." She paused for a few seconds to let them scan the two towers. "It is quite challenging to develop satellites and space instrumentation that can withstand such a violent shaking and such strong sound waves during launch."

"Must be quite shocking," Julia commented.

"You can see it for yourself," said Grace, pointing to a large window.

They approached the window, which looked into another clean room. There was another platform and two more towers of loudspeakers. A complex instrument with large lenses and electronic boards was on it.

"That's part of a scientific instrument that will go on another satellite. It's going to start its vibrational and acoustic test…" she paused while scanning the monitors located to one side, "in a few seconds."

The platform started to move. At first, the instrument clamped on it moved slowly. Then it started to shake faster and faster, more and more vigorously. Horizontally, vertically, in all directions. At the same time, the loudspeakers started to vibrate, generating a profound, deep sound, louder and louder. Although the room was insulated, Laura had to cover her ears with her hands. The instrument was shaking violently, rocking and swinging, trembling and rattling convulsively. Laura expected the instrument to explode in thousands of pieces at any moment. The torture of the instrument lasted for a few minutes. The monitors next to the window were showing graphs being updated in real time. "These screens show the displacement of the various optical elements, lenses and mirrors inside the instrument," Grace explained. All of the graphs were oscillating frantically as if the instrument was experiencing a devastating earthquake.

When the shaking slowed down and eventually stopped, Laura expected to see dangling bits and pieces and cracked lenses, but the instrument looked as if nothing had happened. Grace pointed at the monitors. "All of the optical elements are back in position within a thousandth of a millimetre. Perfect. Perfectly designed." Grace could not conceal the pride in her voice.

"Impressive," Laura commented. She was truly fascinated by such a sophisticated and seemingly delicate piece of technology, designed to easily withstand such a shocking and devastating test.

Grace led the way to the exit of the room, opposite the door through which they had entered. They arrived in another vast clean room, which was even larger than the previous one. There were three relatively small spacecraft, each about two metres in size, located in different areas of the clean room. None of them had visible mirrors or lenses, just electronic boards branching out, and each of them had two large holes in their sides. There were several mirrors distributed around the vast clean room. Laura noticed that these mirrors were reflecting laser beams, some of which were entering the spacecraft through their holes. Laura immediately understood what this was about. She was thrilled.

"So these spacecraft are not for astronomical observations," Sergei said naively, "I don't see any mirrors or large optics on them."

"They are for astronomical observations. Simply, they are not made for detecting light," Laura corrected Sergei, her eyes twinkling with excitement, "their goal will be to detect other kinds of waves from the universe."

"Indeed!" Grace exclaimed. She got closer to one of the three satellites. "This is our most important project. Technologically speaking, it is the most challenging astronomical space mission ever conceived. For the first time, all major space agencies have joined efforts to develop this project. NASA together with the European Space Agency, and the Canadian, Chinese, Japanese, Russian and Indian Space Agencies. All together. Unprecedented." She paused. "Although all of these space agencies are providing the technical requirements, guidance and funding, the bulk of the project is being developed here. We're very proud of this," explained Grace with a spark in her eyes, which were the only visible part of her face.

"Yes, but what is it?" Sergei asked impatiently.

"It's GATEWAY," Grace answered imperiously. "It's a project to develop the largest and most sensitive system for the detection of gravitational waves." Her voice reverberated in the vast area. "It will consist of a fleet of 12 spacecraft orbiting in formation. They will detect tiny distortions of space and time due to the passage of gravitational waves," explained Grace. "If approved, GATEWAY will detect the gravitational waves coming from the merging of the most distant, primeval black holes. Most importantly, it will detect the gravitational waves from the Big Bang… the very first heartbeat of our Universe."

"If approved?" asked Laura, frowning and with a concerned tone.

"The project is not yet fully approved. Although the governments and space agencies are terribly excited about it, before committing they want us to prove the feasibility of the project through these prototypes," said Grace, pointing at the spacecraft in the room. "All the tests in the laboratory have given excellent results, beyond expectation. In a few months, these prototypes will be launched in orbit for additional testing in space and, if successful, the project will be approved and fully funded, jointly by the several space agencies."

"What's the expected cost of the whole project?" Julia asked.

"Twenty billion dollars."

There were a few seconds of total silence.

"Yes, it's by far the most expensive astronomical observatory ever conceived. It gives you a sense of the magnitude of the project and the importance given to it by the scientific community and by governments across the globe."

There were a few more moments of silence as Laura and Sergei walked around the prototypes, inspecting them from all angles.

Julia had crossed her arms and was tapping her foot. "Impressive," she said, "though I'm afraid that we cannot hear more about these fantastic prototypes, as our schedule is a bit tight. May I suggest that we move on to meet Dr Smith," said

Julia, gesturing towards the entrance door they had come from.

"Sure. The fastest route to Roger's office is actually this way," said Grace, heading towards a smaller door on the opposite side of the vast clean room. The door led to a narrow passage, different from all the other corridors they had passed through so far. It had pipes covered in foam rubber and foil, valves, wires and electric panels. At the end of the passage Grace scanned her card to open a small door. Laura noticed that this door opened much more slowly and with a hiss. It looked thicker and heavier than any of the previous doors, and had rubber seals.

The door opened onto a large circular, tall chamber, about 15 metres in diameter and about 20 metres high. Everything inside was painted black – floor, walls and ceiling. The whole area was dimly illuminated with blue lights. It was not cold, but a slight shiver passed through Laura's body.

At the centre of the vast chamber was a small satellite, more or less a cube, a metre in size, with two solar panels deployed on either side.

"This is our cryogenic test chamber," Grace's voice echoed like thunder in the mostly empty space. The pitch of her voice sounded distorted – only the lowest tones were resonating in the large cavity. The effect was that of a voice coming from the underworld.

"Here we test the survival of satellites and space hardware in the harsh temperatures in space. Typically, the side of a satellite facing the sun exceeds 100 degrees Celsius, while the side of the satellite in its own shade cools to –100 degrees. Astronomical satellites approaching the sun can reach temperatures of 300 degrees, while satellites exploring the outskirts of the solar system or in the shade of a planet can freeze to –250 degrees. We mimic such severe conditions in this chamber. The satellite to be tested is placed in the centre." Grace pointed at the small satellite located at the centre. "The whole chamber is essentially a giant freezer, but far more powerful than a household freezer. It can reach temperatures of 230 degrees Celsius below zero. Of course, before cooling, all the air must be sucked out of the chamber. Cooling must happen in near-vacuum conditions, just as in space, else frost would form around and inside the satellite."

Then she pointed at the ceiling. "You may notice that on the ceiling there are a number of large lamps that are now turned off." Laura looked up and, although it was very dark, she could see several dark lamps clustered on the ceiling, their glass dimly reflecting their images. "They can be extremely powerful and can simulate the radiation of the sun in space, and even the extreme radiation and heat that satellites approaching the sun are expected to withstand."

Sergei shifted his gaze to the small satellite at the centre of the chamber. "Is that an astronomical satellite?"

"No, that's just a small telecommunication satellite. It will undergo testing tomorrow," Grace clarified, "the chamber is oversized for it, but of course we use the same test chamber for any satellite. It is designed to hold the largest satellites and space telescopes that we develop." With her hand, she indicated the outline of an immense door on a side of the chamber, about 10 metres wide and 15 metres high. "That door is designed to allow our largest satellites and space modules through."

While Laura and Sergei were looking at the gigantic door, Julia was staring at the smaller door through which they had entered, her arms crossed and her fingers nervously tapping her elbow.

Grace glanced at Julia and said, "Please, follow me through that door on the opposite side, and we will exit not far from Roger's office."

While Julia and Sergei were following Grace, Laura stayed behind for a few seconds, staring at the small satellite, sitting alone in the centre of the wide expanse of the chamber. She felt a little bit sad that the following day it would have to endure such severe testing. Then she thought of how silly she was to feel sorry for a satellite, as if it was a living being.

Removing all the clean room garments was much quicker than putting them on.

"Roger's office is on the top floor," said Grace, while pressing the button for an elevator. As they were waiting for the elevator, a woman's voice from behind asked, "May I join you for the ride?" They turned and saw a young woman dressed casually, wearing sneakers.

"Hi Isabel," said Grace, then she turned to face her guests and added, "Isabel joined SPACEWAVE very recently. You may know each other, as she was studying computer science at Cambridge until recently. She graduated a few months ago."

"I don't think we've met," said Julia, while going in for a hand shake, "Cambridge is a large university. It's nice to meet you, anyway. I'm Julia, Julia Russell."

Isabel nodded, smiling, and turned to face Laura.

"I'm Laura. We may have met at some party, who knows," said Laura, chuckling, as the doors of the elevator started opening.

Sergei also made a goofy attempt to shake Isabel's hand while entering the elevator. "Sergei Vasiliev. Nice to meet you," he said, beaming.

"In which field do you work?" asked Isabel.

"Astrophysics, we are all astrophysicists," responded Julia.

"Then, maybe, you know Jack Lewis?" asked Isabel.

"Of course we do, he is a student at our institute, his office is just next to mine!" exclaimed Laura, "How do you know him?"

"We were at the same college and we are still in touch."

"I see," Laura smiled, while raising an eyebrow, "strange that Jack never mentioned your friendship."

"Well, I wouldn't say that we are close friends, we typically only met in the dining hall and at social events, together with many more students," said Isabel, looking at the display in the elevator. "This is my floor," she said as the doors were opening, "it was nice to meet you." Having gotten out, she turned, gave half a smile, and said, "A curious coincidence to meet you here." The doors of the elevator closed between them.

"We have another five floors to go," said Grace with a smile.

***

As they passed in front of Roger Smith's Personal Assistant, Grace guided the party towards his office's door.

"Roger is waiting for you," said Grace in an unusually loud voice, as if wanting to make sure that Smith's PA would not step in their way.

Grace knocked on the door and swung it open without waiting for a reply. "Hi Roger, our guests are here."

As they entered the office a strong smell of smoke filled their nostrils. Cigar, probably, though there was no sign of an ashtray. A plump man in his sixties was sitting behind a bulky desk. A floor to ceiling window behind him gave a complete view over the wide SPACEWAVE compound, with its many buildings and a wide desert area surrounded by a fence.

Roger Smith was intently looking at the screen of his computer. As the party entered his office, he glanced at them, lazily lifting his eyes from the screen, feigning a smile.

"So nice to meet you, Dr Smith," Julia said, smiling and holding out her hand. "My name is Julia Russell, from Cambridge, UK. This is my student Laura Bellini and this is Sergei Vasiliev, student at the Russian Special Observatory." At the word 'Russian' Smith immediately glared at Grace, who responded with a reassuring nod.

"Yeah, sure, nice to meet you. Please have a seat. How can I help you?" asked Smith while glancing at his watch.

Not the warmest welcome, thought Laura, especially from someone who was supposed to be 'eager to meet them', according to Grace.

"We are astrophysicists, working in the area of exoplanets–" Julia started.

"It has been decades since I worked in astronomy," interrupted Smith, "for the last 25 years I have been in the space industry, and for the last 15 years, I've been busy running this company. So I'm afraid I'm not the best person to talk to about astronomy or astrophysics." His eyes were continually darting to the screen of his computer and every so often he would click on his mouse.

Grace, who was sitting with her legs crossed next to Smith's desk, glared at him and shifted nervously on her chair. She leaned towards the desk slightly and placed her arm on it, as if to rest it, but then started tapping her fingers on the surface. She was successful in distracting Smith from his screen, who responded with an irritated scowl.

"Actually, we are not here to talk about science. Not strictly science," clarified Julia, "I will just get straight to the point: do you know Professor Vladimir Kasparov?"

"No, I don't remember anyone with that name," responded Smith.

"He was an astronomer, at the Russian Special Observatory."

"Was?"

"He passed away a few weeks ago."

"Sorry to hear that," Smith said with no real sadness in his expression and his fingers still typing on his keyboard every now and then. His forehead creased, "Why are you telling me this?"

"Well, his death is still somehow shrouded in mystery. He died in a strange accident at the BTA-6 telescope."

Smith stopped typing. For an instant, he glared at Grace. It was a fraction of a second, Grace had not even noticed, but Laura had seen it clearly.

Julia explained the details of the accident, or at least what they knew about it. "So, the additional strange thing is that the accident happened soon after Professor Kasparov had discovered a connection between our data and data obtained by him 30 years ago, and those datasets were stolen a few days after the accident." Julia paused for a few seconds to see if Smith was starting to connect dots, but he remained silent. "Coincidentally, 30 years ago is also when Professor Kasparov entered into a phase of deep depression, as a consequence of something that happened at a conference." She pulled out the picture and handed it to Smith. "A conference in Paris that you also attended. Do you recall what happened? Anything that might have caused distress to Kasparov?"

Smith sighed, put on his glasses on and asked, "Who is Kasparov here?"

Julia pointed at the young Kasparov in the photo. Smith squinted his eyes and massaged his chin. Laura was not sure whether he was truly making a mental effort or if he was just pretending.

"Yes," he said, looking more intensely at the photo, "I vaguely recall this. It was a conference about the chemical properties of stars. I remember something awkward when he, Kasparov, presented his results. During his presentation, he claimed some discovery. I don't recall what the discovery was about, but I do remember that people thought his claim was based on some marginal features in his data and that the interpretation was questionable and, actually… laughable… yes, laughable, that was the main reaction of the audience. His claim was not even criticised, it was not taken seriously at all, it was just laughed at and dismissed by the audience and the most prominent people."

"Don't you recall what the topic of the claimed discovery was about?"

"Not really. Must have been something associated with the chemistry of some star, I guess. Since I left astronomy all these memories about the scientific meetings that I attended have gradually faded."

"Do you remember what Professor Kasparov's reaction was when the conference's delegates didn't take his discovery seriously?"

"Well, as far as I recall he was embarrassed. Clearly he wasn't giggling with the audience. I remember he made some goofy attempts to reply to the comments, but he wasn't even listened to, he was continuously interrupted by jokes from the delegates."

Laura felt sorry for Professor Kasparov, that he had to endure such humiliation. She looked around and saw that sadness had clouded the expressions of Julia, Sergei and Grace. There were a few seconds of silence.

Smith had turned on his swivel chair to face the large window. His reflection revealed a frowning, thoughtful expression, staring at the blue sky.

Laura exchanged a glance with Grace, who shrugged with an embarrassed expression. Julia cleared her throat, which made Smith re-emerge from his thoughts. He looked at his watch and asked, "Anything else I can help you with?"

"You have been very helpful. Thank you!" replied Julia, standing up. Laura wasn't sure whether Julia was being sarcastic or sincere. Had Julia possibility inferred anything useful out of that short conversation?

On the way out, Laura stopped in front of a faded photo hanging on the wall. Julia approached Laura to look at the photo. It portrayed a young version of Smith, probably around the same time as the conference in Paris, with two other men, a mountain landscape and a telescope in the background. Julia frowned and pointed at one of the two men in the photo, "Arthur," she whispered.

Laura's eyes widened, she could indeed recognise the features of a younger Arthur Cecil-Hood. "They must be close friends," Laura whispered in response.

"Apparently," commented Julia.

Laura noticed that Sergei had engaged Grace and Smith in a conversation about the activities of SPACEWAVE, which gave her and Julia a few more seconds to inspect the photo. Laura pointed at the third man in the photo, skinny, with frizzy hair. "He looks familiar too," she whispered. "Can I see the photo of the conference in Paris?"

Julia pulled it out. "You are right," she said, pointing at a face in the conference photo, "he was one of the participants too."

Julia turned to face Smith. "May I ask you who the person with you in this photo is?" said Julia, pointing at the skinny young man.

Smith hesitated a second. "That's Neil. Neil Thomson."

"Oh, yes, quite a big name in the field of stellar globular clusters. I didn't recognise him so young," Julia exclaimed.

"Yes, unlike me, he continued in academia. He's now retired. He lives not far from here, on the hills near Tucson, next to the Saguaro National Park. Fantastic view from his cottage." Then he anticipated Julia's query, "Sandra, my PA, can give you his address," he said, having already shifted his gaze back to the screen of his computer and started typing. "I'm sure he can be far more helpful than me. You'll excuse me now, I have some important business to attend to. Grace will see you out."

"Actually, we will give them some *hospitality*," Grace emphasised the last word and accompanied it with a rebuking scowl at Smith, "for a couple of more hours here at SPACEWAVE, as Julia has to attend a videocon."

While Julia, Laura and Sergei headed to Roger's PA in the next room, Grace lagged behind. "I'll be with you in a minute, in the meantime, Sandra will find Neil Thomson's address for you." She remained in Smith's office and closed the door behind the three. With a tense expression, she turned to face him and whispered, "Roger, it would cost you very little to be slightly more welcoming to our visitors, especially astronomers. It's evident that you have not preserved any of the 'scientific spirit' since you entered the space industry. But bear in mind that one-third of the satellites and space missions that we develop are for astronomical research. Astronomers, and more broadly scientists, are our customers."

"Astronomers are not our customers. Space agencies and governments are our customers, they deal with scientists and their dreams, we don't. We simply execute and develop what we're asked to."

Grace was about to explode, but Roger didn't give her the time, "Please, don't start again with your lecture that 'our mission is to serve science'…" he said, mocking her, "that 'we have to provide scientists with the tools to further our understanding of the universe'," he waved her off, "and, by the way, you should be making better use of your time, following the progress of GATEWAY rather than acting as a tourist guide for our visitors," and with that he went back to his monitor.

Grace stared at him for a few seconds, her lower lip trembling, her pupils flaring with rage. Then she said, "It's pointless to discuss this with you any further, we have had this conversation too many times," and with that, she left the office.

Her smile was back on her face as she approached the three guests. "Julia, you wanted a quiet place with internet connection for your videocon, please follow me, I'll find you a suitable office."

***

Roger's gaze shifted to the photo on the wall.

The meeting with those astronomers had had an unexpected effect on him. Old memories had resurfaced.

He looked at his younger self. Smiling. Enthusiastic. Except for some of the facial features, he did not seem to share anything with the person in the photo anymore. Was he as enthusiastic in his current well-paid job as when he was an astronomer, barely making ends meet? No, not even remotely. Was he as happy as he was 30 years ago? Was he happy at all?

Enough with the memories! What was the point? He should focus on what mattered now… and the key question now was: did they know or did they not know? Were they simply pretending not to know? He was tormented by these thoughts. Had those people managed to trace the BTA-6 back to SPACEWAVE? Had they made the connection?

The control software.

Yet another of Grace's ideas, to support the scientific community. A variant of the software developed by SPACEWAVE to operate space observatories. Grace had persuaded the company to develop a simplified version to operate ground-based telescopes and ground-based scientific instruments. When she launched it, Grace had praised the initiative as 'highly advanced and sophisticated software at low cost for the broader astronomical community'.

He had never been convinced. Low profit and high liability.

However, while Grace was pleased by her 'charity' project, in her dreamland, in the end, it had been quite convenient…

But now it might be coming back at them like a boomerang. He could not risk it.

CHAPTER 21

Arthur Cecil-Hood was stroking his grizzled beard while waiting at the gate. 'Tucson', it said on the screen, 'Boarding in 20 minutes'.

He had already been allocated a few nights of observations at the Multi-Mirror Telescope, on Mount Hopkins in Arizona, in July. But he had persuaded the director of the observatory, a good friend of his, and the observer who had originally been allocated the night between the 9th and 10th of June, yet another good friend of his, to swap observing runs.

He wanted to be at the telescope at least a few days earlier to properly prepare the observations.

He was already savouring the outcome of those observations. The implications for science. The implications for his career. The implications for much more important aspects of his personal life.

Everything was going according to plan. Perfectly. Nothing in his way. Nothing between him and his greatest achievement. The greatest achievement of the century, of the millennium, of humanity. Straight to success… and more… what he cared about, deep down.

His phone buzzed. He looked at the message.

Plans had to be changed.

He headed towards the ticket counter.

CHAPTER 22

Miguel tried to work on his coding, but couldn't focus. He shot a glance at the picture of his wife and child next to his keyboard, while adjusting his glasses as the frame slipped down his nose. He was sweating and shivering at the same time. He reached out for the thermostat on the wall next to him. His hand remained on it for a few seconds, unsure which way to turn it. Looking around, his office, in the basement of a secondary building within SPACEWAVE, felt smaller than usual.

He could not stop thinking about those people visiting from Cambridge and the Russian Special Observatory. Bringing his palms to his face, he squeezed his eyes shut. His glasses fell on the keyboard in front of him.

His alarm watch went off. Time for his medicines. Yes, that was probably the real cause of his anxiety, the effect of his drugs was fading. He took two pills and injected himself with insulin. Their effect was immediate. He leaned on the back of his chair, breathing slowly and deeply.

A buzz.

A message appeared on his phone

We have a problem. Contact person will meet you to provide detailed instructions. In two hours. Usual place.

He was tempted to reply that it was too late for him, that he had to go home, that he *wanted* to go home. But he knew it would have been a waste of time. Thuban was not to be argued with.

***

Julia had just come out of the office where she had borrowed a computer for her videocon. Laura and Sergei had been waiting for her in a foyer next to the office. Its floor-to-ceiling windows opened onto the red Arizona desert, which now seemed ablaze with the sunset.

Laura and Sergei had planned to read a few scientific articles, but eventually ended up spending most of their time talking about their different experiences as students, and even about their personal lives. They were also starting to get hungry. Laura was nibbling a chocolate bar and Sergei was halfway through a sandwich which they had purchased from a vending machine. They were so engrossed in their conversation that they had not noticed Julia approaching them.

"Sorry to interrupt you. I'm done with my videocon and it's getting late," Julia said, looking outside at the long shadows cast by the saguaros.

Laura and Sergei nodded. They put their snacks in their pockets and stood up.

"So, according to what Grace told us before leaving, there's no need for anyone to escort us out of the building," continued Julia. "Besides all the signs, our badges are programmed in such a way that we are only allowed to pass through the doors that lead us out, so it's not possible to get lost."

They followed the 'EXIT' signs. The doors slid open as they approached them. Laura noticed that all the other doors they were passing by remained closed, with their red lights on. The security badge system was working properly, just as Grace had explained.

They were now in a wide corridor with many doors. Halfway there was another 'EXIT' sign high on the ceiling, with an arrow pointing towards a door on the right. As they approached the door it did not open. The light next to the door stayed red and would not turn green. Julia tried to hold the badge closer to the scanning device. Nothing. Laura and Sergei also tried with no success.

"Maybe this late in the evening the standard exit route is not activated and people are supposed to follow a different route because of some security or safety issues," Laura said while moving towards another door. Its light remained red and the door did not open. Sergei tried yet another door further down the corridor. Red, closed. Laura went to the last door at the end of the corridor. She got closer. Green. The door slid open.

"See?" she said with a smirk, "it seems that the route to the exit is indeed different after hours."

The door opened onto yet another corridor, perpendicular to the first one. They first tried the door indicated by the EXIT signal. Red. It would not open. They tried the door on the opposite side. Red. Closed. They tried yet another door. Green. Open.

The door led them to a large square area with several doors. Red, closed. Red, closed. Red, closed. Red, closed. Laura started to doubt that this area had any way out. Then the last door: green, open.

It led to a long corridor.

Red, closed. Red, closed. Red, closed. Green, open.

Yet another corridor. The various signs no longer indicated the exit, this must have been an area used by employees familiar with the building and usually not open to visitors.

Red. Red. Green.

Another long corridor.

Red. Red. Red. Red. Green.

Laura had a strange feeling. Like being in one of those mazes for mice used in some laboratories to study their behaviour or intelligence.

Red. Green.

Red. Red. Green.

The sequence repeated several times until they entered a narrower corridor. It was darker, just dimly lit, but Laura could see electric panels and pipes running along the walls. It looked familiar. There was only one other door at the end of the corridor. There was no choice this time. Green. The door opened more slowly and looked much heavier than all the previous ones. It led into a large circular area. High ceiling. All black, dimly lit. A small satellite at the centre.

"This is the test chamber that Grace showed us this afternoon," exclaimed Sergei.

"How is it possible that the route out passes through this highly sophisticated testing area? We are not even supposed to be in here without wearing the clean room garments," commented Laura.

"It must be a flaw in the system that regulates the access to the areas," Julia said, scowling. "Anyway, it's not our fault," and she headed towards the opposite door, the one through which they had entered the chamber earlier in the afternoon.

Red, closed.

Laura tried with her badge. Red.

Sergei. Red.

"Well, it seems we have come to a dead end," said Julia annoyed, but maintaining her British stiff upper lip. She pulled out her phone. "No signal."

Laura and Sergei did the same. "Of course! This test chamber is made of thick layers of metal, no electromagnetic waves can pass through it," pointed out Laura.

"This whole test area is probably isolated to avoid interference with the instrumentation," said Julia.

"We should go back to the office area where we came from and call someone through a landline," Laura suggested. Julia sighed, while heading towards the door through which they came in. It had already closed, automatically, just like all the previous doors. Julia nearly walked into it, expecting that it would open just as it had when they came inside. It did not. The light remained red. Not a blink. They looked around. There was no other door, except for the very large portal used to let the satellites in and out, which was sealed well with huge hatches.

They looked around. No other way out.

"I'm afraid we're stuck," said Julia in a calm voice, but there was a slight twitch in the corner of her mouth.

Laura realised that her earlier comparison with a 'mouse maze' was wrong... a 'mouse trap' was more appropriate.

***

The only living thing in sight was a scorpion, crawling on a rock. No trace of Thuban's contact.

The meeting point was in a narrow canyon, less than a mile from the SPACEWAVE compound, well hidden from surveillance cameras and any other tracking systems.

The faint orange tint of dusk was giving way to the dark blue of the desert night. Miguel squinted through the thick lenses of his glasses, but couldn't see far. He realised that the problem was not the darkness, it was his own sight, getting blurrier. Breathing was becoming difficult, and it wasn't his anxiety, it was something different inside him. He decided it would be better to head back to SPACEWAVE, after all he had been waiting for half an hour. It wasn't his fault if Thuban's contact was late.

As he started walking back, his limbs felt numb, terribly numb. He was struggling to climb the path leading outside the canyon. He decided to sit on a rock, to rest and gather strength. Pulling out his phone, he realised that there was no signal. His sight was too blurred for him to make anything out on the screen anyway.

He looked at the dark sky. The myriads of stars that were visible at night from the desert had always given him a sense of awe and comfort. But now the sky appeared to him just a foggy blend of lighter and darker patches. No comfort from the heavens tonight.

***

"It seems that all we can do is wait for someone to find us here. I'm afraid that won't be until tomorrow morning, when people come back to work," Laura commented.

She noticed two cameras that were probably streaming the inside of the chamber to some monitors, but it was unlikely that someone was watching at the other end this late in the evening.

"I guess so. That's very annoying. I had some things to do this evening. All of this because of a stupid 'smart' computerised system," said Julia, unable to keep the irritation out of her voice. It was one of the very rare occasions when Laura saw Julia losing her temper.

"Sorry to interrupt, but haven't you noticed that it's getting colder?" pointed out Sergei while rubbing his arms.

"Yes, you're right," Laura concurred. She realised that she had put on her jumper a few minutes earlier, nearly subconsciously.

***

Simon was sipping beer from a can while lying back on his recliner, looking at the TV channel streaming through his laptop. He was on the night shift in the main control room of SPACEWAVE. This was where all the diagnostics, monitors and control systems were run for all the clean rooms and chambers at SPACEWAVE. It was a large area with several screens, computers, keyboards and electrical panels, each connected to the various test rooms, monitoring and showing the real time status of the various satellites and prototypes being tested. Since most tests were running 24/7, someone was needed during off-hours, to check that there were no emerging criticalities. Everything was automated and was supposed to work smoothly with no need for human intervention. However, the company still wanted one person to supervise at night.

Simon was sitting in a corner of the room. There was really nothing for him to do, except for 'checking'. He considered his job as essentially limited to glancing at all the screens and lights on the electrical panels from the comfort of his chair.

The Arizona Wildcats were due to play in less than half an hour. Nothing would have stopped him from watching the match on his laptop.

***

Laura noticed two digital displays on the wall. One of them labelled 'FRONT', the other one 'BACK'. Both displays were showing the same figure: 14°C. But the numbers were slowly dropping, synchronously: 13°C, 12°C, 11°C,…

"Those displays must be connected to temperature sensors on the satellite. The temperature is indeed dropping. Is it possible that they have started the cryogenic testing of the satellite?" suggested Laura, while pulling up the zipper of her jumper, "Grace mentioned that the test was due to start tomorrow, but maybe it has been moved up to tonight."

Julia snorted. "No, it's not possible. Before starting the cryogenic test they should first suck all the air out from inside the chamber, and I think we are still breathing normally," she said with a laugh, "although…" she was now frowning, "it may be that the chamber is going through a pre-cooling phase. But it cannot drop below about seven degrees, or else water vapour would start to condense on the surface of the satellite, and I'm sure they do not want that. So, nothing to worry about."

Well, seven degrees may be fine for Julia, thought Laura, but it was pretty cold by her standards.

They sat on the floor. Waiting in silence. Watching the temperature display.

10°C

9°C

8°C

7°C

The display seemed to have stopped on this reading for a few minutes.

Then

6°C

5°C

Laura looked at Julia, who was scowling at the display, motionless. She turned to look at Sergei, who shrugged and exchanged a deeply worried look with her.

4°C

3°C

Water droplets appeared, condensing on the floor and walls of the chamber, as well as on the satellite. The blue light that was dimly illuminating the chamber was now reflected by millions of water beads, producing fantastic patterns of light, which were slowly changing shape as the droplets started growing and merging on the surfaces. It would have been a wonderful scene if it weren't so frightening in that context.

2°C

1°C

0°C

The droplets were quickly turning into frost. Frost on the chamber's walls, frost on the floor, frost on the satellite.

They were all holding their breath.

-1°C

Now it was officially worrying. Laura cuddled up to Sergei.

-2°C

Her foot slipped on the ice that had formed on the floor. The inside of the chamber looked like a gigantic freezer. It *was* a gigantic freezer.

***

The Arizona Wildcats and their opponents, the Colorado Buffaloes, were entering the basketball court. From the comfort of his chair, Simon was rubbing his hands in expectation. The match would start in a few minutes.

To appease his conscience he quickly glanced at all the screens and panels in the room, from a distance, while staying reclined in his chair. He noticed that, on the control panel of the cryogenic test chamber, a blue light was on, signalling that the cooling system had been activated. The temperature display was large enough so that, from his position, he could see that the temperature of the chamber was dropping. Strange, he thought that the satellite in there was due for cryogenic testing the following day. Apparently, they had decided to start the testing earlier. He shrugged.

He realised that he was hungry, having forgotten to bring some food with him to nibble on during the match. There were still a couple of minutes before the beginning of the game, just enough to go to the vending machine. He hurried out of the control room.

***

-4°C

…

-5°C

…

The three of them were watching in trepidation as the display showed the temperature dropping.

Laura noticed that Sergei was nervously looking around at all the parts of the chamber, as if trying to find a way out. Then his eyes went back to the display on the wall.

"What's the meaning of 'FRONT' and 'BACK'?" he asked. "Why are there two temperature displays?"

"Front and back of the satellite," replied Laura.

"Front and back with respect to what?"

"With respect to the sun."

"Sun? What sun?"

"You were not listening very carefully this afternoon."

Sergei looked at Laura, frowning.

In that very moment, as if the chamber had been listening to them, as if to teach Sergei a lesson, a blazing light came on from above.

***

Breathe. Try to breathe.

No matter how hard he tried, his lungs would not expand.

Only a feeble flow of air passed in. Not enough.

Miguel was now lying on the ground. He could vaguely feel some rocks beneath him, but his whole body was numb.

He was dying. Unsure why.

Just when everything seemed lost, when all his efforts to inhale seemed in vain, he heard steps approaching. Someone was finally coming to his rescue! He couldn't see anything, his sight was now completely blurred, but he heard the steps stopping next to him.

He felt a puncture in his leg. It must have been a jab of medicine to save him. Finally. Soon his pain would be over.

**

With her eyes squinted, Laura could see that the light was coming from several powerful beacons distributed on the ceiling of the chamber – the 'sun simulator'. Despite the strength of the light, she could see the rest of the chamber, as the deep black colour of the walls and floor absorbed all radiation, with the exception of the satellite, which was now shining brightly.

Her first sensation was of relief. The radiation was warming her up… at least the parts of her body facing the 'sun'.

The temperature sensors were now giving different readings:
FRONT +1°C. BACK -5°C
And they were quickly diverging.
FRONT +5°C. BACK -6°C
…
FRONT +10°C. BACK -7°C
…
FRONT +16°C. BACK -9°C
…
FRONT +23°C. BACK -11°C

Soon the pleasant, welcome warmth became a nuisance, an unpleasant heat.
FRONT +35°C. BACK -13°C

Actually, it was much worse: burning hot on one side of their body, freezing cold on the other side.
FRONT +43°C. BACK -15°C

"We have to roll!" exclaimed Julia

"What do you mea–" Laura didn't have time to finish her question as Julia had thrown herself onto the floor and started rolling.

Of course, thought Laura, they had to avoid one side burning and the other side freezing.

Both Laura and Sergei threw themselves onto the floor and started to roll too. Day and night, day and night with their bodies.

They could not find respite from the sun's blaze. The area behind the satellite was too small… and even if they reached it they would then freeze to death.

FRONT +51°C. BACK -17°C.

Day and night. Day and night.

While rolling, Laura could see her chocolate bar and Sergei's half-eaten sandwich lying on the floor, where they had slipped out of their pockets. It was a horrifying sight. The upper part of the chocolate bar was melting, but the liquid chocolate instantly hardened when it touched the frozen floor. The side of the sandwich facing the 'sun' was being toasted, while the opposite side was growing ice crystals.

FRONT +59°C. BACK -19°C.

Day and night. Day and night.

They wouldn't survive much longer, though Laura.

She noticed a small light blinking on the wall. It was next to a small paraboloid antenna that was pointing towards the satellite, which had another paraboloid antenna pointing back at the antenna on the wall. The satellite was probably communicating with a control system in some control room, probably sending data on its status.

Maybe there was one last hope. She stopped rolling and stood up, staggered towards the satellite and started kicking its antenna.

"What the hell are you doing? These satellites cost millions!" Julia exclaimed.

"I'm not that worried about the cost of this satellite if we're going to die here!" Laura replied frantically, while kicking harder the antenna on the satellite. "If I manage to break its communications then maybe the system will highlight the anomaly to someone, maybe someone might notice…"

While rolling on the floor, Sergei looked from Laura kicking the satellite's antenna to the parabolic antenna on the wall. He stumbled up and joined Laura in kicking the satellite's antenna. But the antenna would not break.

"After all, these satellites are 'designed to withstand tremendous shocks', aren't they?" Laura recalled while panting.

Finally, in desperation, Laura moved backwards and then ran towards the satellite with all her remaining energy, jumped with her knees locked, and landed violently onto the antenna with both her feet. The antenna broke into pieces and the parabola hit the floor with a loud bang, sliding for several metres on the icy, wet floor.

The light next to the antenna on the wall had stopped blinking. It was now on, steadily.

The three of them looked at the temperature displays on the other side of the wall. They were now idling. The reading of the temperature was no longer changing.

"It doesn't mean that the temperature of the satellite isn't changing, it simply means that the satellite has stopped communicating its temperature," said Julia while rolling on the icy floor. Her face was starting to display a frightening mixture of burns and frostbites.

"The question now is: will anyone notice it from outside?" said Laura, who had been standing still for a few seconds to look at the display, while attempting to cover her head from the burning 'sun' with her arms. She knelt. A shiver went through her body as soon as her shins touched the ground. Then she lay down and started rolling.

***

An alarm was beeping.

Simon, annoyed, turned his head. The sound was coming from the station linked to the cryochamber. A red light was blinking.

No, not now, please, not in the middle of the game!

144

Without moving from his position, reclining in his chair, he tried to guess what the problem was. From a distance, he could only assess that it was some fault with the communication system of the satellite being tested.

Nothing serious. He knew how this would go, having experienced this on similar occasions. He would try to phone one of the engineers, who would take ages to answer, half asleep, only to tell him that there was nothing that he could do now and that they would fix it the following day. So he would have spent half an hour of his precious time to achieve nothing, while missing some of the best shots in the game.

He decided to ignore the alarm. He put on his headphones and plugged them into his laptop, to minimise the nuisance of the alarm beeping, and lay back in his chair to watch the rest of the game.

***

Laura was lying on the floor. Julia and Sergei were a few metres away. None of them were rolling anymore. Exhausted.

The sun simulator was even brighter. The floor was colder than ever.

There was no sign that anyone had shut down the system. No one was coming to their rescue.

On the side facing the 'sun' she was feeling the exposed parts of her skin literally burning. The parts of her body touching the floor were frozen, her skin cracking. Her blood was freezing immediately after oozing out of her wounds.

She would never have imagined that her death would be as painful and as ridiculous as this, half-roasted and half-frozen.

This was her last thought before blacking out.

***

That damned beeping was really annoying, so loud that he could hardly hear the voice of the game commentator, even with his headphones on.

145

Enough!

Huffing, he removed his headphones and headed towards the cryochamber control station to see if the alarm could be silenced, or at least its volume adjusted.

He fiddled with the various knobs and buttons on the console, around the monitor. That's when he saw the images relayed from one of the cameras inside the cryochamber.

Something odd.

What the hell!

CHAPTER 23

Echoing voices and sounds.

Darkness.

Some images out of focus.

Flashes of light.

Pain.

"This one is recovering consciousness too," yelled a female voice next to her, with an unfamiliar, strong accent.

She felt some pressure on her wrist – pain! She instinctively pulled her arm back.

"Easy, easy. Calm down," said the same voice with a soothing tone, "let me handle this. This is the first time that I'm treating burns and frostbites at the same time, on the same person." Then, in a whisper, she added, "Just unbelievable…"

Laura could finally open her eyes wide enough to put images into focus.

Julia was next to her, sitting on another stretcher. Part of her face, arms and hands were covered with bandages. She gave her a weak smile.

"It seems that she's ok, more or less," said the woman with the strong accent, who Laura could now see was wearing a paramedic uniform and who was now checking her blood pressure, "despite everything," she added.

"Yes, it seems so," echoed a man also in a paramedic uniform, who was attending Sergei on another stretcher. "I'm sure there's no clinical record, anywhere, of such an odd mix of injuries."

Sergei slowly turned to Laura. "We made it," he said with a feeble voice.

"Yes, we made it," echoed Julia, "and thanks to you, Laura. We owe you our lives."

Laura tried to smile. She looked around and saw that they were now outside the main SPACEWAVE building. The flashing lights were coming from four ambulances parked next to them, and several police cars. There were policemen, paramedics and other people clustered in another area, not far from them.

As she was brought to the ambulance, she saw several other police cars and ambulances sped by at a distance, with their flashing lights on. Strangely, they passed on the grounds just outside the fenced area, reached the asphalted road and then disappeared in the direction of the city.

CHAPTER 24

"Thank heavens you're all doing ok!" said Grace, her face pale, as she got closer to Julia's hospital bed. "I'm so sorry. You could have been killed in that chamber!" she exclaimed. Tears welled up in her eyes. "I don't know how this could have happened. There must have been some bug in the automatised system of our building. Our engineers are already looking into it."

"No worries," said Julia, waving her bandaged hand, "sometimes, the simple old-fashioned systems work better and are safer," she added with a hint of bitterness in her tone.

"You might be right," admitted Grace sighing and shaking her head, "we're probably relying too much on sophisticated, automated systems that might escape our control, without us realising it." She paused as if deep in thought.

Then she looked at a large bouquet that she was holding, lifted it higher and said, "Unfortunately Roger could not come to visit you, but he sent these flowers along with his apologies on behalf of the company."

"Oh, very kind of him," commented Julia, "please, *send* him our thanks," she added. Laura noticed a pinch of sarcasm in her voice.

"Erm… sure, I will." Grace's expression couldn't hide some embarrassment. She started arranging the flowers in a vase next to Laura's bed. "If you don't mind I will take a few of them to Sergei," Grace said, "I understand he is in the other wing of the hospital."

"Indeed," replied Laura. "We managed to see him earlier this morning. He's doing fine too, despite the injuries."

For a split second, a grimace of guilt crossed Grace's features, as if suddenly reminded of the several wounds that the three of them were suffering because of the fault inside her company.

"He really is doing ok," insisted Laura, now sorry for her remark on the injuries, "and we are doing fine too. The doctors said that we should be discharged from the hospital in a couple of days."

Grace nodded, attempting a smile. "If there is anything I can do, please don't hesitate to call me, anytime," she laid a card onto Laura's side table.

As Grace adjusted the flowers, Laura couldn't resist inquirying about something that had been puzzling her since the previous night. "Grace, may I ask you a question about last night?"

"Certainly."

"While we were attended by the paramedics I noticed a few ambulances and police cars, with their flashing lights on, passing outside the fenced area. What were they there for? What happened outside the SPACEWAVE area?" Laura asked.

Grace closed her eyes and sighed. "There has been another accident," she shook her head. "A terrible accident… one of our employees has died."

"What?!" exclaimed Laura while instinctively pulling herself up on her bed, followed by a grimace, as her wounds were still painful.

"How? When?" asked Julia from the other bed.

"His wife called us as she was worried that he was not back home yet. We could trace that he had used his badge late in the evening to leave the fenced area through a secondary, unattended gate. We called the police, who started a search in that area. Police dogs found his body in a canyon less than a mile away." Grace's voice broke. "Sorry," she said, half hiding her face in her hands.

"No need to apologise. It must have been a sequence of very upsetting events for you last night," said Julia with a comforting tone. Then she brought her hand to her scarred chin and massaged it while frowning, "Isn't it a little odd that your employee decided to go for a walk in a canyon so late?"

Grace was attempting to wipe tears from her face. "Sorry?" she asked with a confused expression.

"Yes, really strange," echoed Laura. "Why did he go walking in the desert so late, especially given that his wife was expecting him?"

"I don't know," responded Grace. "Maybe he was taking a walk to relax at the end of the workday. Maybe some jogging. I don't know," she added, shrugging.

"Maybe he was planning to meet someone else… for some entertainment, before going home," said a smiling corpulent man at the entrance of the room. He was wearing a sheriff's uniform. Grizzled moustache and sunglasses, though they were indoors. A skinny man, also in uniform, who was accompanying the sheriff, laughed at his joke, which Laura found in poor taste, especially given the circumstances.

"Sheriff Gonnagel is looking into the case," explained Grace, introducing the man.

"Nice to meet you Sheriff," said Julia. He nodded back.

"What was the cause of his death?" Julia asked.

"He was bitten by a rattlesnake," answered the sheriff. "We're still waiting for the post-mortem examination report, but there's little doubt about it. One of his legs had the clear mark of a rattlesnake bite and, at first glance, he had all the signs of someone who died of lung and heart failure because of snake venom."

"When did he die?" asked Laura.

"At around 9 pm, according to the forensic team. Just about one hour after he had left SPACEWAVE, based on the records of his badge."

"But isn't that strange?" asked Laura.

"What?"

"I'm not from Arizona and I'm not an expert in rattlesnakes, you certainly know much more than me, Sheriff," hesitated Laura, "but… as far as I know, rattlesnake venom takes more than two hours to kill a person. This means he was bitten by the rattlesnake *within* the SPACEWAVE fenced area."

The sheriff looked puzzled. "So what? Rattlesnakes may be hiding inside the fenced area. The fence doesn't prevent snakes from getting in."

"Yes, I agree, but isn't it strange?" repeated Laura. Julia nodded at Laura with a smirk.

"What?" This time the sheriff sounded irritated.

"That he was bitten by a rattlesnake inside the SPACEWAVE fenced area and then, instead of seeking help, he left for a night stroll in a canyon a mile away."

The sheriff removed his sunglasses. For a moment it seemed to Laura that he was trying to make sense of such nonsense, but the totally blank expression of his eyes revealed that his powers of deduction had already been stretched to their limit. His thoughts culminated in a curt "Young lady, I'm the one who asks the questions here!" He hesitated as if trying to find a question to ask. Then he said, "I just came here to ask if you're all right."

"Yes, we are all right, thank you for your concern," Julia replied curtly.

"Good. Give your details to my assistant in case I need further information from you." With that he walked away. His lieutenant looked at him and then at Julia scratching his head. Then he pulled out a small notepad.

As Grace had moved a little bit farther away, Julia whispered to Laura, "Not really a thorough investigation, if I may say so."

Laura nodded and hinted half a smile.

"Do you really believe these are accidents?" Laura whispered back.

"No, I don't."

CHAPTER 25

Although the three of them recovered quickly, the doctors were concerned about the odd combination of injuries, and so they were kept in hospital for observation longer than they had expected.

Roger Smith never showed up. Grace, however, visited them nearly every day, with a disheartened expression. "I feel directly responsible for all of this," she had continued remarking, during one of her visits. "This accident has been a major failure of the company and I take full responsibility. I've set our best engineers to look at the malfunction... but they have not identified any anomaly. So I must admit that we still don't know how it could have happened." Although her apologies appeared sincere, in the last few days her anxiety was clearly also driven by fear of the implications that the accident might have for the company. "Given that, fortunately there weren't any serious consequences, I trust that there's no need to bother the British, Italian and Russian embassies, and more generally it would be good to limit the publicity of the accident. You understand that this story may potentially jeopardise many of our projects, putting jobs at risk," she had said.

"Don't worry," Julia had reassured her, "we don't want to make a big fuss out of it, let's leave the whole story behind us."

In reality, when Grace was not present, Julia had made it clear that she was certainly not pleased with the accident, not only because it had risked killing the three of them, but also because, as a consequence of it, they were stuck in the hospital. In fact, during the entire hospital stay, Julia was champing at the bit to get out, claiming that they were doing fine and complaining that she had work to do.

Finally, they were released from hospital one week after the accident, early on a bright morning.

While Julia took a taxi to SPACEWAVE to collect the hired car, Laura and Sergei had planned to quickly freshen up at the hotel and then hang out together in a nearby mall, to relax and, most importantly, to recover from the shock of the previous week.

Laura wanted to buy some souvenirs from Arizona. She found a dreamcatcher for her sister. She loved the idea of something that could catch bad dreams at night, although she would have liked an object that could deliver good dreams even more, she really needed some.

As she was about to pay, she jumped back frightened. By the till lay the skeleton of a rattlesnake, head to tail, just a few centimetres from her. After the story of the SPACEWAVE employee who died due a rattlesnake bite, she was particularly sensitive to the thought of these creatures, let alone seeing their skeleton. Who on earth would buy the skeleton of a snake as a souvenir?

Laura noticed that Sergei had not bought anything. She suspected that his studentship was not very generous.

"Shall we meet for dinner tonight?" Sergei asked, as they were heading back and approaching the hotel.

"Sure!"

"Of course, ask Julia too."

"Erm, yes, I will."

"My treat tonight. I want to thank you for having saved my life."

"No kidding. But I'll accept the treat."

***

As Laura had expected, Julia did not feel like going out for dinner. Apparently, after a whole week spent in hospital, she had a backlog of 'things' to finish. She would just grab a sandwich. Laura did not insist. Deep inside, she was actually hoping that Julia would not join them.

Laura put on the only vaguely smart dress she had in her luggage. She looked at herself in the mirror and smoothed a few wrinkles on the fabric. She stared at herself, still, for a few moments. Parts of her body were still bandaged, and her face had a few scars. She thought of how foolish she was to worry about her looks after what she had gone through only a few days earlier. But she was determined to overcome those disturbing memories, and this evening she would make an effort not to think about the recent events. Relax and enjoy, she told herself.

She did not usually wear any makeup, but tonight she wanted to put on some mascara, although even that wasn't simple, as her hand was still a little bit shaky from time to time. Maybe also some lipstick, colour... nude... no, scarlet... she looked at it and flushed slightly. No, nude.

It was dusk when Sergei knocked on her door. As Laura opened it, she saw him beaming. He was wearing a white shirt and was a bit out of breath, having probably walked fast from his nearby hotel. He slightly squinted his eyes. As they adjusted to the light inside the room and could properly see Laura, he gaped.

"You... you are..." he stuttered.

"I appreciate it. Thank you," Laura reassured him. "Julia will not join us. She has some things to finish," she added.

"What a shame," lied Sergei, smiling. "This way. The restaurant is not far."

A few minutes later they approached the restaurant. It had a tricolour sign: green, white and red. Laura stopped in front of it and hesitated.

Sergei looked at her. "The hotel receptionist recommended this restaurant and I thought you might fancy some Italian food."

Her mouth slowly curved into a smile, erasing her frown. "What a pleasant surprise. Thanks."

After they had sat at the table, Laura started inspecting the menu, raising an eyebrow. Maybe 'Spaghetti Bolognaise'? She would have a try.

Laura noticed that Sergei had ordered the least expensive course. Her thoughts went back to Sergei's modest means. Laura's PhD studentship was enough to live on, but without many extras. She suspected Sergei's student allowance was lower than hers. Probably enough for a remote area of Russia, but when travelling abroad he was likely struggling with the cost of living in big cities. She felt bad that Sergei was going to spend all his money at a restaurant because of her. She wanted to pay her share, but did not know how to approach the issue without hurting his feelings.

"I would have loved to take one or two weeks off and have the chance to visit this area in the southwest of the USA. You know, Monument Valley, the Grand Canyon, all the way to the Arches National Park," Laura said, smiling and looking up with a dreamy expression, "but I have to be careful, my studentship is barely enough to live on," she laughed, "I cannot afford many extras, if any. I guess you must be facing similar issues..." she left the sentence unfinished, and nodding at Sergei, prompting him to comment.

"Yes, our job is not very rewarding in terms of money. But I don't really care, do you? After all, the most valuable and important things in life cannot be bought with money," Sergei responded, with a spark of enthusiasm in his blue eyes.

"Are you talking about things such as love..." said Laura with a disenchanted half-smile.

"Not really. I'm talking about talent. Playing a musical instrument. Giving shape and life to a piece of stone. The thrill of understanding the laws of the universe..." he smiled. Then he glanced at the restaurant's open kitchen. "Blending different ingredients and masterfully cooking them into a harmony of delightful flavours... that also needs talent." His gaze slowly shifted back to Laura's green eyes. "These are things you cannot buy," he added, "You can buy a better education, true, but there's a limit to what you can achieve if you're not talented."

This was not what Laura was originally aiming at when she introduced the topic, but she was intrigued by where the conversation was going.

"I'm not sure," Laura said hesitantly, "Take us scientists, we may be talented in our field, maybe... but I sense that most of the time we don't really appreciate and enjoy the value and the implications of what we're studying. I find myself always dealing with equations, processing data, developing codes, and most of the time I lose sight of the ultimate goal. Stuck in a lab, cooped up in an office, frantically analysing data, focused on a little piece of a much larger puzzle. I sometimes think that my relatives and my friends relish the outcome of science much more than us... from the outside they can have a broader view, they can enjoy and appreciate the sight of all the pieces coming together. We scientists are too specialised, we have lost the wonder, we no longer see the charm of science."

"Madam," a waiter interrupted their conversation, setting their dishes on the table in front of them. Laura's philosophical thoughts were brought back down to earth by the terrible sight of the pale spaghetti in front of her. She knew it was overcooked without having to taste it. The sauce, too bright a red, was not mixed or tossed with the spaghetti, but sadly lying on top of it. She gave it the benefit of the doubt, maybe this was one of those cases when the taste of food does not match its appearance... no, it was not, she realised soon after her first bite.

Despite all her efforts, her expression gave her away.

"Something wrong?" Sergei asked.

"No... not really," Laura replied in an uncertain voice. Then she sighed, "Sergei, I'm going be completely honest with you... inviting an Italian to an Italian restaurant abroad can be risky. Some Italian restaurants abroad are very good, but some of them adjust the recipes to meet the local taste and traditions, which is understandable... but Italian recipes have some fundamental boundaries that Italians don't like to cross."

Sergei didn't seem taken aback by Laura's remarks. On the contrary, his expression brightened even further, with his glittering eyes looking straight into hers. He had been smiling at her during the whole dinner.

"You mean like pineapple on pizza?" he asked, pointing at the menu.

"Exactly!" she exclaimed, slapping the table. "In Italy pineapple on pizza is forbidden by our constitution."

Sergei's eyes widened and he straightened up. "Really?" he asked with a bewildered expression.

She looked at him with mock-seriousness. Then she burst out laughing and he grinned back at her.

"Ok, thanks, understood. Lesson learnt," he said, laughing softly and shaking his head.

He continued beaming at her, in silence.

Laura beamed back at him, at first a little bit embarrassed, then more sweetly and relaxed. A few seconds, maybe hours, passed, gazing at each other.

Their meaningful silence was interrupted by the waiter, "Is there a problem, Madam? Not to your liking?" nodding at the spaghetti, barely touched.

"On the contrary," Laura replied promptly, "delicious, just too much, I'm on a diet." Laura and Sergei glanced at each other, smiling in complicity.

***

On the way back, the strong scent of the desert plants filled her nostrils, inebriating her with the fragrance of the night. Laura felt the irresistible need to hold Sergei's hand. She was charmed by him… by his intellect, his enthusiasm, his gentle manners, his wholehearted spirit.

They stopped in front of Laura's hotel entrance.

"So, I guess I'll see you tomorrow morning," he said.

"I guess so."

They stared at each other for a few seconds.

Sergei slowly moved towards her.

Laura closed her eyes.

Their lips were nearly grazing when Laura dodged and kissed him on the cheek.

Why? Why did she dodge? She hated herself! She really wanted to kiss his lips. Was it that stupid thing that people call 'feminine instinct'?

"Goodnight," said Sergei, whose expression could not hide a hint of disappointment, while walking away.

"Goodnight."

CHAPTER 26

It looked like the landscape from another planet. The myriad of saguaros rising on the wide, red valley was impressive. Laura had always been fascinated by these tall, armed cacti. Bizarre creations of nature, perfect devices to store large amounts of water in one of the driest places on Earth. Each of them had been slowly growing for centuries. Just one centimetre in any rainy season, and many of them were as tall as a five-storey building.

The house of Neil Thomson was on a hill just outside the Saguaro National Park.

The retired scientist was gentle, calm and welcoming. He offered them a chilled beer, and they sat sipping it in the shade of a veranda overlooking the valley.

"Of course I remember!"

Laura, Julia and Sergei exchanged a glance that was a mixture of relief and expectation.

"It was a peculiar presentation. Most participants probably didn't give it any importance and forgot about it very quickly. But people should have reconsidered it more seriously a few years later." Thomson paused to sip some beer. He laid the photo of the conference on the small table in front of him.

"Kasparov presented extensive monitoring of some stars obtained with the BTA-6 telescope. Interesting stuff, but nothing spectacular. But towards the end of his presentation he showed some peculiar findings." He paused again, to sip some more of his beer. His three guests were still, thrilled, not losing eye contact with him. Sergei nodded, as if prompting him to go on.

"Yes, quite peculiar…" Thomson said, his eyes distracted by the drops of condensation running down the bottle. He parted his lips as though to continue his sentence, but instead brought the chilled bottle to his lower lip, and took another sip. Julia rolled her eyes and tapped her foot impatiently.

He opened his eyes and returned the attentive gazes of his guests. He nodded, as though responding to their implicit prompt. "For one of the stars that he had been monitoring, he showed the finding of some unexpected features in the data." He sipped some more beer. "Kasparov gave a quite far-fetched interpretation of those features that, at that time, caused hilarity among the public."

Laura leaned forward.

"He claimed that those features were possibly traces of the atmosphere of a planet transiting in front of the star. More specifically, he claimed to have detected water vapour in the atmosphere of the putative exoplanet orbiting the star." Thomson paused again. "He also claimed the detection of other features that he could not identify, but that's not the relevant part. You may be aware that at that time exoplanets had not been discovered yet. The potential existence of planets orbiting around other stars was still in the realm of science fiction." He looked at the bottle of beer in his hand with an intense gaze, as if looking through it. A hint of sadness clouded his features. "The claim sparked a wide range of negative reactions among the conference participants. Amusement, indifference, all the way to outrage about the data interpretation. Some of the comments were at the level of mocking him. I recall that Arthur Cecil-Hood was one of those most fiercely and sarcastically attacking him."

Julia and Laura glanced at each other.

"Kasparov was clearly in distress. He was so upset by the audience's negative reaction that he could not formulate a proper response." Thomson raised the beer as if to drink more, but stopped mid-air and then set it on the table. His forehead creased. "I must say that the datasets were quite noisy and that the interpretation was quite daring," he commented, a hint of scepticism crossing his face. "However, in retrospect, when exoplanets were unambiguously discovered, several years later, and many other studies had discovered atmospheres around them, including traces of water, it would have been fair to look back at Kasparov's datasets with a fresh mind. However, the potential scientific implications of that presentation had been quickly forgotten. Kasparov hadn't made any effort to try to revive any discussion of his data either. He must have been emotionally devastated by that event, as he never published anything on those datasets and he more or less disappeared from the scientific community."

"He has now literally disappeared," commented Julia.

Thomson frowned, "What do you mean?"

"He passed away a few weeks ago," Julia informed him about the accident.

"I'm saddened to hear that." He turned slightly to look at the crimson desert hills surrounding the valley in front of them. "He was an outstanding astronomer," he added.

"Professor Thomson," Laura interrupted, "do you happen to recall the name of the star?"

"The star?"

"I mean the star for which Kasparov claimed the detection of water in a putative transiting planet?"

"Yes, of course, it was 70 Ophiuchi." Laura and Sergei exchanged knowing glances. "I remember it very well, as 70 Ophiuchi is a famous star, as you probably know."

Laura and Julia nodded.

"Famous?" asked Sergei raising his eyebrows.

"Yes, of course, young man. It's a binary star. In the late 18th century the astronomer William Herschel proved that the two stars were orbiting around each other... well, around their centre of mass. It was the first test of Newton's Law of Universal Gravitation applied to bodies outside the solar system," explained Thomson, "I remember that this was also one of the jokes at the conference when Kasparov presented his claim. People made fun of him, saying that he had chosen a famous star associated with a famous discovery, expecting that it would make his own 'discovery' famous too."

There were a few minutes of silence. Everyone was looking down. No words were spoken.

"Do you think there are any records of Kasparov's presentation from which we could recover more information?" Julia asked.

"I doubt it," replied Thomson. "At that time electronic slides didn't exist yet and presentations were given on handwritten or photocopied slides physically laid on a projector. I doubt there's any copy of those slides 30 years later and, as I mentioned, Kasparov never published those results in any article."

Laura twisted her mouth to one side.

"Actually... " he continued with a thoughtful expression, "actually... there was a student taking pictures... quite the enthusiast... I don't remember the name... taking pictures of every presentation, so there may be pictures of Kasparov's presentation somewhere."

Laura raised her eyebrows: what were the odds of finding the photos of an unknown student 30 years later?

***

"So what have we learnt?" said Julia while driving back, her bandaged arms tense and straight on the wheel. "Fine," she continued, without giving Laura and Sergei any time to answer, "Kasparov probably discovered an exoplanet ahead of its time, when the scientific community wasn't yet ready. And he probably also detected water in its atmosphere. So what? Water has now been detected in the atmosphere of other exoplanets, it's not surprising news any more. I do not see how this may be a major 'discovery'," making air quotes with her fingers, temporarily lifting her hands off the steering wheel, which, for a moment, worried Laura who was riding shotgun next to her. "Clearly not a 'discovery' that may be behind all these accidents... assuming that these are 'accidents'," again letting go of the steering wheel to make air quotes, once again making Laura nervous.

"Maybe the data contained something else," suggested Laura. "If we could only identify the student who was taking the photos... maybe the photos captured the content of some of the slides."

"Forget about it," Julia commented shaking her head and with a discouraged tone.

The road was going gently downhill, passing through the forest of high saguaros. The sun was low on the horizon, making the colour of the scarlet desert even more inflamed than usual. It was a beautiful evening.

Laura looked at Julia. She did not seem to feel the bliss. With a tense expression, her driving was more sporty than usual. She was constantly accelerating, taking curves at high speed. Laura turned to look at Sergei in the rear seat, who exchanged a worried glance with her and shrugged.

"Julia, we are not in a hurry," Laura ventured.

"There is a problem with the car," Julia's voice quickly got more frantic. "It's speeding up, the brakes aren't working and the wheel won't steer!" she yelled.

Laura noticed that the electronic display of the car was completely jammed.

The car was going faster and faster, skidding and swerving. Julia was clearly no longer in control of the car. It narrowly missed a large road sign. The pole of a second sign grazed Laura's side of the car and smashed the side-view mirror – its shards hit Laura's face. Sergei reached for the parking brake from behind, and pulled it with all his strength, but it had no effect. The car violently hit a large stone on the side of the road, flying over it and making the three of them bang against the inside of the vehicle. The airbags didn't work. The crash had not stopped the car, which quickly gained speed again.

It was moving faster than ever.

In front of them, Laura saw a hairpin bend. How will the car deal with it?

It did not.

It just went straight off the road, down a steep slope. The vehicle hit another massive stone, which made it overturn and roll violently several times.

It eventually stopped when it hit a tall saguaro.

The car, which was now on its side, oscillated for a few seconds, squeaking, leaning on the cactus, which was proudly maintaining its position and not giving way.

There were a few minutes of silence, during which Laura tried figure out what had just happened and whether she was still in one piece.

She heard the back seatbelt being released. Good! Sergei was alive.

Her window had smashed on the ground, with glass shards scattered everywhere. She could touch the scarlet sand of the desert. A liquid was spreading onto the ground next to her. She couldn't immediately figure out what it was. Its colour was not easy to distinguish from the colour of the sand. It was darker. A darker hue of red. She realised that the red liquid was dripping from above her. She turned. Julia!

CHAPTER 27

Laura heard the body bag being zipped up behind her.

A paramedic was soothing her wounds, removing glass shards from her skin. Maybe it was painful, but she couldn't feel anything, anything physical. Everything else was overwhelmed by the excruciating pain inside her.

Out of the corner of her eye Laura saw the bag containing Julia's body being carried onto the ambulance.

The sheriff was still babbling on about something. She could see his lips moving, but couldn't hear anything. After trying to focus, she finally made sense of what he was saying: "Your story sounds a bit weird, to put it mildly." It was the same sheriff they had met in the hospital.

"Of course it's weird," agreed Laura, exhausted. Then, gathering her remaining energy, she managed to burst out, "Everything in the last few weeks has been weird! All these accidents have been weird, and I'm sure they are not accidents, they are part of a pattern, and it's high time the authorities investigated this!"

"That's exactly what I'm doing, my young lady. That's why I'm questioning you," he said, adjusting the sunglasses on his nose. "Within less than two weeks you have been in two locations where two persons have died, not to mention the strange accident you were involved in inside SPACEWAVE."

Laura looked at him in bewilderment.

"Sheriff, are you perhaps suggesting that I may have something to do with the death of that SPACEWAVE employee?... and with the death of Julia, Professor Russell? As for the accident at SPACEWAVE, why would I have been so stupid as to attempt freezing and roasting myself to death?"

"I don't know," replied the sheriff. Laura's eyes widened in disbelief. He continued with a blank expression, "Maybe you plotted something which went wrong, maybe you lost control... who knows."

"I. Do. Know!" Laura emphasised. She could not believe what the sheriff was hinting at. "Sheriff, are you seriously telling me that I'm your suspect for the murder of my supervisor?"

"No," said the sheriff, calmly and plainly, "you are not the only suspect. Your Russian friend over there," looking at Sergei, who was being attended to by another paramedic at a distance, "he is as much of a suspect as you are."

Laura looked at him with a mixture of rage and despair, but didn't say anything. She realised that she would not achieve anything by logically arguing with that man.

"Do not leave town until further notice," he instructed and then walked to his car.

Laura was in complete meltdown. Confusing thoughts and pain were whirling in her mind. Then, out of this muddle, a thought came to her. "Sheriff," Laura called from a distance, "has the post-mortem examination of the SPACEWAVE employee been completed?"

"Yes"

"And?"

"Killed by a rattlesnake bite, as I had thought. Beyond the shadow of a doubt." He smiled with satisfaction and turned his back, completely ignoring any of the puzzling issues raised by her.

***

Tired.

In pain.

Confused.

Shaken.

The pain following the loss of Julia somehow reminded her of the ache of when her mum passed away, though it had been so long ago.

She had not managed to sleep at all. Lying on the bed in her hotel room, she was struggling to sort out her feelings and thoughts.

But one thing became very clear to her. This was too much. Too much to take in. She had to go home.

She quickly threw her clothes and belongings into her suitcase. As she opened the door she found herself in front of Sergei, hand raised, about to knock.

"Hi," Sergei said with hesitation, looking at the luggage in Laura's hand. "Are you leaving?"

"Yes. I was… I was planning to pass by your hotel to say goodbye," lied Laura, looking down. In the confusion of the last few hours, she had totally forgotten about Sergei.

"Where are you going?"

"To the airport. I want to take the very first flight to Italy. I need to go home. Immediately. It doesn't matter how much it costs."

"But the sheriff warned us not to leave town."

"I'm relying on the fact that he's not that efficient and organised. I expect that he has not given directions to the airport or to the border police." She looked at Sergei and his sad blue eyes. "If you're questioned you should simply tell him that I left without your knowing."

There was a pause. Sergei was staring at her, as if seeking more explanations. Laura kept avoiding his gaze.

Then Sergei broke the silence with an expression that did not hide his disappointment, "But… don't you want to know what's behind all these accidents? Don't you want to know if and how these deaths are connected? Don't you want to understand if and how they are linked to your data, to your research?" Sergei's tone was getting more heated, "Don't you want to understand why Julia has died?"

Laura lowered her gaze. Maybe Julia died because of her. Maybe she was *killed* because of her. Maybe all these deaths were linked to her data, to her research. Maybe she was unwillingly and unknowingly responsible. A chill passed through her bones, adding to her sense of guilt… but also her fear… fear of being at the mercy of some dark pattern.

"No, I don't want to know. I just want to go home and leave all of this behind me." She raised her gaze to look at him.

"Sergei, you have been so… so kind… and helpful… and more. I owe you a lot. But I really need to go." She sighed. "I'm collapsing. I'm breaking down." She hugged him tight and broke into tears. It was a soothing moment which lasted a few seconds, or a few minutes, Laura could not say. Then she pulled herself away. She looked at him, smiled and then walked away without saying a word.

***

The airport's ticket office looked more like a travel agency, with posters of exotic destinations.

"The first flight combination I can find for you to either Florence or Pisa… *one way…*" the man at the other side of the counter emphasised the last two words, while raising his gaze from the monitor to look at Laura, "will depart tomorrow afternoon."

"Don't you have anything earlier? Tonight? Any airport in Italy would do," Laura said with an expression that was a mix of supplication and anxiety.

The man looked at her, raising an eyebrow. Then he typed on his keyboard for a few seconds. "There's a flight to Atlanta in four hours and then a connection direct to Mila–"

"That's perfect! I'll take it!" interrupted Laura.

The man paused for a few seconds, looking at Laura.

"All right. Can I have your passport?"

Laura hesitated, then she pulled her passport from her pocket and handed it over with a slightly trembling hand. Would he check her name against some security or immigration list? Maybe she had underestimated the sheriff's efficiency. She looked at the clerk with some trepidation as he typed her name into the system. He looked at the monitor for a few moments, frowning. Laura held her breath. He looked at her. Then he turned back to the monitor.

"You're lucky!" he said, beaming, "You've got the last available seat on the transatlantic flight."

Laura exhaled.

"Give me a minute to complete the ticket purchase," the clerk said, handing back the passport to her.

While the clerk was typing on his keyboard, Laura's gaze wandered over the bright posters hanging in the room. One of them caught her attention. It was an aerial view of the Amazon rain forest at sunset. A glistening, wide river was winding through the jade forest. Likely the Amazon River. A glowing ruby sun was setting in the horizon behind some light clouds. 'Earth's green lungs are waiting for you' was the slogan, written in fancy characters beneath the image. A smaller label clarified that the poster was issued by the Brazilian Department of Tourism.

She stared at the poster, slightly hypnotised.

The river

The forest

The sun

…

Water

Forest

Sun

…

She was hovering over the forest.

The sounds of the jungle's animals were echoing from everywhere.

She flew higher.

Higher.

She could see the entire extent of the vast jungle, breathing as a single body, while relishing the fresh water delivered by the mighty yet gentle river.

She flew higher.

Higher and higher.

She started to see the roundness of the Earth. Only now did she perceive it was a planet, a beautiful, gigantic body bustling with life.

She could now see the sun from outside the atmosphere, no longer red, no longer dimmed, shining in its splendour.

Here, high in space, all the recent events started to revolve around her.

Kasparov's fatal accident

Professor Cecil-Hood

The wiped TNG archive

Schneider's death

The burgled BTA-6 archive

The photo from the conference in Paris

Her stolen data

Roger Smith

SPACEWAVE's dead employee

Snake venom

The freezing burning test chamber

Neil Thomson

The car accident

Julia

…

Water

Forest

Sun

…

A voice was saying something from a distance. She could hardly understand.

"Twelve hundred…"

The voice sounded insistent.

"Twelve hundred dollars, Madam." The clerk was smiling politely. "Yes, it's expensive, but that's the only option if you want to depart tonight."

Laura had not yet fully come back to Earth. She was still staring at the Amazon Forest poster.

"Santiago," whispered Laura, not taking her eyes off the poster.

"I'm sorry?" asked the clerk, furrowing his forehead.

"Santiago de Chile," said Laura more clearly, now looking at the clerk.

"Sorry, I'm not sure I understand."

"Can you please look for the first flight to Santiago de Chile?"

The clerk looked at Laura, now slightly scared, as if dealing with an insane person.

"Santiago de Chile!" insisted Laura, pointing at the monitor and nodding at his keyboard, prompting him to type the new destination into the booking system.

"Erm… sorry… what about your ticket to Italy?"

"Just forget about it!" Then she insisted again, "Santiago de Chile, please!"

The clerk looked at Laura in total bewilderment, not even politely smiling anymore.

"… erm… yes… of course," he said and started typing on the keyboard.

"I'm sorry, but the first flight to Santiago departs tomorrow morning, via Mexico City."

"I'll take it!"

Tomorrow morning… this would give her some time to work it out, she thought. She grabbed her luggage and headed towards the taxi rank.

CHAPTER 28

Sergei opened the door with dishevelled hair, wearing a baggy, wrinkled T-shirt. His eyes widened and his jaw went slack when he saw Laura in front of him.

"I may have half an idea," Laura said, striding into his room with her luggage, "but I need to access my data."

"Wh– What about your flight home?" asked Sergei blankly.

"So what do we know? We know that 70 Ophiuchi is a binary star whose bigger star has a planet orbiting around it," said Laura, ignoring his question. "I have no doubt about it. I fully trust the analysis of my data. I trust it even more now. Now that I know that Kasparov had also found hints of a planet transiting in front of the same star. Someone else must have made the same connection, the connection between my data and Kasparov's finding, and, for some reason, doesn't want us, or anyone, to make such a connection."

Laura narrowed her eyes.

"If I combine the information from my past data and the fact that the planet is transiting in front of its stars, then this solves the major uncertainty about the orbit of the planet, its inclination, and therefore it pins down its mass: it must have a mass about five times the mass of the Earth."

Sergei sat down. "Interesting. But... so what? There have been exoplanets discovered as small as the Earth."

"Yes, I know." Laura said dismissively, then she continued with her reasoning, "Apparently the planet has an atmosphere extended enough that its signatures, when transiting in front of its star, could be detected even with the early instrument used by Kasparov. He must have accidentally caught the planet transiting while he was monitoring the star."

Sergei kept listening intently as Laura paced in the room.

"We haven't seen his data, but if we trust Kasparov's interpretation, and I do, then the features detected in his data revealed that the atmosphere of the planet contains water vapour, implying that liquid water is present on its surface. I mean, given its distance from its sun, as inferred from my data, the planet's temperature should be about right, not too hot and not too cold."

"The presence of water is interesting, but not so extraordinary," Sergei interrupted, "Professor Kasparov was particularly interested in this story as he probably saw his redemption, in the eyes of the scientific community, in your confirmation of an exoplanet orbiting 70 Ophiuchi. However, apart from that, nowadays it is no longer a terribly exciting result. As Julia had pointed out, water has been detected in the atmosphere of other exoplanets."

Laura nodded. "I agree. Water on that exoplanet is unlikely to be at the root of this sequence of strange events. The key must be in those additional features that Kasparov had detected, but which he couldn't identify, and which might be the missing pieces of the puzzle. Someone, for some reason, doesn't want the existence of a planet around 70 Ophiuchi to be known and doesn't want those additional features to be found by others. No one knows what they were, except for, maybe, the person who stole the tapes from the BTA-6's archive and, possibly, that former student who may have a record of Kasparov's presentation, if those photos still exist." Laura raised an eyebrow.

"However," continued Laura, now narrowing her eyes, "we can still try to obtain new data about the planet's atmosphere through a telescope by observing its next transit in front of its sun, 70 Ophiuchi."

Sergei slouched in his chair as if he had lost interest in the whole discussion, "Yes. Right. Sure. Who knows when the next transit is going to occur."

"According to my data, the duration of the planet's orbit around 70 Ophiuchi is 271 days, about nine months, and I also know it is due to transit in front of its sun within the next few days or weeks. So actually we quite soon have the chance to observe it and obtain new data during the transit…" said

Laura, with excitement in her eyes, but which soon turned into concern when she realised, "This may be the reason why all of these accidents have been happening during the last few weeks. Someone who knew about Kasparov's claim 30 years ago must have seen my article published a few weeks ago and they may also have been aware of my additional data taken recently at the TNG telescope. After all, I explicitly talked about it during my presentation at the conference in Florence." She recalled Professor Cecil-Hood's strange look when she mentioned her new data. "That person must be aware that the planet's atmosphere may have interesting features, based on Kasparov's data, and may have calculated that the planet is due to transit soon. The sequence of accidents must have been triggered to prevent people from making these connections and to make sure that no one, or no one else, would observe the planet again during its forthcoming transit." Laura's expression turned from concern to a half-smile, "Ironically, the effect has been to make us aware of these connections."

There were a few moments of silence.

Sergei was staring at Laura intently. His interest now appeared revived.

"Fine. Exciting," he said, "but it's not enough to know that the transit will happen in the coming days or weeks. We need to know *exactly* when it will happen: date and time. We cannot use a large telescope to observe 70 Ophiuchi every night for weeks while waiting for the transit to happen. At such short notice, it will be extremely difficult to find an observatory that will give us access to a telescope even for just a couple of hours."

"Right," agreed Laura. "There are two ways to pin down the exact timing of the transit. One way would be to combine my published data with Kasparov's old data. Kasparov's old data contains the timing of the transit 30 years ago. Combining this with the information about the orbital period from my data would give us the exact date and time of the next transit. But we don't have access to his old data... though someone else likely does," Laura said, scowling.

Sergei leaned forward, "And?" he nodded, prompting her, "What's the second way?"

"The alternative option is to combine my published data with my new data, the data that I have obtained in the past months at the TNG telescope, but which I haven't had time to process. Those datasets have been mysteriously wiped off the TNG archives. I suspect that's part of the same pattern as the accidents. But there's a copy of the data in a hard drive in Julia's office," said Laura with a hopeful expression.

"Now the problem is how to access the data on that disk, but we may have an easy solution…" She pulled out her laptop, switched it on and opened the Skype application. "Yes, he's online."

CHAPTER 29

Jack winced when he saw Laura's Skype icon pop up on his screen, ringing.

"Hi, Laura. Nice to see you!" he said beaming, but his smile quickly faded when he saw Sergei sitting next to her. "Where are you?" he said, now less enthusiastic.

"Tucson, Arizona."

"Arizona? You're still in Arizona? Are you taking a holiday break?"

"Not really," she noticed that Jack was pointedly looking in the direction of Sergei. "By the way, this is Sergei. He is a student at the Russian Special Observatory." Sergei nodded. Jack didn't nod back.

"Isn't that the observatory operating the BTA-6 telescope where that odd accident occurred?" asked Jack.

"Exactly." Laura's face clouded with sadness. "Jack... that's not the only odd accident that happened recently..."

She briefed Jack about the recent events.

"I'm devastated! I'm so sorry. For Julia. And for you!" said Jack with a saddened expression, "But I can hardly believe all these strange events have anything to do with astronomical data," he commented.

"That's what I want to find out. But to do that I need to access the data that I had gathered at the TNG telescope over the past few months. Where are you now?"

"In my office. I work best in the evening, it's quieter. Why are you asking?"

"Excellent. I need you to go to Julia's office."

"I don't like where this is going..."

Laura ignored his complaint, "You need to look for a hard disk containing my latest data. I'm sure Julia labelled it properly. Hopefully Julia's office is open, otherwise..." she massaged her neck, glancing up at the ceiling.

"Otherwise," Jack interrupted her thoughts, "don't worry. As you know I grew up in a rough neighbourhood. I know how to handle certain situations," he added, winking. Then he sighed and promised, "Fine, I'll call you back in ten minutes, with good or bad news," and his scruffy live image was replaced by a photo of him with a plastered grin, combed hair and tie.

***

Laura was pacing inside the room.

Sergei was looking at his phone. From time to time Laura glanced at him. For some reason he seemed uninterested. Maybe he was not convinced that Laura's plan would lead anywhere.

Jack's Skype icon popped up on the screen. Laura rushed to open the conversation.

Jack's beaming face appeared, holding a hard disk in front of the screen. "Mission accomplished, my lady!" he said buoyantly.

"Great!" Laura cried.

"Wow!" exclaimed Sergei, straightening up in his chair and now showing renewed interest.

"Not too difficult to identify." Jack pointed at a label stuck on the drive: *Laura's data.*

"It was in a locked drawer an—"

"Fantastic!" said Laura interrupting him, "Thank you so much Jack! Can you please plug it into your computer and give me access to it."

"Yes, yes, calm down, that's what I'm doing," Jack said, clearly busy typing on the other side, "but…"

"What?"

"It's encrypted. It's password-protected. What's the password, Laura?"

"I don't have a clue."

Both Jack and Sergei looked at her, bewildered.

"I didn't encrypt the disk and I didn't set the password. Julia must have done this. She must have sensed that the data might contain precious information and that someone, possibly someone with criminal intentions, might be interested in it."

"So now what? Don't you have any idea of what the password might be?" Sergei asked.

"Not really. Julia didn't tell me anything about a password, at least not explicitly." Laura tried to recall all her recent conversations with Julia, but couldn't identify anything that could have been a subtle clue for a password.

"Jack, can you see anything on the hard drive that might provide any hints?"

Jack picked up the hard disk and looked perplexed. "Not real– Wait!" He had turned the drive upside down, "There is another label stuck beneath the drive."

"What does it say?" Laura asked, moving closer to the screen and tilting her head in front of it, as if attempting to peek into Jack's office to read the label herself.

"I'm not sure… there are two lines… the first looks like Italian, the second one looks like… Latin," his forehead furrowed, "I do not fully understand…"

"Can you please take a photo and send it to us?"

"Fine," Jack replied, sounding a bit annoyed.

In a few seconds the photo appeared on Laura's screen. The photo showed the bottom side of the hard drive on which a label had two handwritten lines:

Dialogo sopra i massimi sistemi del mondo
Philosophiæ Naturalis Principia Mathematica.
Isaaci. pCXXV

Laura recognised Julia's handwriting and felt a lump in her throat.

"What do they mean?" Sergei asked.

"These are the titles of two of the major masterpieces in the history of science. The first one is the original Italian title of Galileo Galilei's *Dialogue Concerning the Two Chief World Systems*. It's the book in which he discussed the two competing views of the universe in his time. One was the 'Ptolemaic system', widely accepted and approved by the Church, according to which the sun, other planets, and everything else in the universe revolved around the Earth. The other was the 'Copernican system', supported by Galileo through his early astronomical observations, which put the Sun at the centre, and the Earth orbiting around it together with the other planets, a view that at that time was considered heretical. The book was written by Galileo in Italian so that it could be read by the wider public, outside the academic community who then wrote in Latin. As the manuscript contradicted the Church's view that the Earth was placed by God at the centre of the universe, the Catholic Church placed it on the Index, the 'List of Prohibited Books'."

"Fine, but what does this have to do with the password?" Sergei asked.

"I don't know… but it looks like a clue Julia left me. We shared a common interest in the history of science and we eagerly discussed the works of Galilei and Newton and their contribution to the foundations of astronomy and physics. The fact that she wrote the title of Galileo's book in Italian is probably not only out of respect for the original version, but also to make it less likely that people other than me would understand it."

"Ok, but now that you have understood it, can you guess the password?" Sergei insisted.

"I'm not sure…" Laura looked at the image on her screen, massaging her chin and narrowing her eyes, "Wait! The title is incomplete. The full title of Galileo's book is *Dialogo sopra i due massimi sistemi del mondo*, I'm pretty sure of that, so the title written on the label is missing a word: *due*, which is the Italian for 'two'. I'm sure Julia omitted this word on purpose, so *due* must be the password, or at least the first part of it."

"It must just be part of it, I've just tried it – unsuccessfully," Jack commented.

"What about the second sentence? The one in Latin." asked Sergei, getting closer to the photo.

"That's the title of Isaac Newton's masterpiece, *Philosophiæ Naturalis Principia Mathematica*, which in English translates into 'Mathematical Principles of Natural Philosophy'. It's the book in which, among other things, Newton laid down the laws of motion and the laws of universal gravitation, also explaining the motion of planets around the sun. It was written in Latin, as was the custom in the academic community at that time, as I've just told you. It's often simply referred to as the *Principia*, but Julia wrote the full title on the label."

"Is it missing any word from the original title, as with Galilei's book?" Sergei asked with a hopeful expression.

"Not really."

"What's that *Isaaci* after the title?" Jack asked "It looks like Newton's first name, Isaac, but why an 'i' attached to the end? Is that a typo?"

"No, it's not a typo, it's the genitive in Latin, it means *Isaac's*, of Isaac," Laura replied. Then she frowned, "But it's not clear what Julia meant. The *Principia* is Isaac Newton's work, of course, everyone knows that, so what?"

"And what about the final part, *pCXXV*, it doesn't look like a meaningful word... is it some arcane name or a code?" asked Sergei.

"I don't think so. The last part 'CXXV' looks to me like a Roman number: 125. So pCXXV must indicate that we should look at page 125 of the *Principia*."

"Great!" Sergei exulted.

"No, it's not great, it doesn't make any sense," responded Laura frowning.

"Why not?"

"There are several versions and editions of the *Principia*, each with a different layout, so each of them has a different text on that page."

"I see," said Sergei, slumping back in his chair.

"Moreover, even if we could identify which edition Julia referred to, what are we supposed to look for on that page?"

Jack and Sergei's faces were blank, as if their brains were idling. Their gazes were mechanically following Laura, who was now pacing inside the room.

Laura's thoughts were racing chaotically inside her head.

Then, slowly, pieces started to connect with each other. Laura stopped pacing, staring intensely ahead of her, but actually looking at nothing. The walls of the room became transparent. She could see the outside, the red desert, the cacti. Then zooming out, fast, across the ocean, Britain's soft, green hills. Now in Cambridge, the River Cam, down beneath the Mathematical Bridge, and then… there it is, the elegant building… dive inside it, find the manuscript, the precious manuscript, open it… read it… focus… focus… come on… no! It was too long ago, she could not remember.

"Jack!" Laura burst out, "I need you to do me a favour."

"Yes?"

"You're a student at Trinity College, aren't you?"

"Yes."

"Do you know the Wren Library?"

"Of course I do, it's part of Trinity College. It holds some of the most precious collections of–"

"Yes, I know, I know, and it also holds Newton's personal copy of the *Principia*… with his own handwritten notes…"

"Umm… so what?"

"Don't you see it? Julia wanted the password to be deciphered only by her and me. She knew our joint passion for the history of physics and astronomy, that's why the password is encoded in Galileo and Newton's manuscripts. But that was not enough, not safe enough. She had realised that the data on the disk might have been of interest, or under threat, by some obscure and secretive international organisation. She wanted to make sure that, if stolen, the content of the hard drive could not be accessed if taken away from Cambridge." She paused, her eyes shifting between Jack and Sergei, who were gawking back at her – they had yet to connected the dots. She continued, "Julia's *Isaaci* has a double meaning: Isaac Newton's own copy of the *Principia*, and Isaac Newton's own writing. A while ago Julia and I visited the Wren Library. Newton's personal copy of the first edition of the *Principia*, with his own handwritten notes, is usually displayed in a glass case. But Julia had got special permission to consult the manuscript and we spent a couple of hours browsing it together. I remember she was particularly excited about some notes of Newton's, which she pointed out to me to highlight how his thoughts had evolved with time. I bet the second part of the password is one of those notes in Newton's writing that caught Julia's attention, one of the notes on page 125 of his personal copy. So we simply need to access Newton's copy of the *Principia* and look for a handwritten note on page 125." Laura was beaming.

"Erm, 'simply'?" Jack protested. "How do you expect me to access and browse Newton's original manuscript in the Wren Library? Julia had special permission. For me, it would mean submitting multiple requests, likely endorsed by my supervisor and the head of the department, and I would not even know how to justify them. Even if I manage to submit such requests, it's not sure permission will be granted. And anyway it would take weeks, maybe months. To put it bluntly, it's impossible to get access to the manuscript in the coming few days. Of course now, at this late time, the library is closed."

"Well, aren't you a good friend of the librarian's junior assistant?"

"I don't like where this is going…"

"Jack, please! We urgently need to know when the planet orbiting 70 Ophiuchi will transit. It could be in weeks, but it could also be in a few days… it could even be tomorrow. We can only know this by accessing the data on that drive."

Jack rolled his eyes.

CHAPTER 30

"Are you out of your mind?!"

Jack had expected this reaction, but he thought it was worth trying the simple, direct approach.

"You made me come here, in front of the Wren Library, at night, just for this insane request? To give you access to the most precious manuscript in the library?" Tom, the librarian's assistant, was visibly irritated. "You know very well that you need multiple permissions which take weeks, even months! Look, tell your friend that it will be faster and easier for her to wait until the scanned version is made available online, in a few months."

"Yes, yes, that's what I told her, but she was so, so... that I promised her to try. Anyway, I'm sorry, that's not the main reason I asked you to meet me here." Jack moved onto Plan B. "Today I forgot the printout of a chapter of my thesis, with my supervisor's comments on it, in the library. I promised to give him the revised version with the changes he suggested, by tomorrow morning, so I really need those notes tonight, otherwise I'll be in trouble. So I was wondering whether you could let me in for a few secs to get those pages."

"Sheesh! Your supervisor doesn't look so pushy!"

"Well you know, we're in the final rush for the thesis, so he's a bit concerned."

Tom looked at Jack with a doubtful expression. Then he sighed, "Oh well, you owe me a beer." He moved towards the library entrance's alarm panel.

Jack watched his movements closely. He would only get one chance.

"You know that I'm breaching all the protocols, don't you?" Tom said while opening a small window that gave him access to a keypad.

"Yes, I know, and I really appreciate it. Don't worry, I'll be quick and no one will notice."

Taking care not to be seen, Jack moved closer to Tom to get a better view of the keypad.

3-9-2-6-9

Jack saw a couple of red lights turn green and heard the main door lock click open.

They passed through the large door. It was dark inside, so Tom switched on the lights. They walked up a large stone staircase which took them to the main library, a vast room with row upon row of tall bookcases, each with many shelves. In front of some bookcases, there were display cases with glass tops, containing priceless manuscripts.

"So, where did you leave your precious thesis?" Tom asked, yawning.

"I think I was by one of those tables down there," Jack replied, moving quickly down the library to leave Tom behind, who was slowly following him, a bit unsteady on his feet.

Jack could see the wooden display case with the *Principia* in it, no more than ten metres away, but he did not go towards it. Instead, he swiftly hid behind a tall bookcase, so that Tom could not see him pulling a bunch of papers out of his backpack and drop them onto a table.

"There it is!" Jack yelled, faking relief.

"All right, lucky you, grab it and let's leave," Tom said, with an annoyed tone and droopy eyelids.

As they exited the main door Tom reactivated the alarm. "Be more careful next time. And don't tell anyone I let you in the library at night, I would get in trouble."

"Of course!" Jack pretended to zip up his mouth. "Thanks, you saved me, I owe you one!"

They left in opposite directions.

Jack stopped just behind the corner and waited a couple of minutes to make sure that Tom was out of sight. Then he returned to the entrance of the Wren Library. He approached the alarm panel.

3-9-2-6-9

Green.

Slowly, he pushed the door that was now unlocked. It was dark inside again, with just the feeble glow of the moonlight coming in through the high windows. He pulled a torch out of his backpack and turned it on. There were several motion sensors distributed on the walls, but they all had green lights on, indicating that they were deactivated.

He quickly walked up the stone stairs and entered the main library.

With reverence, he approached the case displaying the *Principia*. The manuscript was opened on the first page, displaying the full title

Philosophiæ Naturalis Principia Mathematica
Autore I S. Newton

'*I*' was for Isaac, '*S*'. was for Sir, the knighthood bestowed on him. There were several handwritten notes even on this first page. It was in a wooden case with a glass lid, which also served as a window to view the manuscript. It was locked, but only with a simple padlock. Clearly the custodians were mostly relying on the sophisticated alarm system and the assumption that no one would dare to force the padlock open during open hours. He pulled out a pair of massive cutters from his backpack and broke the padlock. His plan was to replace the padlock with a new one. No one would notice that the old keys did not open the new padlock until the next time that someone wanted to access the manuscript, hopefully not until months later, by which point Tom would not associate the changed padlock with Jack's request that night.

Wearing latex gloves, he opened the window carefully as if accessing a precious treasure. It *was* a precious treasure.

Without the glass, Jack could now see the manuscript even more clearly, in all its splendour. It was faded, torn, but glowing in his eyes. This manuscript had changed the course of humanity. He wondered where mankind would be without the knowledge of these fundamental laws of nature, which regulate everything, literally everything.

He remained in awe for a minute, while lightly stroking the first page, feeling unworthy to touch the unique manuscript. This should be regarded as a 'sacred scripture', not only for science, for all of humanity.

Focus. He had to do this. He had to look through this fragile book. Pulling his left sleeve up, he revealed the page number written on his forearm. 125.

He slowly started turning the pages. Nervous and sweaty. Fortunately the latex gloves were keeping his sweat from the pages, which would have ruined them.

He flinched as the lights came on. The noise of a slamming door came from the main entrance hall, followed by the sound of rapid steps on the staircase.

He quickly hid behind a bookcase. Then he looked between the books, trying to see who was coming. It was Tom. While walking towards him, he was mumbling something.

"… Jack…"

Had he discovered him?

He seemed to be talking to himself.

"…all his fault… with his absurd requests at night. Not only did I lose the keys to my room, but apparently I also forgot to reactivate the alarm… if my boss found out tomorrow morning he would have sacked me on the spot."

Jack felt relieved for a few seconds. Tom had only come back to look for his keys. But he immediately froze when he saw that he had left the window of the *Principia*'s case open! If Tom noticed it, it would be the end.

Jack kept monitoring Tom's movements from behind the bookcase. Tom had stopped walking and was scanning the area where Jack had pretended to find the printout of his thesis. He was now looking in his direction, squinting his eyes with a concerned expression. Jack hid further behind the bookcase.

Had Tom seen him? Or, even worse, had he noticed the *Principia*'s case open? He was sweating. Why had he agreed to do this?

He was expecting Tom to appear in front of him at any moment.

"There they are!" Tom had found his keys.

Jack exhaled as he heard Tom's steps retreating. The lights went off. He heard the main door being slammed.

The relief was short-lived. The lights on the motion sensors turned red – Tom had reactivated the alarm.

Now what? He was stuck! One of the sensors was right next to him. He could not move. Would he have to stay still until the following morning, when they would open the library? And risk being discovered anyway, when they would find the window of the *Principia*'s case unlocked and opened. Either way, he was in an awkward position, and he would not manage to be still for several hours, that's for sure!

He waited motionless for a few minutes, hoping that Tom had gone far enough, hopefully was even in bed.

Then he decided to act. He had to be fast.

He swiftly moved towards the *Principia*. The alarm went off immediately – loud.

All the lights were automatically switched on.

He would have about five minutes, just enough to find the page, take a picture, put everything in order, and run away.

He hastily turned the pages, much less carefully than before.

Quick! Page 75. Quick! Page 92. Quick! 103. Qui– An excruciating sound. He had torn a page! It was as if someone had torn his skin.

He paused. His blood froze. His heart was pounding, not sure if it was because of the scar he had just inflicted on the most sacred manuscript in science, or because of the loud hammering alarm, which was insistently reminding him that the police were approaching.

He started turning the pages again, fast but more gently, trying to remain calm, though he was on the verge of panicking.

Page 125!

Without even looking at what was on the page, he took a picture and immediately sent it to Laura. He rearranged the manuscript open to the first page. Closed the glass lid of the case. Put the new lock on. In that very instant he heard many voices shouting, and hurried footsteps. The police were storming in. He had grossly underestimated how long the police would take to reach the library. He should have just run away. Stupid!

He immediately hid in a recess of a bookcase. From behind the bookshelves he could see several policemen and policewomen running around, giving directions to each other, searching everywhere. It wouldn't be a matter of minutes, but seconds until they discovered him.

His phone started ringing. He had forgotten to silence it. It was from Laura. Damn it! Tonight she had been the cause of endless troubles. He declined the call and silenced the phone. Maybe the police had not heard it.

"Was that your phone?" one policewoman asked. Jack froze.

"No. It must be Martin's," he heard a policeman respond, "I recognise his ringtone, he must be here searching among these bookcases." Jack heard footsteps moving away. Only a brief respite, he thought, the police will soon find him. His heart was pounding out of his chest.

At some point, he heard the voice of the head librarian and Tom. They were talking with great agitation. They both sounded very upset.

He saw Tom passing by near the bookcase where he was hiding. He had that one single chance, just an instant. As soon as Tom had passed beyond the bookcase, he got out behind him and said, "Tom! What's going on?"

"Jack? What the hell are you doing here?!" Tom exclaimed.

"Well, I was passing by, after having finished the chapter of my thesis in the common room. I was heading to my room when I heard the alarm and the police… I was curious, especially since we were here not long ago, and so thought I would come in to see."

"Well, that was a bad idea, it seems we have an intruder, and he or she may still be in the library."

A few policemen hurried past them, taking no notice of them talking.

"You should leave the building, it's not the right time to poke your nose in. Leave the police to their work, they have to comb every room, every corner."

"All right, all right, sorry, I didn't mean to interfere," Jack said, heading towards the exit while Tom departed in the opposite direction.

His pace was calm, giving away nothing about his nerves. He just hoped that no one would notice the sweat on his forehead.

He was a few metres from the exit, when a male voice from behind yelled, "Hey, young man!"

"Yes?" Jack said while turning around calmly. A policeman was staring at him.

"Can I check your bag?"

Jack hesitated a second. "Of course, Sir," he replied with a fake smile.

The policeman grabbed his bag and started searching inside. He pulled out the torch. "What's this?"

"I would say it's a torch."

"I know it's a torch," the policeman replied, with irritation in his voice, "but why do you have it with you?"

"It's the torch for my bicycle. I guess about half of the people here in Cambridge carry bicycle torches with them. You may not have noticed, but Cambridge has the highest density of bicycles and cyclists of the whole of the UK and–"

"Yes, yes, I know," the policeman interrupted curtly.

He continued searching, pulled out a bundle of papers and, waving it, asked, "Is this part of this library?"

"I wish it was!" Jack scoffed, "That's a chapter of my thesis."

The policeman scowled. He put the papers back into the backpack, coldly handed it back to Jack, and sprinted away.

Jack left the library and exhaled. Fortunately, in a moment of lucidity, while hidden behind the bookcase, he had thought to remove the cutters, the gloves and the broken padlock and had hidden them in a nook of the library. He would collect them later that day, during regular opening times, when things calmed down.

***

There was just one handwritten word on the printed page of his personal copy. One word inserted by Newton inside a paragraph. To make sure that the editor saw and understood the correction, Newton had written the same word again in the margin:

aequalibus

There was no doubt about it. That was the missing word: *aequalibus*. One of the forms of *aequalis*, Latin for 'equals'.

Laura turned towards Sergei, "The full password is *due aequalibus*, 'two equals'."

Laura felt a lump in her throat. She could not help but think that Julia was referring to the two of them. She had said they were 'two equals' quite a few times. It had a double meaning. Despite their different characters, they had a similar approach to the world. But it also meant their relationship had evolved from student and supervisor, to become equals.

Skype was ringing on the computer screen.

"Jack is calling you," Sergei pointed out.

Laura opened the conversation.

"Laura!" Jack burst out as soon as he saw Laura's face, "You cannot imagine the mes–"

"Yes, Jack, I really appreciate what you have done," Laura cut short Jack's complaints, "I believe we have the password."

"I hope so! I was a hair's breadth from being arrest–"

"Are you in your office, with the drive?" Laura again interrupted Jack's remonstrations.

"Yes," Jack replied curtly, his eyes flickering with irritation and frustration.

"So, try '*due aequalibus*' to access the hard disk."

Laura held her breath while waiting for Jack's response from the other side of the ocean.

"It works!"

"Yesss!" Laura and Sergei jumped out of their chairs and hugged each other jubilantly.

Jack immediately glared at them. His mouth twisted. "Sorry that I cannot join your celebrations over there," he said, his voice dripping with sarcasm.

"Jack, thanks!" said Laura, releasing Sergei from her embrace. "Please leave the drive connected for a couple of hours, so that I can transfer the data to my laptop here. Thanks!"

She closed the Skype connection and launched the data transfer from Jack's remote computer to her laptop. She was so exultant that she hadn't even given Jack time to say goodbye, and his blazing eyes were suddenly replaced by the picture of his beaming face.

She turned to Sergei. "I'm so happy! I feel I'm accomplishing what Julia was expecting from me."

"Julia would be proud of you!" he said, "It was good that she made a copy of the data on another drive before the original was stolen."

"Yes, she was farsighted."

The two grinned at each other. Laura was ecstatic. She felt an irresistible impulse to kiss Sergei. They got closer. He leaned towards her. She would not dodge this time.

While she was feeling the warmth of his lips on hers, a sudden chill passed through her body.

She stepped back.

"Sergei, how do you know that the original hard disk was stolen and that Julia had made a copy? I don't think I ever told you that."

Sergei remained speechless for a couple of seconds.

Then his warm smile slowly turned into a sly smirk. "Thank you!" he said calmly, with a cryptic expression.

"Thank you for what?"

"Thank you for deciphering the password," he responded, now with a perfect British accent, his strong Russian accent completely gone.

He reached into his bag and pulled out Laura's original drive.

"How did you get that?!" Laura tried to grab the hard disk, but Sergei lifted it high in the air, out of her reach.

"Who *are* you?" Laura yelled angrily.

"I didn't lie to you about my name. My name is Sergei. And I really am a PhD student in astronomy. But I'm not enrolled in Russia. I'm a British student. My parents are Russian and that's how I know Russian, but I was born and grew up in the UK."

"Why did you lie?"

"While pursuing my PhD in the UK, I quickly realised that an academic career takes too long. Too long before I could get a decent position in academia... at least too long for me. I don't think I'm an outstanding scientist with a meteoric career," he said, laughing at himself, "I thought I would be better off exploiting my more unusual asset: being bilingual in English and Russian. Russia is a rapidly growing economy with which most western countries are keen to boost trading activities, legal or less legal. People who can speak both English and Russian are highly valued."

Laura was listening, confused, she wasn't sure where this was going.

"But my Russian was quite rusty. I needed some way to brush it up. So I had the idea of exploiting my PhD studies. I convinced my supervisor that a period of secondment in Russia would be a good thing for me. That's how I ended up at the BTA-6 telescope. Kasparov naively agreed to supervise me, believing I was genuinely interested in pursuing science with the BTA-6. There I gained the trust of the local staff and I was given the additional role of IT system manager. As such, I could have access to all the computers and the accounts of the staff."

"Are you... somehow involved in Kasparov's death?" Laura asked, stepping back, horrified.

"No," he answered, laughing loudly, "I don't have a clue about how Kasparov's weird accident happened. However, soon after his death, Kasparov received an email. I was in charge of passing all Kasparov's email correspondence on to the police. I noticed this message from a British professor, a well-known professor, Arthur Cecil-Hood."

Laura felt her stomach shrink as she heard that name.

"He was asking Kasparov to access some data taken 30 years ago. I thought it was polite and appropriate to inform him that Kasparov had passed away. It was also an opportunity to introduce myself to him, you never know when such a connection might be useful."

Laura was disgusted. She could not believe that this deceitful person in front of her was the same sweet and good-hearted Sergei that she had known until a few minutes earlier.

"Cecil-Hood replied asking whether I had access to the old tapes containing Kasparov's data and if I could ship them to him. He was willing to pay ten thousand pounds for the 'inconvenience'. Wow! Ten thousand pounds, for some dusty old data forgotten by everyone. I didn't think twice about accommodating the British professor's request." Sergei was grinning with satisfaction, as Laura's disgust grew.

"But the fact that someone was willing to pay so much was intriguing. I thought that those dusty datasets may not be so worthless after all, they might hide information that could unlock something big. But I did not have a clue what that could be. That's when I made the connection with the very last message sent by Kasparov before his death... his message to you and Julia."

A shiver ran up Laura's spine.

"The message in which he was referring to the data taken 30 years ago," he said, raising an eyebrow. "It didn't take a Sherlock Holmes to understand that he was referring to the same data Cecil-Hood was interested in. So I realised that you and Julia might hold the key to unlocking the mystery behind it."

Sergei was a flood of words, he sounded proud of having connected things and hatched a plan. He was openly bragging about it.

"That's when I faked the burglary in the BTA-6 archive. On purpose, I retained one of Kasparov's tape reels, which I did not send to Cecil-Hood together with the other tapes. I left it on the floor of the BTA-6 archive so to give you and Julia a clue about what the datasets were about, and to connect them to your research. Which you did. You identified that 70 Ophiuchi was the star in common between your research and Kasparov's data."

Laura had willingly been a part of Sergei's diabolic plan.

"So…" Laura interrupted Sergei, with a knot in her stomach, "you did not care about Nikolai. When you said you were concerned about him being unfairly convicted, you were just pretending. You simply staged everything to make me and Julia help you!"

"Poor guy, that Nikolai," Sergei feigned sympathy, "I feel sorry for him, he probably got framed for Kasparov's death, whether an accident or not… I don't know." Then, turning his sad face into a sneer, he added "But yes, I used his conviction as an excuse to bring you and Julia to the BTA-6."

Sergei's boasting confession was like a poison.

"Then you told me about the hard drive with your new data of 70 Ophiuchi, which Julia was hiding in her office," he said, his smirk becoming diabolical. "I realised that your data might be the key to solving the puzzle. So, I rearranged my flights to attend the meeting of the American Astronomical Society in Phoenix, and allow for a two-day stopover in London. I came to Cambridge and it was not too difficult to break into Julia's office and take your hard drive."

"*Steal* my hard drive," Laura corrected him.

"Whatever," Sergei said with a dismissive tone. "But I hadn't expected that Julia had encrypted the hard disk and password-protected it. The original drive has the same clue as the copy." Sergei turned the device upside down to reveal a label with the identical clue as the copy of the hard drive found by Jack. "I didn't manage to decipher it, I couldn't even get the first part of the password. But you, you have brilliantly solved the riddle, congratulations!" He waved the hard drive around with a satisfied smile and then put it back in his bag.

Laura felt betrayed and powerless. There was no way to confront him physically.

"It wasn't easy to pretend for so long," he admitted, "I had to be sure that nothing was leaked about my true intentions and not to give away, with you and Julia, that I was actually a British student on secondment. I sensed that Julia was very suspicious of me."

Laura remembered how cold Julia had been about Sergei's proposition to join them in Arizona.

"I had to be careful not to speak in English with my Russian colleagues when the two of you were present, or else they would have questioned why I was mocking a Russian accent, while they knew my English was spotless."

Laura recalled the various instances when Sergei had inexplicably switched to Russian when meeting his local colleagues amid conversations in English. She had been puzzled about it, but only now did she realise how stupid she had been to not see that it was a flag – a red flag that something was wrong, terribly wrong with Sergei.

"But in the end all these efforts were worth it!" he concluded with satisfaction. He pulled his bag onto his shoulder and headed towards the door, under Laura's flaming eyes. As he passed in front of Laura's laptop, which was downloading the datasets, he glanced at it with disinterest. He then abruptly stopped, stepped back and grabbed it.

"What are you doing?" yelled Laura while sprinting towards him.

"I just want to make sure I have no competitors."

With one arm he easily kept Laura at a distance, who was trying to grab the computer. With the other hand he dropped the open laptop on the floor and started stomping on it with his boot.

"Nooo!" screamed Laura. "Please!" she implored him while desperately trying to reach out for the device.

Sergei only stopped when a loud crack terminated the computer.

Laura kneeled, powerless in front of her laptop. The smashed screen was flickering. Keys were scattered everywhere and splinters of electronic circuits were poking out the the keyboard. Anger gave way to discomfort. Her eyes welled up.

"I think I'm done here," said Sergei with a grin of complacency, as he opened the door, "and, by the way… thank you!" He winked and walked out.

"You will not get away with this!" she managed to cry behind him, "Julia will…"

She did not finish her sentence. Julia was no more.

***

Jack banged his fist on the keyboard.

The image of Laura hugging that Russian student was still vivid in his mind. He kicked a box full of books next to his desk.

Never mind, he thought. Now he had some more urgent business to attend to.

I have the hard drive with Laura's latest data.
Too risky to transfer its content via the internet.
Transfers of large volumes of data are monitored.
Better to ship the whole drive.
Please provide an address.

Message sent.

***

One of the tears slowly slid across the screen and slipped into one of its cracks.

She was still knelt in front of her smashed laptop, staring at it, motionless.

Her phone rang, a few times. She didn't even glance at it.

It rang again. Laura grabbed it and carelessly answered the call.

"Laura! Sheriff Gonnagel just informed me about Julia, I'm shocked!" Grace exclaimed at the other end, "What a tragic news. I'm so, so sorry!" She paused, as if to give Laura the chance to comment.

"It must have been really devastating for you," Grace added with a grave tone.

"Yes, it was a blow…" replied Laura with a low voice, "it *is* a blow."

"My darling, I can believe that," Grace sighed and paused for a couple of seconds. "Is there anything I can do for you?"

"Not really, thanks," responded Laura. The broken screen of her laptop flickered more intensely and then went black. "Actually… there's something you might be able to help with…"

"Anything!" Grace interleaved eagerly.

"My computer broke, and I would urgently need–"

"Say no more. In less than one hour someone will bring you the best laptop we have in stock."

***

Jack's phone buzzed.

Thuban.

It hadn't taken long for him to reply to his message, very curtly. It was a simple, anonymous PO Box. Not unexpected.

Jack would send the hard drive the following day. But first, he had to do something.

Laura had finished downloading the data. He grabbed the drive and left the Institute.

***

Fortunately, the copy of her disc in Cambridge also had a backup of all her scripts and applications, so, together with her datasets, she had fully restored the functionalities of her previous computer.

Laura didn't sleep at all. She spent all night processing her new data and combining it with her previous data. The new laptop that Grace had provided to her was much faster than her old one. By seven in the morning she had the answer. The planet would transit in two nights. Much sooner than she had expected. There was no time to waste.

There was no doubt that Cecil-Hood had also figured out the date and time of the transit, by combining her past data with Kasparov's. Moreover, with his many high-level connections, he must have easily found a big telescope with which to observe the transit.

Sergei would soon figure out the transit time too, by combining the data on her stolen drive with her previous, published data. He would also find a telescope to observe the transit. He had mentioned some friends observing at several telescopes. Surely, one of them would lend him half a night as a favour.

She, she was not so well connected. But she had one single chance.

She picked up her phone and searched its contacts.

"Hello? Steve? Laura here."

"Laura! So nice to hear from you! How are you? And where are you?" replied an upbeat voice on the other side.

"I'm in Tucson, but I'm taking a flight to Santiago in a few hours."

"Really? How long are you staying? Are you coming to observe? Maybe we can manage to meet each other!" Steve replied with an enthusiastic voice.

"Actually, Steve, we shall meet. Are you on duty at the telescopes these nights?"

"Yes, indeed. The nights are long now in Chile, quite tiring. I just woke up," he said giggling, "last night's shift was quite demanding."

"I need a favour. A really big favour," Laura said with a heavy tone.

"Anything for you, my dear!"

Laura was sure Steve would soon regret saying that.

***

Jack had just shipped the hard disk to Thuban. He smiled while tapping his fingers together.

His phone rang. Laura?

"Laura, what's up? Have you figured out the date of the exoplanet's transit?"

"Yes, it's tomorrow night."

"Wow, so soon! You were right in wanting to access to your data the earliest possible. Are you planning–"

"Jack," interrupted Laura with a lump in her throat, "Jack, can I trust you?"

Jack hesitated for a few seconds.

"Yes, of course."

"Jack, please be honest. I need someone I can trust."

"Of course you can trust me."

"Thanks. I really need this." Laura was calm, but her tone was grave. "I need a favour from you. Can you please give me your code?"

"Which code?"

"The code that you developed to analyse data taken during transits of exoplanets in front of their star. The one you use to detect the signatures of exoplanet atmospheres."

CHAPTER 31

Chilly.

She was outside the aeroplane at Santiago airport.

T-shirt and sandals. Laura had forgotten that it was now winter in Chile.

When she had prepared her suitcase for Arizona she had only packed light summer clothing. She had not expected that she would have to travel to the other hemisphere. Just before taking the connecting flight to Antofagasta, she bought a jumper, boots, and a coat at a shop inside the airport, probably paying them five times more than at the discount retailers where she was used to shopping at. She was likely using up all her savings during this trip. But now that was the least of her worries. If all of this went wrong, her savings would be irrelevant.

Steve was waiting for her at the Arrivals Hall in Antofagasta. Laura beamed as soon as she saw him. He did not smile back, which was unusual for him, given his always joyful character.

"Laura, I cannot do this! It's just impossible!"

Laura hugged him and felt that he was stiff and tense.

"I assure you it's terribly important!" Laura implored, fearing that Steve might change his mind.

Steve kept complaining throughout the entire ride. "You know that I may lose my job. You know that such a sudden change in the telescope schedule can only be granted by the director of the observatory."

They were speeding through the lunar landscape of the Atacama Desert.

"On top of that, for all four telescopes! I'm sure this has never happened in the entire history of our observatory!" In Steve's distress, and his attempts to look at Laura while grumbling, he nearly swerved off the road on several occasions.

"You are right," Laura said, trying to calm him down, "but, in the end... do you have a plan?"

Steve remained silent for a few moments, his features tense. "Maybe."

An orange flash blazed from the top of a mountain. A flat-topped mountain. Paranal.

The glare was the sunset, reflected off one of the domes of the 'Very Large Telescope'. This was actually a set of four large telescopes. Each of them had a huge mirror with a diameter of eight metres. The reason why its name was singular, and not plural, was because the four telescopes were also conceived to work together, synchronously, as a single, much larger telescope.

Laura could see the shape of the four domes, silhouetted against the lapis blue sky, more clearly as they approached the observatory. This was part of ESO, the European Southern Observatory, an international organisation running many telescopes in Chile.

***

On Mount Graham, in Arizona, the Large Binocular Telescope was already tracking 70 Ophiuchi.

Sergei had started his observation at twilight. His friend Peter had five nights of observing time and had agreed to allow Sergei to use two hours in the early night for his 'extremely important observation'. Of course, in principle, this was not permitted. Only the director could change the schedule at such short notice. However, the telescope operator was a friend of Peter's. No one would find out.

Sergei was staring at the monitor that was displaying, in real time, the data coming from the instrument attached to the telescope. According to his calculations, by using Laura's data, the transit of the planet should start soon after twilight. The signature of the planet should show up at any moment now.

***

On the tallest of Hawaii's inactive volcanoes, Mauna Kea, Professor Arthur Cecil-Hood was sitting in the control room of the Gemini telescope, rubbing his hands together.

Everything was perfect.

Kasparov's archival data provided by that English student –what was his name?… Sergei? Yes, Sergei– had enabled him to identify the exact date and time of the planet's transit 30 years ago. Together with the data published by Julia and her student, Laura, this had been enough to predict the next transit of the planet with accuracy.

Initially he had managed to secure observing time at the smaller Multi-Mirror-Telescope in Arizona. However, later, he had convinced the director of the larger Gemini telescope, a good friend of his, that this might be the discovery of the century and was worth a few hours of telescope time. Confirmation from his friend had come only minutes before boarding his flight to Arizona, so he had quickly transferred to a flight to Hawaii.

Looking at the screen in front of him he could see the image of 70 Ophiuchi relayed from the tracking camera. The monitor of the scientific instrument was already actively displaying the data being acquired.

While stroking his goatee, Arthur anticipated the taste of success.

He was confident that this would be the greatest discovery of his career.

Simply the greatest discovery, ever.

The world will see.

She will see.

CHAPTER 32

In the control room of the Very Large Telescope Observatory, the perplexed gazes of Steve's colleagues were shifting between him and Laura.

He had come up with an excuse: that the engineers had identified a technical issue with the four telescopes and that, in order to fix it, the four telescopes had to track a bright star, say, 70 Ophiuchi, for a few hours. In the meantime the data of the star could be taken, because why not? 'It would be a waste of time... and, as a fortunate coincidence, there's this friend of mine who is visiting, and she is interested in bright stars of that type. She can make use of such engineering time, so that it's not totally wasted?'

Raised eyebrows, narrowed eyes, sneering... none of his colleagues seemed convinced by his story.

Laura realised that she wasn't helping to make Steve's story more convincing either. She knew that, but she could not help it, she was too nervous. While pacing in the large control room, all the while anxiously looking at the monitors, she continuously and impatiently glanced at her watch. Not really the attitude of someone who happened to be visiting just by chance. The overall atmosphere was incredibly awkward.

The control room of the Very Large Telescope was not like most other telescope control rooms around the world. It was more like the control room of a space centre, with several consoles, panels and various arrays of monitors, all required to control the four telescopes and the many scientific instruments attached to them. In contrast to other observatories, the control room was not located beneath or next to the telescopes, it was in a building about one hundred metres away. This was to prevent the heat produced by the building from introducing turbulence in the air next to the telescopes, which would have affected the quality of the astronomical images.

Laura was now looking out of the window. Although it was night, she could clearly see the four domes, lit by the glow of the Milky Way. They were perfectly aligned. The four large telescopes were all in position, tracking 70 Ophiuchi.

***

On Mount Graham, in the control room of the Large Binocular Telescope, Peter, Sergei's friend, was now very annoyed. He had reluctantly agreed, more because of their friendship than because he truly believed in the potential discovery.

It wasn't the first time that Sergei had 'fantastic' ideas that turned out to be a waste of time.

"Look Sergei, I've been patient enough," Peter said, putting a hand on Sergei's shoulder, "you asked for two hours. We have been staring at this star for more than three hours now and nothing has happened. There's no trace of the putative exoplanet that was supposed to transit. You got more time than you asked for. I now need to go back to my official observing programme."

"I don't understand!" exclaimed Sergei, "It should have already started transiting a few hours ago! Let me check…" Sergei opened his laptop to check his calculations. "Yes, the transit should have started at 3:08 Universal Time, that is 20:08 Local Time. So, why? Why is there no trace of the exoplanet transiting?"

In the meantime, Peter had taken another chair and set it in front of the console by pushing Sergei slightly to one side.

Sergei ran both his hands through his hair while staring at the screen of his laptop. "Wait. Together with the several datasets, there's also a script on Laura's hard drive." He opened it. "It seems like a script developed by Laura to analyse exoplanet data and derive their orbital parameters. It should give exactly the same time that I have obtained with my calculation. Let me run the script on the combined set of Laura's old and new data sets."

The output of the calculation appeared on the screen:

Transit time: 23:17

"What?" Sergei exclaimed.

"You messed up your calculations, didn't you?" said Peter with a wry smile, while typing on the keyboard of the console.

Sergei hastily looked at his watch. "The planet is due to transit in twenty minutes!" He saw that Peter was setting up the scientific instrument for his own observing programme. "No! Wait!" yelled Sergei, "The exoplanet will transit in a few minutes!"

"I'm sick of your stupid requests!" Peter dismissed Sergei without even looking at him, focused on typing his commands.

"I swear! It's going to happen in a few minutes!"

"Sorry, Sergei, telescope time is precious, I can't afford to waste any more of it."

Peter instructed the telescope operator with the coordinates of his target.

Sergei's face flushed. "You don't understand, you're wasting a once-in-a-lifetime opportunity!"

"Enough, Sergei."

Sergei raced to the telescope operator, violently pushed him out of his chair and started typing the coordinates of 70 Ophiuchi back into the telescope guiding system.

"Are you out of your mind?" Peter yelled at Sergei and sprinted towards him.

Peter tried to pull Sergei away from the telescope control panel. While still typing on the keyboard with one hand, Sergei aggressively elbowed Peter's face with his other arm. Peter fell to the ground, his nose bleeding. He jumped up and seized Sergei, pulling him away from the control panel. Sergei reacted even more violently, freeing himself and punching Peter, who in turn furiously pushed him to the ground. The two fought fiercely, until several technicians, called by the telescope operator, burst into the control room, separating and immobilising the two of them.

The telescope operator looked at Peter. "Should we call the police?"

Peter was panting and trying to stop his bleeding nose from dripping with a tissue. "Just kick him out of the building. I don't want to see his face ever again."

"You stupid idiot! You have no idea what you're doing…" Sergei kept yelling at Peter as he was taken away.

***

Laura grabbed her laptop and dashed out of the control room, under everyone's baffled eyes.

Steve looked around with a smile plastered on his face and, while nodding, casually walked toward the exit. As soon as he was out of the control room he saw Laura walking towards the telescopes. "Laura!" he called to her in a stage whisper, "Laura! Where are you going?"

"I cannot stay in that aseptic control room any longer," Laura said, shaking her head, "I have to stay next to the telescopes."

"You cannot go to the telescopes! Not now! Not unaccompanied! It's against the protocol!" Steve protested.

"Keep tracking 70 Ophiuchi and keep acquiring data, please," Laura kept walking at a fast pace.

"Damn it!" Steve kicked a stone, a big one, which hurt his toe. He limped back into the control room. Everyone looked at him. He forced a smile.

***

Laura was now among the four large telescopes. All of them were pointing in the same direction, working in unison, as a single huge telescope.

She entered the dome of the telescope closest to her.

The night sky was brighter than ever and its glow, filtering through the dome's slit, was bathing the telescope's frame.

She placed the laptop in a hidden area of the dome, with the screen dimmed as low as possible, as to not affect the sensitive instrumentation attached to the telescope. The laptop was connected to the data acquisition system, which was streaming the data in real time.

The inside of the dome echoed the soft pulsing of pumps, which were injecting cooling fluid into various instruments through pipes coiling around the telescope. They were like steel arteries conveying lifeblood to this huge, technological creature. Laura stroked the frame holding the huge mirror. These four mighty, scientific beasts were now tamed by her, meekly following her orders. Now they were all turned to 70 Ophiuchi, which she could see shining through the dome's slit.

Strangely, her attention was caught by a star in the constellation of Draco, which was grazing the horizon. Thuban. She did not know it was observable from such low latitudes. It was deep crimson. Its rapid and vigorous twinkling had something sinister about it.

She focused back on 70 Ophiuchi. The planet would soon start transiting in front of the star. She had the impression that 70 Ophiuchi was shining brighter, as if to facilitate the observation and reveal the secret that it had concealed for millennia. She could feel the pounding of her heart growing louder inside her. It was pulsing with the telescope pumps – the two of them were a single, symbiotic system.

***

On Mauna Kea, Professor Arthur Cecil-Hood was enjoying the data coming from the instrument attached to the Gemini telescope. Soon the planet would be in front of its star. Everything was proceeding perfectly. It would take a while before the signal of the planet's atmosphere would reveal itself.

Arthur decided to leave the control room and go outside the observatory to take a refreshing stroll around the rim of the dormant volcano.

The firmament was glistening, brighter than ever, as if to celebrate his forthcoming glory. He slowly turned while gazing at the whole sky, receiving the ovation from the entire starred vault.

Unexpectedly, out of the corner of his eye, he saw something dreadful. The nightmare of all astronomers – clouds. Approaching fast.

***

Laura went to her laptop. Jack's software, slightly adapted by her, was processing the data coming from the instrument in real time. Laura was mentally picturing the planet passing in front of 70 Ophiuchi, all the molecules in its atmosphere imprinting a characteristic signal on the stellar light that was passing through it, then reaching the large mirror of her telescope and being funnelled into the instrument.

She stared at the trace of the signal on the screen.

It had some very weak ripples. Barely distinguishable from the noise, but slowly becoming clearer and sharper.

Maybe… yes… there it was… water! Beautifully confirming Kasparov's finding! Laura's thoughts went out to him. His only fault: being ahead of his time.

But Laura's goal was not simply to restore Kasparov's reputation. There must be more.

She looked at the graph more closely, squinting her eyes.

Maybe… it was very feeble… hardly noticeable… but slowly becoming clearer with time… possibly… two marginal additional features… slowly becoming sharper… ye– yes… there was no doubt about it. Indisputable.

She stopped breathing.

Awestruck.

She felt numb.

Lost awareness of her surroundings.

This was too much for her mind to take in.

This was more profound than the Copernican revolution.

CHAPTER 33

Laura was jolted from her trance by the flashing of blue and red lights outside, illuminating the inside of the dome through its slit. The hypersensitive instrument, designed to perceive the faintest light from the boundaries of the universe, was now being blinded, no longer capable of detecting the light from 70 Ophiuchi. Laura peeked out from the door of the dome, unsure about what to think, but fearing the worst. The lights were coming from the control room. Several police cars were parked next to it. A small crowd of people had gathered next to them.

Four police cars departed in the direction of the telescopes. One of them stopped next to the dome where she was hiding. Two policemen got out of the car and switched their flashlights on. Laura frantically looked around – there was no place to hide. Then she looked up – the Nasmyth platform. The Very Large Telescopes had a different structure with respect to the BTA-6 telescope that she had visited just a couple of weeks earlier. The large primary mirror focused the light onto a secondary mirror located about ten metres above it. The secondary mirror reflected the light back onto a third mirror, which folded the beam on the side of the telescope, towards the Nasmyth platform, where massive, scientific instruments were located. Laura spotted the stairs leading to the platform. She rushed up and hid behind one of the large instruments.

Moments later steps echoed inside the dome and light beams scanned the inside. She shifted further behind the instrument, part of which was slowly rotating to compensate for the effect of the revolving sky.

"Can I see the image of the young woman again?" asked one of the two policemen, who had a hoarse voice.

"Here it is," responded the other policeman, who sounded very young from the pitch of his voice, "but what's the point? There's no one here. Why are we even searching for her?"

"She is a fugitive. There's an international arrest warrant on her head, big stuff. She seems to be involved in multiple murders." A shiver passed through Laura's body. "The captain warned us to be careful," continued the policeman with the hoarse voice, "she may be very dangerous."

"I wouldn't have been able to tell from her photo, she seems harmless. Looks can really be deceiving."

"Yep. Stay alert. Raise your gun."

Laura heard their steps getting closer, beneath the platform.

"Wow!" exclaimed the younger policeman, "I had never seen one of these large telescopes up close! Impressive."

"Yeah, impressive," responded the other policeman with a bored tone. "Look there's laptop here. It's on. There are some graphs being displayed."

Laura squeezed her eyes shut – in the rush she had forgotten that her laptop was open. She mentally scanned the windows that she had left open on the screen… nothing that could give her away… No! The name of the script! She had modified Jack's code and renamed it by adding `Laura.1`, and it was displayed on the header of the window running the script!

"So what?" remarked the young policeman, "It must be part of the control system."

A few seconds, seemingly infinite, passed. Was the policeman inspecting the screen of her laptop? Had he spotted the window with her name?

"Umm… maybe," said the elder policeman, followed by steps.

Laura exhaled.

The beam of one of the flashlights hit a corner of the instrument behind which Laura was hiding.

"What's up there?" asked the young policeman.

"It seems like a platform attached to the telescope."

The beam disappeared.

"Look, there are stairs, let's take a look."

Metallic steps resonated through the dome. Laura frantically looked around. There was nowhere to hide on the platform –

they will soon find her! The sound of steps grew louder. Laura pushed her body closer to the instrument, but realised it was pointless. The moment they got on the platform they would see her! She was trembling. As her foot shifted, she noticed that there was a gap beneath the instrument. She lowered and saw that the aperture between the big device and the platform was about 30 centimetres… maybe, just enough. She squeezed herself into the gap, just as she saw the feet of the policemen landing on the platform. The beams of the flashlights were scanning the platform and the instruments. For a moment the beam hit the spot where she was standing a few seconds earlier. From her position she could see, in the semi-darkness, the feet of the policemen walking on the platform. Just next to her, the moving part of the instrument kept rotating very slowly. A massive cable wrapper, holding thick wires, was sluggishly coiling around the instrument through a system of multiple segments on wheels.

One of the policemen got closer and his feet stopped a metre from her face. She held her breath.

"It's fantastic to see the telescope from this perspective, isn't it?" said the young policeman.

The other policemen moved to join the younger colleague. His foot stopped no more than 20 centimetres from her face. She squeezed herself further beneath the instrument.

"Yes, I must admit that from here it looks even more impressive."

"I think that the one up there is called the 'secondary mirror'. A friend of mine is a student in astronomy and he explained a little bit about modern large telescopes to me. Look, if you stare at it you can see the stars reflected from the large mirror beneath. Isn't it fascinating to see the starred sky compressed in there?"

Laura felt something pulling her. The space was barely big enough for her to turn her head. The cable wrapper had hooked onto the hood of her jumper and was very slowly dragging her towards a narrower recess between the instrument and the platform.

"Umm… I don't think those are stars, I think they are the reflection of the faint lights inside the dome."

Laura tried to free her hood from the cable wrapper, but it had been clamped by two of its segments during its slow coiling.

"Don't be a fool, those are stars!"

The cable wrapper was pulling Laura towards the very narrow slit. Laura tried to take her jumper off, but it was now too tense around her chest and the hood was pulling her neck just beneath her jaw.

"I've never seen green stars… come on, those are the reflected lights from inside the dome."

Her chest started to be squeezed between the instrument and the platform. The hood was getting tighter around her neck. She tried to tear the jumper but the fabric was too thick and, on second thought, even if she succeeded, the policemen were just next to her and would have heard the ripping sound. She frantically looked around. There were a few tools scattered on the platform. A cable cutter was within reach, but it was just behind the policemen's feet. Reaching for it would have implied exposing her arm and passing her hand in between the policemen's feet. One of the policemen had lowered his flashlight so that it was now illuminating the platform beneath them – the cutter's blades were glittering under the flashlight's beam. They would certainly see her arm if she tried to grab it.

"Anyway, there's no one over here," said the elder policeman. Laura saw his feet going towards the stairs.

The feet of the younger policeman shifted, giving her hope. But something started buzzing. The policeman's feet stopped. The buzzing continued for a few more seconds. "Hello honey!" It was his phone, "I'm sorry that I had to leave in the middle of the night, we're searching for a very dangerous criminal… Yes… of course, honey… yes…" He was not moving. The cable wrapper was slowly, but steadily pulling Laura… stronger and stronger… her chest was being pressed harder between the instrument and the platform, the hood was gradually strangling her. "Yes, babe… but, can we talk later? You know that when

I'm on duty… No! No! Of course I love you! I didn't mean to dismiss you…"

Laura was struggling to breathe.

***

Just outside the control room, Julien Blanchet, the director of the Very Large Telescope, could not believe that such a mess could have happened in his absence of less than 12 hours. All observing programmes had been cancelled and replaced by a putative urgent global calibration, involving all four telescopes, to tackle some non-existent technical issue. And then the Chilean police had burst into the control room searching for a Cambridge student under an international arrest warrant. Keep calm, fix one issue at a time, Julien kept telling himself.

"This is an astronomical observatory, do you realise that your lights are affecting our observations? Are you aware that a night of observation with the Very Large Telescope costs over $200,000, which you're now wasting with your lights on? Shall I send the bill to your police department? Or shall I send it directly to the Chilean government? I guess they are the ones that will eventually pay."

The police captain gave Julien a stiff glare. "Sergeant, switch off the lights," he ordered. The sergeant hesitated for a moment. "Quick!" The captain yelled nervously. Then, tensely, he continued, "We know that this student, Bellini…" he looked down at the piece of paper in his hand, "Laura Bellini, is hiding here."

"Why are you searching for her? And how can you be so sure that she is here?"

"She is involved in a double murder."

Julien froze for a couple of seconds, but kept a steady, blank expression on his face. He could not believe that a student could be involved in a murder, let alone two.

"The sheriff of Tucson, in Arizona, had ordered her not to leave town," the captain continued, "but she took a flight to Santiago."

"If she was really under an arrest warrant, then how come the authorities at the airport allowed her to leave Arizona and take a flight to Chile?" Julien asked defiantly.

The captain continued, ignoring Peter's remark, "We have traced that she then took a second flight to Antofagasta. The airport's CCTVs recorded that she was picked up by a van from your organisation, licence number…" he paused first looking at the sheet in his hand and then lifting his eyes in the direction of a van with the logo of the European Southern Observatory in front of him and reading its plate aloud, "AX12DFC." Then, without moving his face, he slowly shifted his eyes towards Julien, menacingly.

Julien kept his face inexpressive.

A few metres away Steve was listening, still, eyes wide open, all colour drained from his face.

Julien scowled at the other police cars parked in front of the four telescope domes. "Captain, there are delicate instrumentation and devices inside those domes and attached to the telescopes. Your men's search risks causing irreparable damage."

"My men know how to search properly."

"Most importantly," continued Julien ignoring the captain's remark, "you are on land belonging to the European Southern Observatory, an international organisation that has international diplomatic status. You have no jurisdiction here. If you are planning any search on this premises you need a formal request from your government to the Director-General of the European Southern Observatory. Do you have this?" Julien asked with a smirk.

The captain glared at Julien intensely, unmoving.

***

The hood strangling her was also blocking the blood circulation to her head. Her compressed lungs could no longer expand.

"Honey, please, don't say that…" the young policeman was not moving. "You know I always think of you…"

To die or to be arrested? If she was arrested, she would obviously also lose access to the amazing data that she had just obtained. But what was the point of having mind-blowing data if she would no longer be alive? Yet, without those datasets the world would never know about the discovery!

Her hips were now also being constricted between the instrument and the platform. Something hard was pressing on her flank from one of her jeans' pockets. She reached out for it, squeezing her hand between her body and the instrument. It was her phone. She managed to pull it out of the pocket. The screen had cracked, but it was still functioning.

She tried to shift her head trying to find a position which would loosen the grip on her neck and allow some air to pass through her throat. However, her head and her entire body were now totally compressed in less than 20 centimetres between the instrument and the platform, completely stuck. The only part of her body that she could move was her right arm.

While glancing at her mobile, she recalled that she was logged onto a university Skype account on her computer, which was different from her own personal Skype account on her phone. With her free hand she frenetically looked for the Skype application. She opened it and called her university account.

A loud sound started resonating in the dome.

"What the he– Sorry babe, I really have to hang up, we have a situation here…"

The policeman's feet moved towards the edge of the platform and, on their way, hit the cable cutter, which skidded further from Laura.

"What the heck have you done! You've triggered an alarm!"

"Hey, calm down, I've done nothing!"

"I'm coming!"

As Laura heard hasty metallic steps descending the stairs, she extended her arm to reach for the cable cutter, but it was now too far away. She stretched, making her hood strangle her even more, but despite all efforts was a few centimetres short from reaching the tool.

"It's not an alarm, it's coming from that laptop," said the elder policeman from beneath the platform.

Laura looked around her, searching for something to extend her arm. The ringing of the Skype call on her laptop was echoing loudly within the dome. She looked at her smartphone, on which the Skype application was flashing while calling the account on her computer. She grabbed it and extended it towards the cable cutter – she hit it, pushing it even further away.

"Look, it's a Skype call," said the younger policeman.

Laura tried to calm down, but the seam of her hood had now entered deep into her throat and she could no longer breathe. She stretched her arm out again. The phone in her hand was trembling. She gently laid it on the cutter and slowly moved it.

"Who is calling?"

Having managed to move the top of the tool towards her, she grabbed it from the part closest to her, one of the blades. She spun the tool around and grasped it by its handles. While her head was starting to feel dizzy because of the lack of oxygen, she managed to cut the thick bottom of her jumper and then rip the rest, relieving her chest – but her lungs would not expand. The tear had stopped at the very thick finish of her hood, which was still tensely strangling her.

She grabbed the cable cutter again and placed the blades on either side of the hood's neckline, which was wrapped around her throat. The blades pierced into her skin, between her neck and her jaw. She paused for a split second – then she closed the handles of cutter and chopped the fabric – and her flesh with it.

The sudden flow of oxygen in her lungs was overwhelming.

"The call is coming from Laura Bellini, the wanted woman!"

***

The captain clenched his jaw. "It will not take long to get a warrant to search on these premises."

"Until then, you're kindly excused."

"Are you telling me that we should leave?"

"Precisely, unless you want to cause a major diplomatic incident."

The captain narrowed his eyes. Then he strode off towards his car and shouted to his men to do the same.

While the police cars were leaving, Julien scowled and turned towards Steve, who was praying that some yet-to-be-discovered law of physics would make him vanish instantly.

***

"Where is she calling from?"

"I don't know, but it means we're clearly on the right track. Should we respond?"

"Not sure, she would hang up as soon as she realises we're not the person she was expecting. But this means that an accomplice of hers is hiding here!"

She heard a beep. "To all units, to all units," it was the walkie-talkie of the policemen, "leave the area, immediately, we're heading back to the base."

"Damn it!" yelled the elder policeman. A beep from the walkie-talkie, "Unit 32 here, we have found a trace! I repeat, we've found a trace!"

"Leave the area unit 32, immediately – captain's orders!"

"But–"

"Leave the area, now! You risk causing a diplomatic incident."

Laura, reached for her phone. Stretching her arm made the wound on her neck hurt, but she barely noticed, she was too focused on breathing again and trying to gather her thoughts. She quit the Skype call. The loud ringing stopped resonating in the dome.

"The Skype call has ended. Umm... Whatever. We've done our best, let's leave," said the elder policeman.

"Shall we take the laptop with us?" asked the younger policeman.

"Maybe... it has the record of the Skype call and it may contain files linked to the fugitive."

"But… you heard the story about the diplomatic incident."

"You're right, I'm not sure what kind of trouble we risk finding ourselves in. Leave it and let's go."

Laura exhaled in relief. The policemen steps faded in the distance and she soon heard their car departing. She slowly descended the platform and peeked out of the dome's door – all the police cars were leaving the observatory.

A few minutes later, a car and a large van with the logo of the European Southern Observatory were heading towards the telescopes, lights off. She was not sure what to do. Steve had not communicated anything to her. She decided to hide behind the dome.

A hint of dawn was starting to lighten the horizon, suffusing the sky with a slightly lighter blue tint. In the meantime, the four large telescopes had not stopped observing, still obediently tracking 70 Ophiuchi.

The car and the van stopped about ten metres from the dome where she was hidden. No one came out of the van, but two men came out of the car. She could recognise that one of them was Steve. The other one was an older, taller man.

"Laura Bellini, I know you are here," said the tall man with a loud voice and a French accent. "Please, come forward, immediately."

Laura remained in the darkness behind the dome, holding her breath, her mind racing. Her laptop was still in the dome, still collecting and processing data from the instrument. She hadn't copied the data anywhere yet and was afraid that, should her laptop be confiscated, she would not be able to access that precious data.

"Laura, please, we need to talk, urgently," the tall man insisted.

Laura realised that she didn't have many options. She was surrounded by hundreds of kilometres of desert. Running away would have meant certain death.

She came out of the shadows, trying to compose herself by closing her torn jumper. Only then did she realise that both the jumper and her shirt were soaked with blood. It was coming from the cut on her neck.

As the tall man saw her, he approached her. With a flashlight he inspected the cut in her neck and touched it gently. "It's a large cut, but it's not too deep," he said with a reassuring tone. "Most of the bleeding has already stopped. Fortunately, whatever caused the wound, didn't cut any vital blood vessels… you wouldn't be standing here if that were the case. Steve, take the emergency kit from the car, it will suffice."

Steve dashed towards the car.

The tall man looked at Laura narrowing his eyes. "My name is Julien Blanchet, I'm the director of the Very Large Telescope," he said calmly, but with a severe expression. Laura looked down.

As Steve returned with the emergency kit, Julien started applying some disinfectant to her neck. His expression was getting stricter. While still soothing her wound, he said, "Steve confessed that you induced him to disrupt all the operations, of the entire observatory," his voice was getting louder, "of all four telescopes, to undertake an observing programme of yours."

Steve looked at Laura with a saddened expression. "Laura, I'm sorr–"

"You should apologise to the Observatory," interrupted Julien harshly, "and to all the astronomers whose observing programmes have been cancelled tonight because of you! Shame on you!"

Steve lowered his eyes.

Julien applied some medical strips to close Laura's wound. He then covered it with a large plaster, pressing hard. It seemed to Laura that he had pressed harder than needed.

He stepped back, distancing himself from Laura. His glare shifted between her and Steve, "Tonight all protocols have been broken. Precious observing time has been lost. An unauthorised person," he said, looking pointedly at Laura, "has been let into the Observatory premises. This will have major diplomatic consequences that will reach the highest levels. All of this because of the two of you."

Then he scowled at Laura and continued, "Steve has acted recklessly by blindly following your requests and he is to blame for this. But you, Laura, you too are to blame for this mess."

Laura was looking down, feeling guilty, especially for having involved Steve and putting him in such a difficult situation. What on earth had she been thinking? How could she have thought that her plan would have had no serious consequences? The fact was that, amid the excitement for the scientific discovery, she had not thought through the practical implications of her actions.

"Fortunately for you, Laura, I knew Julia. Very well."

Laura's eyes widened, surprised. Her thoughts went back to Julia. She was not sure whether she was failing Julia in front of the astronomical community with her reckless actions, or she was fulfilling Julia's scientific legacy with one of the most important discoveries of the century.

"She talked to me about you," said Julien.

Julia had talked about her? With the director of the Very Large Telescope?

For the first time, Julien softened his tone, as if now distancing himself from his institutional role. "She thought very highly of you. Scientifically and as a human being." He paused. "And that means a lot to me."

There was a moment of silence. Laura's eyes welled up, but she fought back her tears.

Julien broke the silence, "Now, we need to find a way to get you out of here… and out of Chile. The Chilean police are after you. I managed to push them out of the Observatory's boundaries, but I'm afraid it will not take long before they get a warrant that allows them to enter and undertake a major search."

A shiver passed through Laura's bones. The idea that she was now wanted by the police and that she might be put in jail would have been something unimaginable to her only a few days back.

"I'm sure that, along the road to Antofagasta, there's a police checkpoint just outside our fence, and that they are monitoring the whole area around our land. So it's nearly impossible for you to leave the observatory without being caught by the police…"

A second, deeper chill passed through her.

"Nearly," he emphasised. "Early in the morning," he glanced at the feeble light of the dawn that was starting to make the Andes' skyline visible towards the east, "we are supposed to send a couple of electronic boards to the ALMA observatory, our sibling observatory, close to the border with Bolivia. Those boards are only twenty centimetres long, but…" he smirked, glancing at the van, "I thought they would also appreciate a few dozen old computers that have been sitting in our storage room for years."

A man in the van's driver seat smiled and waved.

Julien explained the rest of the plan.

Then he looked at 70 Ophiuchi. "Your star is now barely observable and will soon set. You should start copying your data," he said, pulling a memory stick out of his pocket and handing it to Laura. "During your journey you will not be able to take your laptop with you. No luggage either, I'm afraid."

He gave her a small smile with a nod, which Laura took as unspoken approval, mixed with concern.

"Good luck, you'll need it." He got into the car, followed by Steve, who was still visibly shaken. He started the engine and, before departing, he lowered the window and said, "And, Laura," while pointing at 70 Ophiuchi, "I hope your data delivers what you are looking for."

CHAPTER 34

She felt the van slowing down. The trip in the back had been a pain. Several hours of sitting in the dark, on the hard and cold metal floor, behind a huge pile of old computers, with bits and pieces falling on her at every bump. But it had worked. Julien was right. The police at the checkpoint had opened the back door of the van, but did not even try to inspect the mass of computer carcasses and wires that was hiding Laura.

The van had come to a stop. Someone opened the back door and started to pull out the computers. A friendly face appeared from behind a cracked monitor. "Hello! You must be tired and hungry." She helped Laura out of the van. "My name is Céline de Windt and I'm the director of ALMA, the Atacama Large Millimetre Array."

Laura looked around squinting her eyes, still adjusting to the sunlight after so many hours in the dark. She was in another part of the Atacama Desert, now surrounded by several buildings.

"Yes, I know ALMA," commented Laura, "it's an array of 56 antennae dishes, but I don't see any here."

"We are at the Operations Centre," explained the woman, handing Laura a sandwich. "We operate the antennae dishes from here, but their actual location is on a much higher site, on the Chajnantor Plateau, at an altitude of 5000 metres," explained Céline.

"It doesn't feel like low altitude here either," Laura said.

"Yes, we're at quite an altitude, but still not so high as to prevent working in relatively normal conditions, in terms of oxygen."

Laura was not so convinced. Maybe she was so distressed and tired that even that slightly lower oxygen content of the air was having an impact on her. After all, she hadn't slept for more than 30 hours.

"Now, about the plan," continued Céline, frowning, "Julien explained everything to me. There's no way for you to leave the country via air. Your name is certainly on the 'wanted' list at every airport."

Laura lowered her gaze, ashamed that she was now hunted, a fugitive, and causing so much trouble.

"However, as far as we know, here in South America the arrest warrant has been issued only within Chile. The border with Bolivia is very close. If we manage to get you there, then you can reach La Paz and take a flight to Europe."

She pointed to a jeep, which was being loaded with various boxes by a man, who waved when he saw them looking at him.

"José has to deliver some hardware parts to the ALMA high site, where the antennae are located. He can do an unofficial 'detour' and take you beyond the border. He doesn't speak a word of English, but I have instructed him properly. Julien told me that he was trying to find someone to help you in Bolivia… but I shall be completely honest with you, we don't have any collaborators over there, so I have little hope that Julien could find any additional help. I'm afraid that once you are in Bolivia you'll be on your own."

Laura felt lost and overwhelmed, but had understood that such a plan was the only way out of her current situation.

Céline glanced at Laura's torn jumper and her bloodstained shirt. "I wish I could find some clean clothes for you, but there's no time", she said looking at the jeep, "I'm afraid you have to leave." Then she prompted her, "The sooner you cross the border, the better."

Céline approached her. She made as if to hug her, maybe she perceived how fragile Laura was in that moment, but eventually, she just squeezed her shoulder and said, "Good luck!"

José was holding the door of the rear seat open. Laura got into the jeep. It was full of wooden boxes of various sizes, including on the front passenger seat and next to her in the rear seat. José did not waste any more time and immediately drove the jeep out of the ALMA compound.

Laura realised that, confused as she was, she hadn't thanked Céline. She turned to wave at her, but she was already out of sight.

***

The jeep was moving on the steep uphill road in the lunar landscape of the Atacama Desert. Dormant volcanoes were looming at the horizon, one of them lightly smoking.

The wooden box next to her was moving slightly with the jolting of the jeep.

Half an hour later Laura saw a deviation with a sign, 'Bolivian border', but José did not take that road and kept speeding ahead.

"Why didn't you take the road to Bolivia?" Laura asked, concerned.

"Todo bien, todo bien," said José, smiling and looking at Laura through the rear mirror.

In the distance, she could see the white and silvery ALMA antennae dishes spread across the Chajnantor Plateau. She wondered what kind of molecules they were observing in interstellar space.

She thought that maybe José wanted to deliver the boxes to the ALMA site first. But the jeep kept going straight ahead, leaving the ALMA antennae behind.

Another deviation appeared along the road, again with the sign 'Bolivia'. But José missed this one too, and kept speeding ahead.

"Where are you going?" Laura asked leaning forward and glaring at him. "Where are you taking me?"

"Todo bien, todo bien," repeated José, this time not even looking at Laura in the mirror.

Laura was getting anxious.

The box next to her seemed to be moving more. She convinced herself that it was because of the humps and bumps along the road.

Abruptly the jeep took a left turn into a barely visible track, which soon became indistinguishable from the landscape. The driver had not slowed down despite the jeep now being off-road. They were dashing through rocks, gravel and sand, pits and humps. The whole jeep was shaking.

The driver put on a mask with a can attached to it, and passed another one back to Laura, signalling that she should put it on as well. Laura nervously looked it. The thought that she was being abducted crossed her mind. In case the can attached to the mask contained some sort of narcotic, she pretended to put it on, but removed it as soon as the driver turned to look at the road ahead again.

Everything was shaking around her. The jeep was speeding uphill in harsh terrain, desolated and wonderful at the same time. She started to feel numb. The sky looked a deeper blue than ever. The lunar landscape looked brighter, nearly blazing.

The jeep was passing between rocks, large rocks with iridescent colours, so bright that they looked alive. Like living things. One of them started to unroll itself. Beautiful large, colourful coils. The huge snake looked at Laura with its bright yellow slit eyes. Wonderful and yet dreadful. It opened its mouth to reveal long fangs, and hissed loudly. All the other rocks along the way were unrolling into magnificent snakes, each with different coloured, gleaming patterns. Their stares were terrifying. Their fangs reflected the blazing sun. As the jeep passed they rose up, majestically, hissing. Then, like a perfectly synchronised war machine, they started attacking the jeep in unison. Their fangs cracked the windows, pierced the tyres, opening the metal body of the jeep like it was paper. Laura was screaming – terrified. She looked at José. He was still driving calmly, as if oblivious to what was happening around them, or possibly complicit. Did he take her there knowingly?

Suddenly a huge black snake erupted out of the box next to Laura. She could see its flaming eyes, just for an instant, as the snake pounced on her neck. The pain of the fangs piercing her flesh and of its powerful jaws crushing her throat was unbearable. She felt the snake coiling around her, cracking her ribs and squeezing the air out of her lungs. She desperately wanted to cry for help. Trying to expand her lungs… to suck air in… there was no way… the mighty black snake was strangling her.

The driver was still driving calmly as his jeep was wrecked by the pack of snakes.

Laura made one last attempt to breathe.

Everything went black.

CHAPTER 35

"Señorita."

"¡Señorita!"

The woman's voice sounded upset.

Everything was still black. Muted sounds and voices echoing around.

"Estúpido... ¡Mira esta pobrecita!" The woman sounded as though she was complaining to someone.

Laura felt something hard press on her face.

She heard a familiar male voice moaning in response. "Le dije de ponerse la máscara de oxígeno. ¡Se lo dije!"

The voices were resounding in her head. She felt numb.

Something pierced her arm, making her scream. She sat up frantically looking around, trying to figure out where the snake was attacking her from. But all that she could see was a group of people, gathered around her. The person closest to her was wearing a stethoscope, with a concerned but also reassuring face. He gently pressed her down. "Calm down. You lacked oxygen. You were hallucinating. I need to give you some medications," with that he gave her another jab.

"Where am I?"

"You are in a small village next to the border with Chile."

"Am I in Bolivia?"

"Yes, a small village in Bolivia."

"But the driver did not take the route to Bolivia, I thought he wanted to kidnap me."

She saw that José, the jeep's driver, was among the people around her.

"He did not take the official route to Bolivia. You could have been identified and detained by the border police along the main route, so he took a route off-road. In doing so you stayed at a high altitude for too long, with little oxygen, not enough to keep you conscious."

Laura felt ashamed that she hadn't understood anything, including when José had passed her the oxygen mask.

"I need to reach a city with an airport," she said, trying to stand up.

"You need to rest…" the doctor tried to warn her.

"Don't worry. I'll take care of her," said a warm and friendly familiar voice.

Laura's eyes widened, "Grace? What are you doing here?" She was the last person Laura was expecting to see in this remote part of the Earth.

Grace was beaming at her, but her smile was mixed with an expression of sorrow and sympathy when she saw Laura struggling to get up. She helped her to her feet.

"I'll explain to you on the way, we don't have time to waste," Grace said with a reassuring tone, but not hiding a sense of urgency. She accompanied her to an SUV. Laura was still weak and dazed. Grace assisted her onto the passenger seat of the large vehicle, under the concerned eyes of the group of people. Grace hurried to the driver seat and their SUV sprinted northbound.

"Julien informed me about the plans," Grace said while entering the main road to La Paz.

"I wasn't aware you were in touch with the director of the Very Large Telescope," said Laura, still disoriented.

"Of course I am. We have been providing control software to several telescopes around the world. It's one of the activities I'm proud of," Grace replied with a knowing smile. "Readapting advanced control software originally developed for satellites to ground-based telescopes, at little cost, to serve a large scientific community." Then her smile faded, "Some of my colleagues don't share my eagerness to support scientists." Laura understood whom she was referring to. After a moment of silence, Grace clarified further, "Roger, you met him, Roger Smith, the head of SPACEWAVE, he never liked this idea. 'Little revenue'. 'Not worth it,' he would say. He only cares about profit."

She paused for a few seconds.

"Anyway, yes, of course, I know Julien, as well as Céline. When I heard that you were in trouble I wanted to help."

"By coming all the way from Arizona to Bolivia?"

"I was actually already in South America on some other business, so it didn't take me long to get here. I still feel bad and somehow responsible for what happened to you at SPACEWAVE and therefore I felt the obligation to help. Especially when I heard about the additional complications. I may be the only one who can help you out of this situation."

"What do you mean by 'additional complications'?" Laura asked, frowning.

"Well…" Grace hesitated, "Julien and Céline thought that the arrest warrant was restricted to Chile, while it has actually been extended to the whole of South America."

Laura felt her breath failing her again for a moment.

"So Julien and Céline's assumption that once in Bolivia you would be free to leave for Europe was wrong," Grace said with a sigh. "Border police at any airport here in Bolivia, and in the rest of South America, have photographs of you. There's no way that you can leave the country from any of the airports here in Bolivia, or from anywhere else in South America."

Laura sank in her seat. "So why are we going to La Paz?"

"Because actually we're not," Grace said while taking a left turn into a secondary road. "At SPACEWAVE we also develop and have access to a number of high-tech air transportation systems, many of which are developed for the Department of Defence. Some of these systems do not need an airport or even a runaway to land."

They were now off-road. Grace was driving the SUV uphill on a path that was barely distinguishable from the surrounding deserted landscape. She hadn't slowed down at all, the SUV was sprinting on the uneven, rocky terrain as if they were on a motor way. Laura guessed that Grace was in a hurry because of a rendezvous with a chartered private plane. The jolting of the SUV speeding over humps and bumps was a toxic mixture together with the lack of oxygen, as they were reaching higher altitudes.

About one hour later they reached a vast, flat plateau covered with snow. It was so extended that Laura could not see the end of it in any direction. The horizon was flat and white. The light of the sun, reflected by the snow, was blinding Laura, who was struggling to keep her eyes open.

About half an hour later Grace stopped and turned off the engine. They were in the middle of the white expanse. Absolute silence. Nothing to be heard, nothing to be seen, anywhere. Just white. Peaceful, quiet, flat white, everywhere. Laura squinted her eyes, trying to see if an aircraft was approaching from any direction. This immense flat area was ideal for aircraft to secretly land, she thought.

Grace was silently staring in front of her through her sunglasses. Laura looked in the same direction, but couldn't see anything.

After a few minutes Grace got out of the SUV and slowly walked in front of it, still looking ahead. Laura got out as well. The altitude of the plateau made it freezing cold. As she set her foot onto the ground she realised that the snow had a very strange consistency. She bent to pick up a handful. It was not snow. It was salt. It was an endless expanse of salt.

Shivering, she approached Grace, who was still looking ahead of her. Impassive.

"You don't give up easily, do you?" said Grace with a flat tone. She removed her sunglasses, still staring at the salt expanse. The blazing light did not seem to bother her at all.

"I beg your pardon?" Laura asked, confused.

"You don't give up easily. Of course you don't." Grace was in a sort of a trance, as if talking to another Laura, an imaginary Laura in front of her.

"I know your kind," she continued, "flying below the radar, unnoticed, apparently shy and harmless, even dull at moments. But no. Not at all. Within your shell you're smart, you're shrewd, you're determined."

Laura was bewildered. She was not sure where this was going. Was she having some other sort of hallucination because of the altitude?

Then, as though coming out of her trance, Grace turned towards Laura, the real Laura, the one that was standing next to her.

"Actually, part of me admires you, and I would like you… if I did not hate you!"

Grace's words startled Laura. "Wh– why… why do you hate me?" she stuttered, "I don't… I don't understand. I haven't done anything to you."

Grace looked at Laura in silence for a few moments. Then she asked, "Have you found what you expected to find?"

"What do you mean?"

"Have the datasets that you collected last night revealed it?"

"How do you know about the data that I collected last night? How do you know what it's supposed to reveal?"

"I know a lot of things about this story… and I know a lot about you, too, thanks to your friend, Jack."

"Jack?" Laura hoped she had misunderstood.

"Yes, Jack, your friend."

"Has Jack been spying on me for you?"

"Spying is not really the right word. 'Intelligence' is more appropriate. He has been providing a lot of information about you and Julia, about your activities, your discoveries, your movements. Quite efficiently, I must say."

She was shivering, no longer from the cold, the altitude, but from the shock, the shock of discovering that she had been deceived by so many and for so long. Who could she trust? She felt that Julia was the only person she could really trust. But Julia was no more.

"So, have you found what you were looking for?" Grace interrupted Laura's train of thought.

"Erm… What do you mean?"

"In the data that you collected last night, did you find what you were looking for?"

"Ye– yes… actually more."

"I had no doubt about it. You're smart. You're brilliant. I was sure that if you had access to such a powerful machine, the Very

237

Large Telescope, you would make good use of it. That's why I was trying to prevent it."

"Bu– but why? Why?" Laura stuttered again.

"I know what you have discovered. A hint of it was already in Kasparov's data 30 years ago. Just a hint. Not even Kasparov had realised."

"How do you know what was in Kasparov's data?"

"Remember that conference group photo? That photo taken 30 years ago. The one that Julia showed to Roger Smith."

"Yes?"

"I was the student who took it," explained Grace, now looking again at the blue and white horizon. "I was an enthusiastic student, taking photos of everyone, of everything… including most presentations."

Grace was again in a sort of trance, as if brought back to that conference 30 years ago.

"I remember Kasparov's presentation. It is impressed vividly in my memory. I had taken photos of his presentation, the slides with which he illustrated his data and his claims. In the following weeks, I kept looking at those photos. I was struggling to understand why he had been attacked so harshly, why he had been ridiculed so ruthlessly. I was young, I was very open-minded. To me, his data looked convincing. His claim that he had detected water in the atmosphere of a transiting exoplanet did not seem as ridiculous to me as it was to the rest of the participants." Sadness crossed Grace's expression.

Then her face lit up. "I was fond of astronomy, I was fond of science, I enjoyed doing scientific research, really! Roger was my supervisor. At that time he was an enthusiastic astronomer too." Then her smile turned into a frown. "But then he got an excellent offer from a big company in the space industry. He convinced me to follow him. Our careers in the space business took off. I discovered that I was talented in leading and managing large space projects, and I started to enjoy this new dimension. But I have always tried to keep my connections with the scientific community. In contrast to Roger, who became increasingly obsessed with revenues and profit, I have always felt like I had the mission to make the scientific community benefit from the space projects that I am developing. I have always kept myself up to date with the scientific developments, with the new frontiers of science and their challenges."

Then she turned her gaze back to Laura. "That's how I came to read your article. When I saw that you and Julia had claimed the detection of an exoplanet orbiting around Kasparov's star, 70 Ophiuchi, the infamous star in his presentation, I froze." She remained still for a few seconds. "I dusted off those old photos and inspected the data that he had displayed in his slides. There was no doubt that his claim of water was fully justified. 30 years later the scientific community should have apologised to him. But then…" she said, now with a glint in her eyes "… then I inspected the data shown by Kasparov in those photos in more detail. I saw those additional signatures. Those features that Kasparov could not explain. They were weak. Marginal. But I could clearly recognise them!" Grace's expression had turned dark. "No one else should find out!"

"Why? Why not?" screamed Laura.

"This would be an epochal discovery, with implications going far beyond science, impacting society, sinking deep into human minds, into human souls," Grace sighed. "There is no doubt that governments would want to invest in new observatories and facilities to know more and follow up on this discovery."

"And why wouldn't you be happy about that?" Laura asked, confused.

"You are as stupid as you're smart." Grace was shaking her head. "Have you seen the prototypes of GATEWAY in our labs?"

Laura nodded, confused, "Yes, a neat piece of cutting-edge space technology with a fantastic scientific goal."

"Indeed, a neat piece of highly advanced technology. The most ambitious scientific space observatory ever developed. For the very first time in history, all the major space agencies in the world have joined forces to fund a joint space mission. Twenty billion dollars, dwarfing any past astronomical facility. An unprecedented endeavour, never achieved by anyone in the past." Grace was looking up at the sky, in rapture.

"Yes, you have achieved something great, fantastic. But I still fail to find the connection with 70 Ophiuchi," Laura commented, even more confused.

"Either you are pretending, or you are much more naive than I thought," Grace said with a tone of contempt. "Should the discovery on 70 Ophiuchi be known to the world then the GATEWAY project would be shut down, don't you understand that?" Grace had started shouting. "Funds would be redirected to facilities aimed at observing the exoplanet orbiting 70 Ophiuchi and searching for similar exoplanets."

"But, Grace… I cannot believe it…" Laura was stuttering, "I cannot believe this is the reason why you want to hide this discovery." Instinctively she touched the pocket in which she had put the memory stick containing the data obtained the previous night. She immediately regretted it.

"Give me that," Grace ordered.

Laura reached for the memory stick inside her pocket. The friction of the skin with the fabric of her jeans was painful. She realised that the coldness and dryness were so extreme on this site that the skin on her hands and her lips had cracked. She gave the memory stick to Grace, who immediately broke it, simply snapping it with her hands. Laura did not even try to stop her. Grace was physically much stronger than her, and Laura felt weak, exhausted.

"Needless to say that the laptop that I gave to you is set to completely erase its contents about…" Grace glanced at her watch, "about now. So there should be no trace of the data that you acquired last night."

Laura sighed.

"Grace," she started with a soothing tone, "I am sure that the governments would find resources to support *both* GATEWAY and any new astronomical facility to follow up on the 70 Ophiuchi discovery. They are both fantastic new avenues for science."

Grace laughed loudly, "You are so naive! Your ingenuity is really astounding!" Her expression changed from amusement to bitterness and disgust. "Governments don't care about science. They don't understand the importance of knowledge. They think science is just something that keeps a bunch of nerds busy. They don't understand how deeply science has shaped humanity, our lives, our souls. They fill their mouths with words such as 'scientific research' and 'knowledge' to dazzle people, and when it's convenient to support their plans. In reality, they have completely different priorities... basic, fundamental scientific research and knowledge are very low on their agendas."

"It's not like that! You're exaggerating, you're raving!" Laura protested.

Grace glared at Laura. Then she addressed her with a calm, firm voice, "Do you know that governments spend much more on weapons and armies than on scientific research? Humanity prefers to invest more in self-destruction than in its welfare. Would you put your trust in humanity and its governments?"

Laura lowered her gaze. She had to admit that Grace had a point.

"Do you understand now why I had to prevent the discovery? It's a matter of 'either/or', governments will never give us 'both'." Grace had apparently calmed down. Her expression was now a mixture of sadness and pain, as if she had gone through a colossal internal struggle. "I had to stop it."

Grace's eyes seemed to be glistening, but no tears came out. She took a deep breath.

"Based on your published data, I quickly realised that the next transit of the same exoplanet in front of 70 Ophiuchi would be soon, though I couldn't determine exactly when. But I had to prevent anyone else from attempting the same observation as Kasparov. I had to prevent anyone else from finding the same signatures. I had to prevent anyone else from finding indisputable proof with modern instruments and modern large telescopes." Grace was deep in the flow of her memories. "My first, main worry was Kasparov. I was afraid that if Kasparov read your paper he would attempt to replicate the same observation that he had performed 30 years ago, but now with modern instruments, to confirm his old result and to identify those additional features."

"So?" Laura had goosebumps all over her body, not sure whether because of the cold or because of the way Grace's monologue was unfolding.

"I had to stop him."

"So?" Laura was now horrified by what might come next.

"I stopped him," Grace said curtly.

Laura froze. "So his accident at the telescope... was not an accident. You... you... did you kill him?"

Grace's face became stiff. "He was not the only one."

Laura was in shock. She was in front of a murderer.

"I had to silence anyone who could connect the dots. Anyone," Grace said with a completely flat tone. "I am sorry for Julia. It was a great loss for science."

Laura was in tears.

"But I'm equally sorry that you didn't die in the same accident. It would have finished everything there, without you and me having to go through further pain."

Laura was looking down. One of her tears dropped on the ground, melting the salt crystals, which attracted Grace's attention. Then her gaze followed the white patterns of salt all the way into the horizon.

"Impressive, isn't it? The largest expanse of salt on Earth. El Salar de Uyuni," Grace said, completely changing the topic. "Magnificent. Magnificent and deadly. More deadly than a desert. Deserts can host forms of life. No form of life can survive here. This is the patch of Earth closest to a lifeless planet."

She looked at Laura, scanning her flushed skin and her cracked lips. Then she turned to look at the sun, which was setting lower on the horizon.

"I'm not sure how you will die. Hypothermia? Dehydration? Probably a fatal combination of the two. Lack of oxygen will help accelerate your death, so it shouldn't take long."

She reached out and said, "Give me your phone."

Laura pulled her mobile out of her pocket and passed it to Grace without arguing.

"I've used it to track your position during the past weeks, exploiting our network of military satellites." Laura was already so shattered by the several shocking revelations in the last few minutes that finding out that her phone had been used to track her did not upset her any further. "It has served its task," continued Grace, "I don't need you to keep it any longer. There's no signal here, but just to be sure that you cannot contact anyone and no one can contact you." Grace put Laura's phone in her pocket. She walked towards the SUV. Salt crystals crunched beneath her feet. She slammed the door and drove away, without looking back.

Laura watched the SUV disappearing into the horizon.

Shivering, she looked around her. White and blue, everywhere.

CHAPTER 36

Arthur Cecil-Hood was analysing the data he had just collected. It was too bad that the clouds had stopped his observations. Never mind, despite that, the data was good enough. Yes, although marginal, the result was there. He felt a little bit ashamed for having attacked others when presenting marginally significant results. He was now in the same position. But this was a different story. Such a groundbreaking result would justify it.

He was planning to announce the result at the major conference that would take place in Rome a few months from now. He had been invited to give a plenary talk. It would be the perfect venue. Most importantly, *she* would be there.

Fully focused on this project and on the calculations required to carefully prepare the observations, he had been out of touch with the rest of the world for the last few weeks, not even reading emails. It was time to reconnect. He would first check the programme of the Rome conference, to verify on which day he was scheduled to talk. Optimally, it should be placed at the beginning of the conference, so that people would talk about his discovery and congratulate him for the rest of the event. Most importantly, he would enjoy *her* appreciation.

He searched the website of the conference. Browsing its online programme, he saw that it included a slot for an obituary. Someone in the astronomical community must have passed away. With little interest, just out of idle curiosity, he clicked on the link of the obituary to see who this was about. As the page opened, he did not even need to read anything. He just saw the photo.

The ground opened up beneath him.

CHAPTER 37

Her foot pressed harder on the accelerator.

She wanted to leave everything behind her. No regrets. Mission accomplished. Problem solved.

The sound of the salty ground being crushed by the tyres reverberated inside the SUV.

Suddenly a wave of heat. At the same time, the electronic control panel of the SUV jammed completely. The engine went off. The mighty SUV came to a stop. Powerless.

Silence.

Absolute, still silence.

Grace looked at the passenger seat next to her. Laura's phone was there. She had forgotten! She had completely forgotten that she had put a backup plan in place in case Laura escaped. Grace realised that she had now been caught in her own trap.

The sun had set. She looked at the endless expanse of salt, which now was tinted flamingo pink.

Now what? She thought, terrified.

***

Vega

   Altair

   Spica

   Antares

   The Southern Cross

   The Magellanic Clouds

Spotting all the stars, all the constellations, all the nebulae, one by one, trying to remain conscious. Laura had only walked for a few metres and then stopped. She had no clue which direction to take. Now lying on the salty bed, she was looking at all the stars on the dark, blue vault above her, as if she wanted to see them all before dying. They were not glittering. They were still. As in meditation. Saddened to see their beloved friend dying.

She was looking at them, smiling, reassuring them that she was no longer in pain. She was not cold. She was not thirsty. There was no pain from the frostbites on her skin. No ache from the cracks in her lips. She no longer felt her body. She was peaceful and joyful. This is how she wanted to die, comforted by the light of her adored stars. And this infinite bed of salt, which was supposed to be her deadly prison, turned out to be the perfect setting for the last moments of her life. It reflected the blue and white tints of the night sky. She was cradled by this magnificent, immense azure glow. Could it be any better?

She knew this was not the end. Nature had given her, everyone, immortality. Her waves, her energy would live forever. Nothing would stop them. They would pass through everything, they would endure everything, they would permeate the whole universe.

She looked at the constellation of Serpens, including the Eagle Nebula, her favourite. A marvellous dance of stars born out of the glowing ashes of their ancestors. She had always dreamed of herself floating in such breathtaking scenery. Someone was likely doing so in that very instant. Her waves would reach it in less than 6000 years.

She turned her head to look down. Thuban was again grazing the horizon. But it was not as bright and flaming as the previous night. It was feeble, barely visible. As if it was dying together with her.

She squinted her eyes. There was something strange next to Thuban. Another star? A new star? Maybe she was hallucinating again. She tried to focus more. There were actually two stars. Two new stars grazing the horizon next to Thuban. They were getting brighter and brighter, so bright they were now blinding her.

The steady silence was now broken by a crunching noise. The sound of cracked salt crystals.

The lights and noise came to a halt next to her.

Steps were approaching. The shapes of two people were now in front of her, apparently scrutinising her. Her eyes were still adjusting to the glare of the lights.

"Need a ride?" said a familiar voice with a teasing tone.

CHAPTER 38

It was painful.

The blood was slowly flowing through her limbs and skin again. She nearly missed the numbness and peace of when she was lying on El Salar, detached from all physical senses, in harmony with the universe. Half awake, she could feel that she was now wrapped in a blanket. Eyes closed. Shivering despite the warmth outside. Whatever she was sleeping in, it was jolting and rocking. There was an echoing of soft humming.

She opened her eyes slightly. It was dark. She was in a car. A jeep. The inside was dimly lit by the starred sky. She was lying on the rear seat. She could discern the silhouette of two people in the front seats. The one driving was bulky. The one on the passenger seat looked slimmer and from behind she could see that he was wearing glasses. The shape of those glasses looked familiar, very familiar. There was a strange smell, which she struggled to identify – cigar?

"What's the plan for her?" said the skinny person.

Laura could clearly recognise his voice – Jack!

"Don't worry, where we're heading they'll take care of her," said the bulky person at the wheel. That voice. That voice was familiar too… Smith! Roger Smith!

Smith was Grace's boss. Jack had been a snitch for Grace. They were part of Grace's lot! So they had not rescued her, they had just collected her for some other evil plan. She felt even colder. Terrified!

What could she do? She was feeling weak. She looked at the door handle. Opening the door and jumping out of the jeep would have been pointless. She didn't know what speed the jeep was going, not sure whether she would survive jumping out, but even if she did, they would have hunted her down and quickly found her.

She slowly sat up and looked out of the window. Although the moon had not yet risen, Venus was up and giving enough light to illuminate the landscape. They were no longer on El Salar. The jeep was dashing through an uneven rocky desert. She looked back and saw that the large trunk of the jeep was open and was accessible from the rear seat. Peeking into it, she saw a few tools, some for jeep maintenance and repair, others for working on the ground, including two spades. Laura wondered why her abductors had left such objects within her reach. Maybe they didn't expect her to recover her senses so quickly. Maybe they didn't think her capable of using those tools as weapons. Men. Silently, she picked up one of the spades. It was heavy. She was still very weak. She looked in front of her at the silhouettes of the two men, with anger, with rage. She looked at Jack's shadow, recalling when he told her that she could fully trust him. Despite her fury, she was lucid. She would aim at Jack first, as he was not the one driving. Smith would need a few seconds to stop the jeep and react, giving her the time to hit him too.

She lifted the spade, gathered all her strength and violently hit Jack's head.

The blow was loud. Jack hit the window and collapsed.

"What the–" cried Smith.

Laura was lifting the tool to hit him too, but Smith swerved to avoid a massive rock and she fell on her side, losing her grip on the spade, which slid out of sight on the bottom of the jeep. She desperately groped the floor, searching for the spade. The jeep decelerated rapidly, Smith was braking hard to bring it to a halt. Laura knew she only had a few seconds left. Once he was no longer occupied with driving she would be no match for Smith's mass. Her hand brushed against something metallic. She grasped it. That was it! She sat up in the dark, lifted the heavy spade, trying to keep her balance against the strong deceleration of the vehicle, while Smith was still pushing on the brakes and swerving to avoid the rocks. She gathered all her strength and – something suddenly grasped her hand. A dark shadow rose in front of her. It pushed her back so hard that she fell on the rear seat. The shadow jumped on her, blocking her arms. It was heavily bleeding on her.

"Have you gone out of your mind?" he yelled.

Laura was panting heavily. Then, with a feeble voice, she said, "I trusted you. I trusted you and you betrayed me."

CHAPTER 39

"I understand how you may feel betrayed."

Jack was now sitting next to Laura in the rear seat, while Roger was driving, visibly upset.

Jack's head was half-covered in bandages. Blood had seeped through them, but the stain was no longer expanding.

"Are you pitying her? She nearly killed you!" Roger Smith remonstrated loudly, "And she was about to kill me too!"

"Well, she must be distressed and baffled," Jack defended Laura.

Laura was sitting in a corner with her knees tucked into her chest, confused and frightened.

Jack looked at her and started explaining, "A couple of months ago I was approached by a person from an untraceable contact. The messages were signed 'Thuban', but it was obviously not their real name. This person offered me a lot of money to provide intelligence about you and Julia, about your research, your astronomical observations and your findings. I was very concerned about the intentions of such a person. I was sure they were up to no good, given that they were not asking you openly for this information, but seeking it surreptitiously in exchange for large sums of money. My first instinct was obviously to decline. But on second thought, if I had declined I was sure Thuban would have simply asked someone else. I realised that the only way to find out about Thuban's plan, and therefore protect you and Julia, was to play the role of the greedy student and gain Thuban's trust by providing all the information that I was asked for."

He sighed and continued, "I became Thuban's spy. I was a perfect spy. I reported everything, everything about you, about your whereabouts, about your research, your notes, your data, everything. I was careful not to omit anything."

Laura's eyes flashed angrily.

Jack sighed, "Don't be mad at me. I was afraid that Thuban had hired more spies, or additional intelligence channels, and would have found out if I had omitted or lied about anything."

Laura turned to look outside. Her eyes, reflected in the window, were tired, saddened and scared. But they glittered as she looked at the tip of the moon that had just risen over the horizon.

Jack continued his story. "When you asked me to retrieve the copy of your hard drive from Julia's office and you managed to decipher its password, I realised that this was the one chance I had to locate Thuban and possibly identify him, or her. I told Thuban that I was in possession of the hard drive and of its password. I made up the excuse that it was unsafe to transfer its content over the internet and suggested that it would be better to ship the whole hard drive. Thuban agreed immediately, but I suspected that she did not buy the story of the data transfer problems, I sensed that she just wanted to get possession of the hard drive. I was not sure why at the time, but now I know… she wanted to make sure that it was destroyed."

Laura didn't say anything, still staring at the moon.

Jack continued, "Unsurprisingly, I was given the address of an anonymous post box. But before shipping the device I opened it and inserted a GPS tracker. With this I could follow the journey of the hard drive, from Cambridge to a courier office in Phoenix, then to Tucson, and then… to SPACEWAVE. In the meanwhile, I had already boarded a flight to Tucson." He smiled. "Thuban's payments had been generous enough that I could afford last-minute business class tickets for the first time in my life." He had a pleased, half-dreamy expression, but soon he returned to the story and the frown came back. "As soon as I landed in Tucson the signal from the GPS tracker had disappeared. I immediately went to the authorities and told a sheriff the whole story. But he didn't take me seriously. He must have thought I was a lunatic. He simply dismissed me, commenting that 'Stargazing is not a crime', implying that he had understood nothing from the entire story."

Laura's brows knitted together and she spoke for the first time since she had attacked Jack. "Was this sheriff a corpulent person with a grizzled moustache, and always wearing sunglasses?"

"Um… yes, exactly."

"I'm not surprised by his response," Laura replied. "Go on," she pressed Jack. She was now more intrigued than upset by the story. "How did you manage to find out Thuban's identity?"

"I recalled that a good friend of mine at Trinity College, Isabel Gibson, who got her PhD recently, had been hired by SPACEWAVE."

"I think I met her when visiting the company in Arizona," commented Laura, as a hint of frown creased her brow.

"Indeed, she told me so when I contacted her," confirmed Jack. "She immediately connected my story with some weird and obscure activities that she had been asked to investigate at SPACEWAVE. Isabel encouraged me to talk about my story directly with the head of the company, Roger." Jack nodded towards Smith, who was still driving without speaking a word. "I was hesitant, as I wasn't sure how high up Thuban was within SPACEWAVE and whether the top executive levels were involved. Isabel reassured me that she was positive Roger was not involved in such nefarious activities, as he was the one who had asked her to investigate."

Jack was interrupted by Smith's deep voice. "I must confess that at the beginning I was only worried about the implications for the company. When you and Julia told me about the fatal accident at the BTA-6 Russian telescope, I immediately recalled that it was one of the telescopes to which we had sold our operating system, the one Grace was so proud of. I was worried that there was a major flaw with the software provided by us, or that there were other issues which would have been associated with SPACEWAVE, jeopardising the entire company. So I started an inquiry, but I did not want to involve Grace, as she was hypersensitive about that project. I resorted to asking Isabel, who had just been hired and still only had very few connections within the company. While investigating the software delivered to the BTA-6 telescope, Isabel unveiled a much more disturbing pattern of clandestine activities inside the company."

"Indeed," Jack continued, "that's why Isabel immediately encouraged me to talk with Roger. I decided to tell him everything I knew about Thuban, the unusual requests and the link to SPACEWAVE." Jack glanced at Smith again, whose dark silhouette was nodding. "He responded immediately. We traced the last location of the GPS tracker before the signal was lost. Its last signal came from Grace's office. There we found some fragments of the smashed hard drive. There was no doubt at that point that Thuban was Grace."

Laura's hair stood on end. She had already found plenty of evidence that Grace was two-faced and that she was behind many, if not all, of the mysterious events she had endured. But having other people confirming this so clearly, and through an independent source, was shocking. She had not been hallucinating, it was not a figment of her imagination, it was all real.

Smith continued the tale. "Grace was nowhere to be found. According to her personal assistant, she had left without notice for an unexpected meeting at an unspecified location." He paused for a few seconds. "The SPACEWAVE's IT system is set up in such a way that, if need be, the head of the company can access any file and any information in the systems. Grace had managed to encrypt a few files, making them inaccessible to me, but they were no match to Isabel's IT skills."

Jack smiled, as if proud of his friend. Laura frowned.

"We found out that, for some reason unclear to us, Grace had been obsessed with 70 Ophiuchi," Smith explained, "She had been trying to prevent anyone from observing it with any telescope, and had been destroying any data associated with this star. And she..." Smith hesitated a moment "... she attempted to silence people with any knowledge about 70 Ophiuchi, to the point..." he sighed "... to the point of silencing them forever."

Laura felt a chill crawl up her back. Grace was a murderer. Yet another shocking confirmation of something she had already known, something she had experienced first hand, when Grace left her to die on El Salar.

"She used the telescope control software that SPACEWAVE has sold and installed at several astronomical observatories as a Trojan Horse. It was used to remotely access the whole control system of the BTA-6 telescope, and to guide the incident that killed Kasparov. She also attempted to prevent you from observing 70 Ophiuchi at the TNG telescope. You managed to observe and obtain data anyway, but she used the same Trojan Horse to access the TNG archives to erase all your data."

Laura's pupils dilated as she started to connect the dots.

"She intercepted a message from Professor Schneider to Kasparov, in which he mentioned your data and their connection with his old data collected 30 years ago."

Laura recalled her chat with Professor Schneider at the Accademia in Florence.

"To silence Professor Schneider she exploited an experimental weapon that we have been developing with the Department of Defence. It consists of a fleet of satellites capable of producing a microwave beam so powerful that it can shut down electric equipment and… it can also hurt people by burning their insides, to the point of even being lethal. She had Professor Schneider tracked through his phone and asked to hit him during one of the testing sessions of the space weapon."

"Asked? Whom? Do you mean that Grace didn't act alone?" Laura asked.

"Of course not! Although Grace is exceptionally smart, the whole operation was far too complex to be implemented by a single person. Grace forced a few people in SPACEWAVE to act on her behalf, by accessing the telescopes software, the military tracking system, and the space microwave beam experiment."

"Forced? How could she force them?" Laura asked again.

"Well, Grace identified people in key positions and with useful expertise who were also vulnerable and whom she could blackmail by exploiting her executive position. I mean people with families who could not afford to lose their jobs, or people who desperately needed their visas to be renewed for themselves or their families. Of course, none of them was willingly complicit, most of these people had deep regrets… sometimes to the point of being close to breaking down. Grace was careful to identify those 'collaborators' who were becoming potentially problematic for her operation… and she did not hesitate to eliminate them."

"Does this have anything to do with that employee who was bitten by a rattlesnake in a canyon not far from SPACEWAVE and, mysteriously, hadn't managed to get back to seek help?" Laura asked.

"Unfortunately yes. Except that he was actually…" Smith let go of the steering wheel for an instant to make air quotes "…'bitten' *inside* SPACEWAVE."

"What! There was a rattlesnake inside SPACEWAVE?" Laura was baffled.

"Not exactly, its poison was inside. When Grace realised that Miguel was breaking down, she managed to insert rattlesnake poison into the insulin doses that he was regularly taking to treat his diabetes. So, unknowingly, he injected himself with the poison. Then she sent him a message and requested that he should meet a contact person at a known point in the canyon not far from SPACEWAVE. By the time Miguel realised something was wrong with him, the poison had already started to affect his muscles, heart and lungs to the point that he could not get back to the compound to seek help."

"But the police found the marks of the rattlesnake bite on his leg!" pointed out Laura.

"That was pierced by Grace into his leg while he was probably already unconscious. We found the skull of a rattlesnake in Grace's office, like those sold in souvenir shops, with well-preserved fangs," intervened Jack.

"But killing Miguel eventually turned out to be a flaw in Grace's plan," Smith remarked.

"What do you mean?" asked Laura

"Miguel was her man for using the SPACEWAVE control software as a Trojan Horse inside observatories. When Grace killed him she did not expect to need his help any longer. But she regretted that when she discovered that you were about to observe 70 Ophiuchi at the Very Large Telescope, on Paranal. She could not prevent it at that point. And she could not access the telescope archive either. We checked with the Director of Paranal that the datasets you obtained last night are indeed safely stored in their archive."

Laura sighed in relief.

She recollected the entire sequence of strange accidents over the past few weeks, trying to place each of them in the tale that she had just heard. "Was the car accident that killed Julia also caused by the microwave beam from space?"

"No, in that case it was, how can I put it, much simpler, unfortunately. Grace hacked the rented car's electronic system through its satellite link, making it easy to control the functionality of the brakes, accelerator and steering wheel." Smith didn't add more details, as if sensing that the accident in which Julia lost her life was a touchy topic for Laura. "If it is any consolation, the microwave beam eventually and ironically boomeranged back on Grace–" Smith tried to explain.

But he was abruptly interrupted by Laura, "I don't seek revenge!" she corrected. Then her curiosity prevailed, "What do you mean by boomerang?"

"She wanted to make absolutely sure that you were silenced, forever. So in addition to her plan of leaving you to freeze and starve to death on El Salar, she had activated an additional parallel stratagem, which would ensure your death even in case you managed to escape that harsh environment. She had programmed the satellite fleet to lock on your phone and hit you with their deadly microwave beam tonight. But in her perfectionism, when she left you on El Salar, she took your phone to prevent you from contacting anyone, even though there's no network signal for your phone... She probably just wanted to be 100% sure. However she must have forgotten about the pre-programmed satellite fleet. When the time came, it hit the holder of your phone – Grace."

Laura felt a mixture of chill and relief that that night she had escaped a double attempt to murder her.

"So, is she dead?" she asked.

"We don't know. The way we tracked you, and indirectly Grace, was by following your phone signal. It was last detected in the northwest of El Salar. We headed towards that specific point. We found Grace's SUV, whose electronics had been completely fried by the microwave beam. Your phone obviously had the same fate." Jack pulled Laura's recovered phone out of his pocket and showed its screen, which was completely jammed.

"And Grace?" insisted Laura.

"She was not inside the SUV and nowhere to be seen nearby. Apparently, the roof of the vehicle had partially shielded her from the beam, so she survived. But at that point the SUV was unusable. Her phone, or whatever communication system she might have had with her, would also have been irredeemably burned by the microwave beam. So she must have started walking on El Salar, heading for the surrounding desert. I must say that the probability of surviving at this temperature and at this altitude is getting slimmer with each passing hour."

"Haven't you tried to search for her?"

"It's a nearly impossible task for us, especially at night. We don't have a clue which direction she may have taken. She was careful to erase her footprints on the salty ground. Without any functioning electronic device on her, we don't have any way to track her with our satellite network either."

"And anyway we were much more worried about you," interrupted Jack. "We had seen from your phone signal that there was a stop of about half an hour at a location in the middle of El Salar. We suspected that Grace had left you there. So we headed straight to that point, where we found you, just in time."

"Shouldn't you warn the authorities about Grace?" Laura hesitated. She did not mean to imply that she was eager to see Grace persecuted. "I mean, to rescue her."

Smith sighed, "I wanted to keep this whole story hidden from the authorities and try to sort it out internally. It will be a huge blow for the company when all of this mess emerges. Anyway, yes, human life is far more important. We have informed the authorities. But they didn't seem too keen to start the search for Grace. They said that finding Grace in this area during the day would be like looking for a needle in a haystack, let alone at night. They promised to start a search tomorrow morning, but I'm afraid that even if they do manage to find her some time tomorrow, it will be too late."

Everyone was silent for a while. The noise of the wheels crushing the desert stones in their path was the only sound inside the jeep.

"Roger," Jack broke the silence, "do you have any clue why Grace chose 'Thuban' as her code name? Do you think it has any esoteric meaning?"

"I think it's much simpler, just an emotional link – Thuban was the star that she had researched for her thesis." He paused for a few moments. His lips curved into a tender smile for the first time, "Actually I remember that, when she was a student, she often joked that Thuban had been the polar star 4000 years ago, when civilisation started, and that studying Thuban would one day enable her to lead humankind out of its modern self-destructive madness and towards civilisation again. I guess that, although a joke, this was a thought that had been in the back of her mind since, for all these years." His smile slipped, "I'm sure deep down she meant to do good. She must have been led astray by her obsession for perfection and her mission... which I still fail to understand." He paused a few instants. Then he lifted his gaze, trying to look at Laura in the rear mirror, "Laura, all of this mess seems associated with 70 Ophiuchi, what's the big deal with it? What have you found in your new observations?"

"Yes, I'm curious too," added Jack, "What did your observations at the Very Large Telescope reveal?"

No answer came from Laura.

He turned to look at her. She had finally fallen asleep.

CHAPTER 40

He was staring at the reflected image of the Wren Library.

The spell was broken by a passing boat. A young couple was on it, giggling. He was punting, clumsily, and she was gently laughing at him.

The boat had left behind a trail of golden and crimson leaves, floating on the River Cam.

The slow spinning of the leaves hypnotised Arthur and brought him back into his bewitchment.

Everything here in Cambridge reminded him of her. All the moments they had spent together. Every hour, every minute, every second. Etched into his memory. Carved in his soul.

Too painful. He stood up and slowly walked towards the Institute.

***

Laura thanked the radio-astronomy team and left the meeting room, beaming. She had spent the last few months working with them. It had been quite fruitful.

On the way to her office she met Jack, who looked baffled.

"There you are!" he exclaimed, a little annoyed. "Still with the radio group?"

"Yes," replied Laura, curtly but smiling.

"But, if I may ask… what the heck are you doing over there? You'll be presenting your results at the Rome conference next week, you should be getting ready by working on the data that you collected in Chile, at the Very Large Telescope."

"Those datasets were ready to be presented the very moment they were gathered that night, thanks to your real-time data processing software," she responded with a smirk and gave him a light, grateful kiss on his cheek, "though adapted by me," she added with a wink and dashed away.

Jack lightly shook his head as his eyes followed her departure.

On the way to her office, Laura passed in front of Julia's former office and noticed the door half open. Her office had not been reallocated yet. The director had resisted assigning it to anyone else, as if pretending... as if wishing Julia was still there.

Laura curiously peeked through the half-open door and saw a man sitting in Julia's chair. At first she did not recognise him, his appearance had changed so much since they had met in Florence. Shabby. Unkempt beard. He looked like he had aged ten years in those few months, as if some disease was consuming him. His eyes were empty, as if his soul had been sucked out of him. He seemed in a trance. His eyes were slowly wandering across the various objects in Julia's office.

"Professor Cecil-Hood, nice to see you again. How... how are you?" Laura asked with some hesitation.

He slowly raised his eyes towards her, ignoring her question. He stared at her for a moment, with a feeble smile, deep in thought. Then he spoke. "I wished one day we could have jointly supervised a smart student like you... jointly... together with her."

Laura was baffled, and it showed in her expression.

Arthur's face became even paler. "It was just a dream... the worst kind, those dreams that can never come true." He lowered his eyes and shook his head. "I've done it all wrong. I realised it when it was too late, blinded as I was by my stupid arrogance. I tried to win her over by impressing her, by aiming high, by showing her what I was capable of achieving in science. That was not what she wanted, that was not what could win her heart. I only realised it when it was too late."

He sighed.

"Now I'm empty. Totally hollow."

He looked around again, "I was hoping that here, in her office, my soul could revive. But no. On the contrary, the sight of Julia's belongings is just a source of additional agony. But it is a self-inflicted pain that I'm eager to feel, to punish myself for my stupidity and my arrogance."

He stood up with a grimace, as if the pain had become unbearable. He pulled a small memory stick out of his pocket and handed it to Laura. "This contains the data that I collected on 70 Ophiuchi at the Gemini telescope. I'm sure you'll find it interesting."

Laura was taken by surprise. Before her trip to Chile she was aware that Sergei had the information required to decipher the mystery associated with 70 Ophiuchi, and that he might have attempted to pursue further observations during the transit of the exoplanet. She had heard about his failed attempt and the story of the tussle at the Large Binocular Telescope in Arizona. But she had completely forgotten that Arthur was probably after the same discovery. It seemed he had managed to solve the puzzle and obtained data. She was really curious to know what was in his data, but hesitated. "But... but Professor, don't you want to publish the data yourself?"

Without saying anything else he walked away, not looking at her, as if ashamed.

From the window, Laura watched him leaving the Institute. She felt sorry for him. He had spent most of his life aiming high not for himself, but to attract his beloved. Although convoluted, this dynamic had produced fantastic scientific results. Motivated by his love for Julia, Arthur Cecil-Hood had achieved an impressive scientific record, his research was recognised as cutting-edge by the astronomical community, the very top. Throughout human history, passion for loved ones had created masterpieces in art, music and poetry... why should scientists be any different?

She looked at the USB stick. She could not resist any longer. She plugged it into her computer and downloaded the data.

It wasn't the same kind of data that she had taken. Fascinating. Unexpected. Together with her own data, Arthur's additional data completed the picture. She felt even more excited. Excited and ashamed at the same time. Excited about the discovery. Ashamed of mankind.

**

Arthur was now at the top of St Mary's belltower. He had come here with her several times when they were students, when they were together. From here, the highest point of this old Cambridge church, he could see dozens of other places where they had been together, when they had been in love, so many years ago.

Yes, this was the last thing he wanted to see.

The last place he wanted to be.

CHAPTER 41

The prickling contrast between the warmth of Rome's sun and the gentle nip of the frosty, autumn air was delightful on her skin.

She had spent over half an hour simply sitting on a bench, eyes closed.

The pealing of the bells from St Giovanni's Basilica reminded her that it was time to go. As she opened her eyes she was dazzled by the white marble of the church's magnificent façade reflecting the bright Mediterranean sun.

Behind the massive basilica was the Lateran University, one of the Catholic Church's main universities. It was hosting this year's Symposium of the European Astronomical Society, one of the largest gatherings of astronomers in the world.

Shortly, she would announce her findings in the brief slot that the organising committee had allocated to her in the programme. Hers was the second presentation in the morning.

She indulged herself for a moment, reluctant to stand. It was not her old fear of talking in front of a large audience – that was completely gone, overcome forever. She was simply enjoying the moment.

She inspected the façade of the basilica and all its parts. The columns, the pilasters, the arches. The statues of angels, saints and popes. Wasn't it ironic? She would reveal her discovery to the world from the womb of that institution, the Church, that had once made the centrality of Earth in the universe a pillar of its doctrine, to the point of persecuting anyone daring to question this dogma. Would the announcement of her discovery be another blow to the Church? She admired the beauty of the basilica's façade once more. No, it would not be a major blow. The Church had evolved, had learnt to live and grow with science. It would adapt and embrace the discovery.

She took a deep breath, stood up, and headed towards the side of the basilica. She turned the corner to enter the square facing the large entrance of the Lateran University, which was flanked by the banners advertising the symposium. From a distance she noticed some unusual commotion by the entrance. She could make out cameras, journalists and TV crews. "What's going on?" she whispered to herself.

"I suspect they're here for you," a familiar voice remarked next to her.

Laura jumped out of her skin. "Jack! You startled me!"

"Sorry," said Jack, his smirk showing that he didn't really mean it, and that he enjoyed the effect of his sudden intrusion on Laura's thoughts.

"Do you mean they are still after the story of SPACEWAVE and Grace? I thought that had died down."

She knew that Smith had managed to bury most of the story and stopped it from becoming a major international scandal. The local press in Arizona had understood that there had been some personal problems between employees that resulted in some tragic accident, but did not grasp the magnitude and scale of the underground operation that Grace had developed. In Chile, the authorities had not been keen to publicly admit that an internationally wanted 'criminal' had slipped through their fingers. In Bolivia, Grace had disappeared. The chances that she had survived were close to zero, but her body was never found. The local news media simply reported that an American woman got lost in the high-altitude desert and rescue teams had been searching for her for a few days. Laura and Jack had been interviewed by a few journalists in connection to Grace, but they had managed to conceal the scale of the story. There was no need for it to be disclosed. It was now all solved and under control by Smith. Revealing the full, true story and the associated tragic events would have irredeemably damaged SPACEWAVE, with catastrophic effects on its employees, and the numerous space projects that the company was developing.

"You're right," confirmed Jack, "although various parts of the story have emerged publicly in the different countries, they were simply reported briefly in the local news. No journalist has connected all the dots on a global scale."

"So, if that isn't it, then why are they here?" insisted Laura, looking at the crowd of journalists and raising an eyebrow.

"I guess they're interested in what you're going to announce this morning," Jack said grinning.

"How do they know that I'm going to announce anything important? My talk is scheduled as a short presentation with a very dull title," asked Laura, putting her hands on her hips. She had been cautious not to give anything away to anyone about her discovery. Not even Jack was aware of the magnitude of her discovery, though he might have had an inkling.

"Well, maybe someone... leaked something and generated some expectations on social media," replied Jack, winking.

Laura gave him a gentle slap on the nape of his neck, frowning and smiling at the same time. "How do you know that I'm going to announce anything exciting?"

"Just guessing."

"And why do you think that I'm keen to announce it to all the media?"

"Come on, Laura, you have been in the shadows for too long. You deserve some limelight."

Laura was about to object, but couldn't find the words. In the end, it was true that she was proud of her discovery and that she was curious to see what the reaction of the scientific community would be, but also the reaction of the general public. It would be foolish to think that it would not make the headlines and that it would not have an impact on people.

"Come with me. It's better if you enter the venue through a side entrance." Jack gently nudged her towards the far side of the large building.

He guided Laura through a side door and then through a few narrow corridors. They reached a small door. Jack signalled for her to wait, slipped through the door and closed it behind him.

Laura waited for a few seconds. Then she cracked the door open and peeked through it. The door was an auxiliary entrance to the large lecture theatre where the plenary sessions of the conference were being held. Delegates were taking their seats, as the first session was about to start. The room was quickly filling in. Laura noticed that the media were setting up their cameras. The first speaker of the morning was already on the stage. She noticed that the organisers of the symposium and the chairwoman of the first session were visibly nervous, hastily conferring, and scanning the audience. Clearly, they were looking for her, as she was scheduled to give the second presentation of the morning, but was nowhere to be seen. The massive presence of the media, atypical for this kind of conferences in astronomy, was probably adding to the tension.

Laura saw Jack approaching from the far side of the theatre, where most of the journalists were clustered. He entered and closed the door behind him. "It's better that you stay hidden here until the beginning of the session, or else you risk being assaulted by the journalists. I may have overdone the rumours about your presentation," Jack said with a grin.

Laura didn't say anything, but rolled her eyes. Only a few months ago this tension and expectation around her would have caused her terrible distress and anxiety. Now she was just annoyed. Annoyed that the organisers were worried and agitated because of her.

A few minutes later they heard the voice of the chairwoman echoing through the loudspeakers of the lecture theatre.

"Welcome, everyone, to the first plenary session of the morning."

Jack and Laura peeked into the theatre again. People were still drifting into the room, taking the few remaining seats, then sitting on the stairs or standing by the sides of the theatre.

"Please take your seats as we are about to start," prompted the chairwoman. She was still searching the audience, trying to spot Laura. "This session is dedicated to exoplanets and we begin with a review by Andrew Foster about the 'Search and characterisation of rocky planets'."

Professor Foster, an elegant elderly man, went on the stage. The first slide of his presentation was already projected on the large screen. "Good morning, everyone. I'm grateful to the organisers for their kind invitation to give this review."

As Professor Foster started his introductory remarks, Jack opened the door and guided Laura towards the first row of seats. Every seat was taken, so Jack indicated for her to sit on some steps next to the wall. The chairwoman noticed the movement, saw Laura, and sighed in relief.

Foster's presentation lasted for about half an hour. There were not many questions at the end. Many eyes in the audience were already focused on Laura.

"If there are no more questions then we can move to the next talk of the morning, by Laura Bellini," said the chairwoman and made a gesture inviting Laura to come on the stage while Professor Foster went to sit in the front row.

Laura walked up onto the stage, with confidence, chin held high. Her insecure and hesitant self was just a faded memory.

All the journalists who were still idling outside hastily entered the lecture theatre. Everyone's gaze was turned on Laura.

The chairwoman approached her together with one of the organisers. "Laura, we don't have your slides in our system for projection," she whispered with a worried expression.

"Don't worry, I have my presentation on my laptop," said Laura, patting the computer that she had just placed on the podium, "I just need to connect it to the projector," she added, grabbing a cable and plugging it into her computer. She had barely finished her sentence when her first slide was already projected onto the large screen. It did not show the title of her presentation, as is customary, but three photos.

She looked out over the audience and started addressing them with a loud, confident voice, "Although I only have ten minutes, I would like to start my presentation with a tribute. A tribute to three persons who are no longer with us, but without whom the discovery that I'm going to present would have not been possible."

She looked at the first photo on the screen.

"Julia Russell. An outstanding scientist. A wonderful mentor. She was the one who had the genial intuition to develop the original program that eventually resulted in the discovery that I am going to present." Only in the last few months Laura had appreciated how visionary Julia had been. And only recently had she realised how stupid she had been to not fully appreciate the project that Julia had conceived. She wished she could tell Julia... she wished she could thank her... she wished she could hug her. Laura paused for a few second. She wanted to say more, a lot more, but did not want to publicly reveal her profound feelings for Julia.

"Arthur Cecil-Hood. A brilliant mind who gave so much to astronomy during his career. He had the idea to obtain the data that greatly expanded the scope of my results. He put passion in his work." Her gaze shifted to Julia's photo. "We will greatly miss his invaluable contribution to science."

Then she looked at the third photo.

"I'm sure that most of you don't know this person," she used the laser beam to point at the black and white photo.

"Vladimir Kasparov." She looked at the many puzzled faces in the audience.

"He was an exceptional Russian scientist, whose findings and intuitions were hastily and unfairly dismissed by his colleagues about 30 years ago."

Some people in the audience shifted in their chairs, loosening the collar of their shirt.

"Yet, this whole story started with him."

Laura moved onto the next slide, which showed a faded photo of a young Kasparov giving a presentation at a conference, behind him a graph projected on the conference screen. Smith and Jack had retrieved it from Grace's office.

"At a conference in Paris, about 30 years ago, Kasparov presented data on the star 70 Ophiuchi. He had monitored the star with the BTA-6 Russian telescope for several months. He noticed that, in some of the observations, the data suggested some peculiar features," Laura pointed at one of the tentative features identified by Kasparov on the graph in the photo. The signal was indeed marginal, embedded in a lot of scattered data.

"He interpreted one of these features as water in the atmosphere of an exoplanet transiting in front of the star." She could see some of the people sneering or raising their eyebrows. There was also some giggling. Laura glared at the audience.

"No one believed him," she said loudly, with a hint of anger. "He was even mocked."

Then she lowered her voice and, with a quiet, forgiving tone, she added, "I don't blame the delegates who were harsh on him. At that time planets outside our solar system had not yet been discovered, let alone the atmospheres around them. At that time it may have sounded like science fiction to them."

She paused for effect.

"Kasparov's claim was quickly forgotten by most."

Laura scanned the audience, whose eyes were glued on her.

"Totally unaware of those early claims, Julia Russell and I obtained several datasets of 70 Ophiuchi." Laura changed the slide to show the result of the datasets collected by her and Julia at the TNG telescope, including those which had been erased by Grace from the archive, but recovered from Laura's own hard drive.

"Our data unambiguously shows that 70 Ophiuchi *does* have a planet orbiting around it with a period of about nine months." The full set of data from the TNG was now beautifully showing the movement of the stars as a consequence of the small gravitational pull of the planet orbiting around it.

"This was not an exceptional finding per se. But Kasparov saw an early release of these results, which we published a few months ago, and immediately connected our findings with his claim 30 years ago. The exoplanet that we have identified around 70 Ophiuchi is most likely the same that had transited in front of the star 30 years ago, leaving the imprint of water in its atmosphere found in Kasparov's data. He probably did not want to make a big fuss about it, but for him our findings must have been a sort of vindication in the eyes of the scientific community."

She looked at the audience sternly, as if they were somehow representative of the same scientific community that had denigrated Kasparov.

"He tried to contact me and Julia about it... but unfortunately he lost his life, in a tragic... accident."

"Julia and I tried to reconstruct what he had found 30 years ago. By combining Kasparov's and our findings, we could estimate that the exoplanet in front of 70 Ophiuchi has a mass of about five times that of the Earth."

Laura noticed that some people in the audience had stopped taking notes, eyes wide open and leaning forward.

"Sadly, our quest cost Julia her life." Laura lowered her eyes. She did not want to give any more details away. It was too painful for her and revealing all of the tragic events associated with it was not relevant to the scientific discovery.

She stood still, eyes closed, for a moment.

Some low murmurs started to rise from the public. She could more distinctly hear the whispering of a delegate sitting in the first rows, "Is this it? Exoplanets with masses similar to the Earth and with water in their atmospheres have already been discovered around other stars. Sorry about the peculiar and sad events linked to it, but this discovery is well below the expectations that the rumours have generated."

She opened her eyes with an intense glare. "Yet," she continued more loudly, "yet, I wanted to understand the additional features that Kasparov had spotted in his data." She slightly narrowed her eyes.

"From my data I could determine the date and time of the next transit of the exoplanet in front of its star. I... erm... convinced..." she hesitated a second, "I convinced the European Southern Observatory to give me access to the Very Large Telescope to observe 70 Ophiuchi at the time of the transit."

People in the audience sat up on their chairs.

"The observation was, how shall I put it… quite successful." She grinned and moved to the next slide.

"This is the data!"

There was a simple graph. Everyone hastily and eagerly studied it. Some squinted their eyes, others adjusted their glasses. Whispering and muttering rose from the audience. Sounds of amazement came from some individuals.

"Yes," Laura tried to be heard above the sounds from the conference delegates. "Yes, impressive, isn't it? The data is self-explanatory and the implications are obvious."

She pointed to one feature in the data.

"This is the clear signature of water in the atmosphere of the exoplanet, confirming unambiguously what Kasparov had already found. At its distance from the star, the temperature of the planet is adequate to have liquid water on its surface."

Then she moved the pointer to indicate two additional, clear features.

"These are the signatures of molecular oxygen and methane…" she paused, enjoying a little bit of drama for the media, "together with water, they are an unambiguous bio-signature."

She surveyed the stunned faces in the audience.

"Each of these elements separately can have different origins, but together they only have one explanation – life."

Now, all the journalists gasped.

"Yes, there is life on this exoplanet. Oxygen produced by the photosynthesis of some form of vegetation and methane coming from the waste of some sort of microbes or some sort of… fauna."

Laura gave a few moments to let the news sink in.

"That's not all."

She saw some people clutch the armrests of their seats.

"As you may know, my colleagues in Cambridge have a leading role in the development of some cutting-edge radio-astronomical observatories. As soon as I had found evidence for life on this exoplanet, I asked them to monitor the radio emissions from that direction."

She moved to the next slide. It showed another graph with several blips.

"This is the radio signal coming from the direction of 70 Ophiuchi. You can certainly notice a complex pattern of various signals. Some of them periodic. Very narrow in frequency. Some of them are faster, appearing every few seconds, while others repeat after several hours. One may wonder whether they come from some 'pulsar', rotating compact neutron stars in the background. However, you may notice that the frequency of the signals changes with time. It changes synchronously with the orbit of the exoplanet."

Laura paused for a few seconds for the delegates to deduce the obvious implication of this additional finding.

"These radio signals come from the exoplanet."

She waited for a moment for the media to understand the ramifications of this statement.

"There is intelligent life. There is intelligent, technologically advanced life on the exoplanet. We're not alone."

The pen of a journalist fell from his hand and rolled down the stairs. The sound of it hitting each step echoed across the entire theatre.

"These periodic signals are likely associated with some sort of radar or communication systems of the civilisation on this exoplanet."

She looked onto the sea of gaping, stunned faces. Motionless, as if hypnotised. The graph was reflected in the multitude of wide open eyes.

Laura took advantage of this moment, in which the audience was pondering about the implications of the discovery, to look at the structure and decorations of the large lecture theatre. She hadn't had a chance to look at the whole of the theatre yet, amid the pressure and arrangements around her presentation. It was a little awkward to be looking around during her presentation, but it was her instinct in that very moment. For the first time, she noticed that the entire wall behind her was decorated with a huge mosaic depicting Christ. She had not seen it before because the mosaic was so huge that one had to step back to take in the entire scene. The mosaic was so vast that it dwarfed the large screen beneath it, on which the slides were being projected. Laura focused on Christ's face. She wondered whether she should feel some regret for having stripped humanity of its centrality so near to *His* house. She looked at Christ's expression more closely, trying to detect any hint of resentment. No. Not really. Quite the opposite. It seemed that he was smiling. Yes, definitely, He was smiling at her.

The giggling of a baby, coming from outside the room, distracted her from her intense eye contact with Christ. Her gaze went back to the audience. No one was moving. Not a word.

"There's more."

The chairwoman gawked.

"In parallel, Arthur Cecil-Hood observed 70 Ophiuchi during the transit of the exoplanet too. But he used another instrument, with a different configuration, observing a different band. Very generously, he gave his data to me before… just before leaving us."

She lowered her gaze for a few seconds.

Then, she moved to the next slide, showing another graph with Arthur's data. "The data clearly shows that carbon dioxide is detected in the atmosphere of the exoplanet. But the amount of carbon dioxide is tiny."

Laura paused to scan the audience and see whether anyone had already guessed the implication of this additional finding. She continued by guiding them, "The civilisation of this exoplanet has managed to develop a technically advanced culture without harming their environment, in harmony with their planet… unlike other civilisations, which are devastating their own."

Laura saw a few delegates sinking in their chair.

Laura could not help dwelling on this point further. "Apparently, that civilisation does not have the same self-destructive instinct as our…" she paused… "our 'civilisation'," she repeated, "which needs a vicious, unintelligent form of life, a virus, to temper its crazy and stupid self-annihilation."

Many of the audience members, who had not blinked once throughout Laura's entire presentation, lowered their eyes. Laura sensed a collective shiver run through the audience. What were they feeling? Shame, for belonging to the human race? Some raised their gaze to stare at her. Maybe they felt hope. Maybe not everything was lost. She stood proudly before them. Her generation could rescue this messy planet from self-destruction. Awakening humanity's intellect and defeating stupidity, like David defeated Goliath. Yes, it was hope she saw in their eyes.

"This is it. Thank you for your attention."

Everyone was stunned, with shocked faces. Even the chairwoman of the session was silent, open-mouthed.

"Any questions?" asked Laura.

At that point the chairwoman blinked; unsteadily, she stood up. "Y– Yes, sorry… any… any question?" she asked the audience, stuttering.

Not a word. Absolute silence. Even the journalists were speechless. Everyone was deep in thoughts, as if still processing the magnitude of what they had just heard.

"Well, if there are no questions, I guess I shall leave the stage to the next speaker."

Laura took her laptop and confidently walked off the stage. She stopped halfway down the steps and looked at the audience. "Oh. I forgot to mention one last curiosity." Everyone's eyes widened. "70 Ophiuchi is a double star. So the exoplanet has two suns," she smiled. "It must be a lovely planet to live on."

She looked up, closed her eyes for an instant and then walked towards the side door through which she had come in.

Jack followed her.

As soon as they were behind the door Jack burst out with enthusiasm. "Laura, that was… was… amazing! Spectacular! I had guessed something, but I wasn't expecting that your discovery would be so far-reaching. This will change everything for humanity!

Our mindset will change forever, forever! Thanks to you!"

"I'm glad that you appreciated my presentation," she smiled.

In the meantime, from the lecture theatre, some initial, timid clapping quickly triggered an avalanche of applause and jubilation from the public.

"It seems I'm not the only appreciative one," commented Jack while peeking through the door. "There's a standing ovation for you out there."

The clapping was mixed with the overlapping voices of delegates and journalists trying to ask questions over the din. "How far is the planet?" "Is it possible to decipher those radio signals?" "Can we know more about the forms of life?"

Jack shut the door and turned to Laura. "Eh, where are you going?"

Laura was walking away towards the exit door. She turned, looked at him and smiled. "Right, I forgot something." She ran back towards him. She hugged him and kissed him passionately on the lips.

Then she loosened the grip of her arms around him, looked him in the eye and asked, "What was the question?"

Jack had gone wobbly at the knees. He stuttered something incomprehensible.

"Where am I going?" she continued, "Well, I'm leaving this session. I'm no longer interested in exoplanets. I'm going to change my area of research."

Jack's jaw dropped, "Wh– wh– what?!" he exclaimed, agog. "Are you insane? Your thesis will be more famous than Stephen Hawking's. Your discovery has placed your name in history. You... Y–"

"Yes, yes, I know," she interrupted, "but I don't care. I have now gained confidence in myself. I know what I want to do and what I do not want to do. And, although I have greatly enjoyed it, I do not want to study exoplanets anymore."

"And what do you want to do?"

"Gravitational waves. I want to study gravitational waves. I want to get involved in GATEWAY, the space project that Grace started.

What she did was appalling, but her space project is fantastic."

"Are… are you sure?" Jack asked with a baffled expression.

"Yes. That's my true passion. I feel it. I feel them. Don't you feel them?" asked Laura with a smile, while walking away.

"Feel what?"

Laura did not reply and left the building from the same side door through which they had entered.

Feel what? Jack kept asking himself. Feel what?

Of course.

Waves.

Row